NEW YORK TIMES BESTSELLING AUTHOR
BECCA FITZPATRICK

hush, hush

- Volume 1 -

created by
BECCA FITZPATRICK

adapted by
DEREK RUIZ

artwork by
JENNYSON ROSERO
with
DAVID PINOS and MEL JOY SAN JUAN

lettering by
DAVE LANPHEAR
with
BILL TORTOLINI

special thanks to
JENN MARTIN and CATHERINE DRAYTON

Sea Lion Books   president: **DAVID DABEL** v.p. publisher: **DEREK RUIZ** marketing: **GLADYS ATWELL** art director: **DAVE LANPHEAR**

hush, hush

Graphic Novel

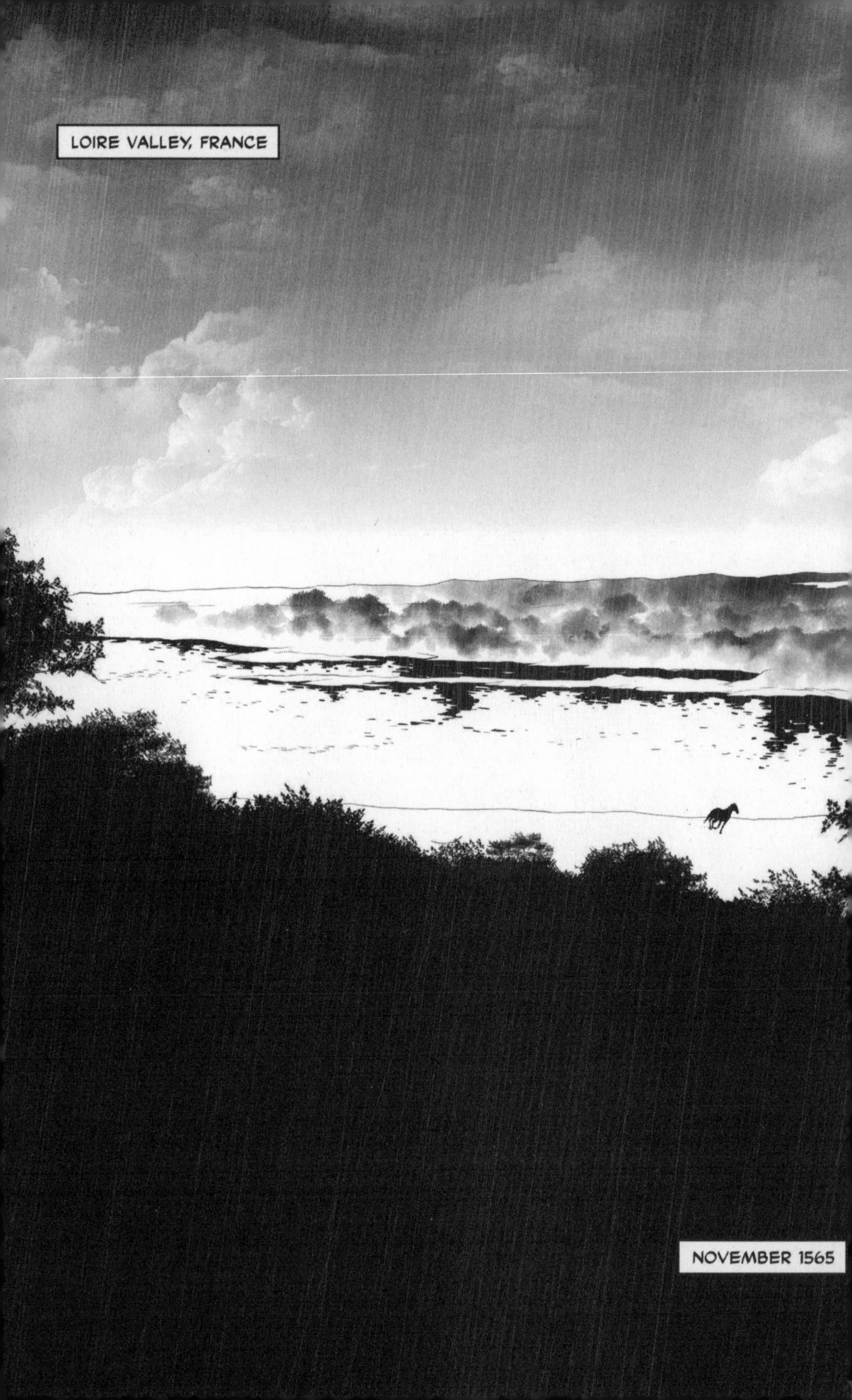
LOIRE VALLEY, FRANCE
NOVEMBER 1565

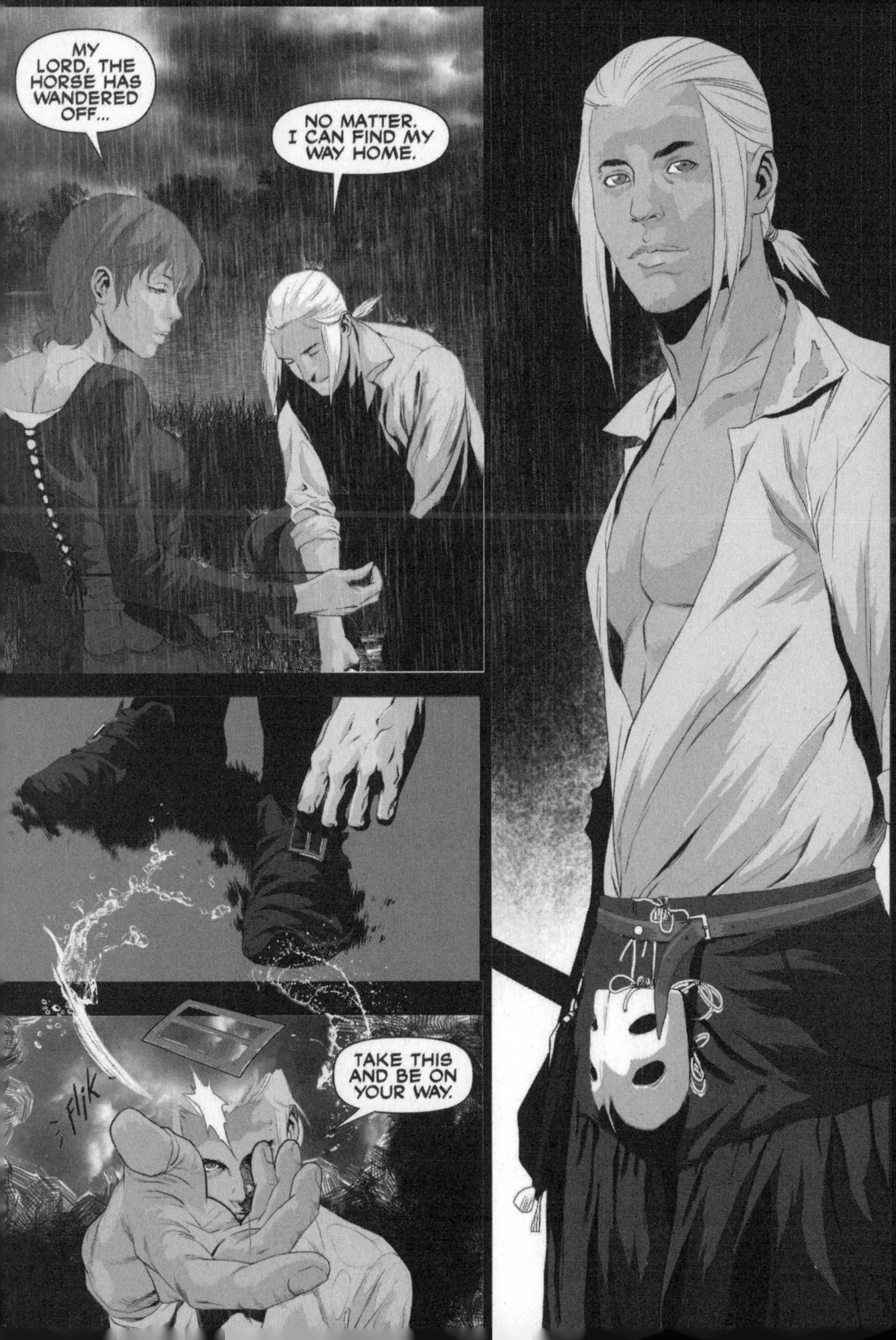
MY LORD, THE HORSE HAS WANDERED OFF...
NO MATTER. I CAN FIND MY WAY HOME.
FLIK
TAKE THIS AND BE ON YOUR WAY.

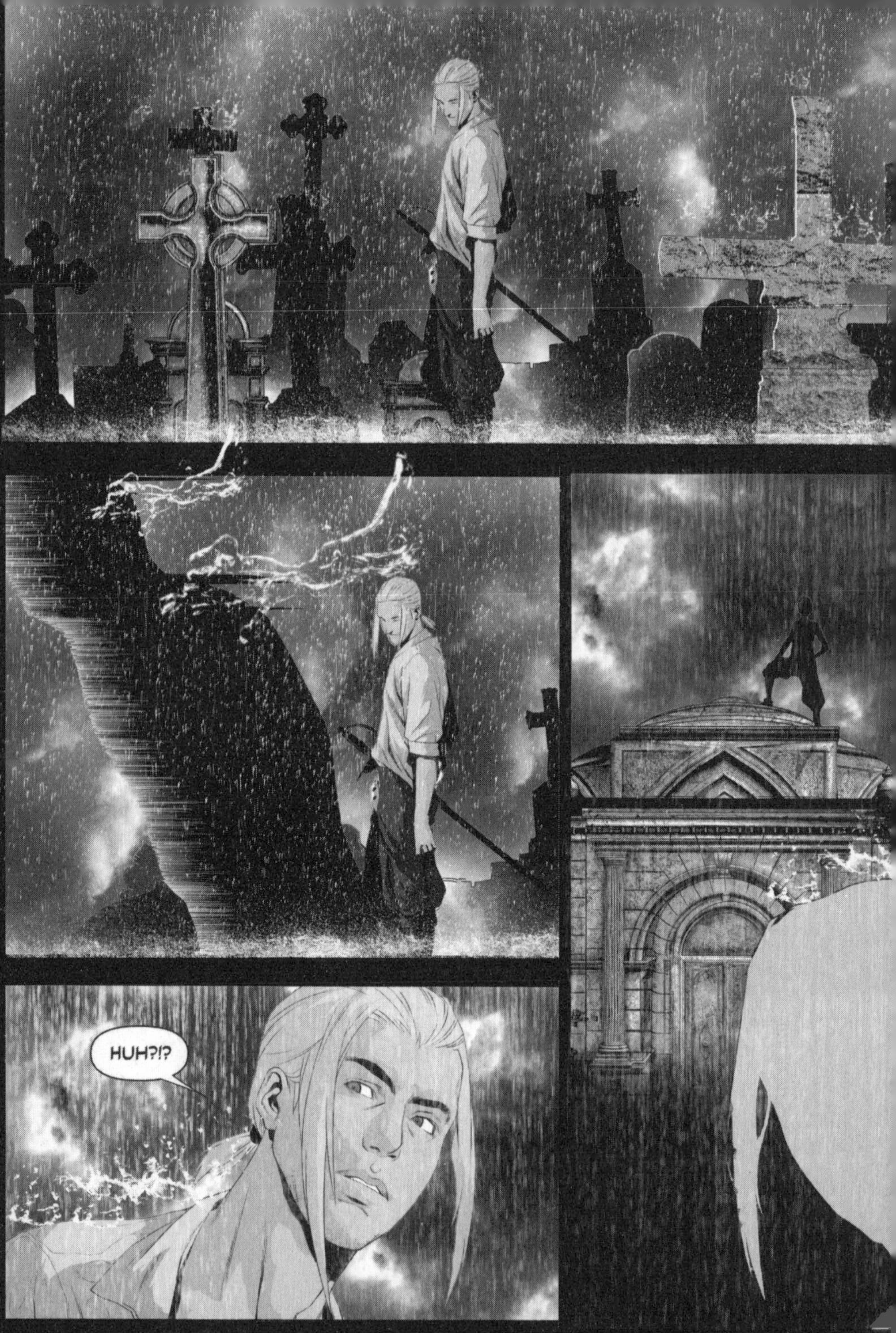
HUH?!?

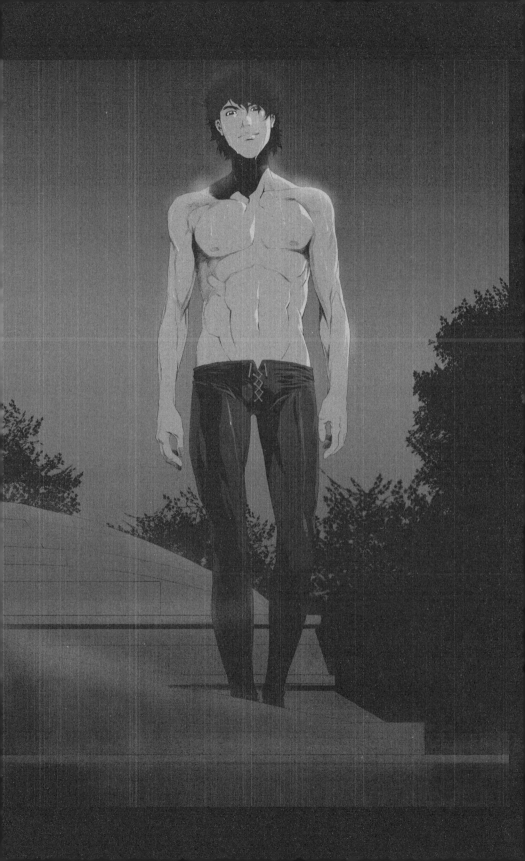

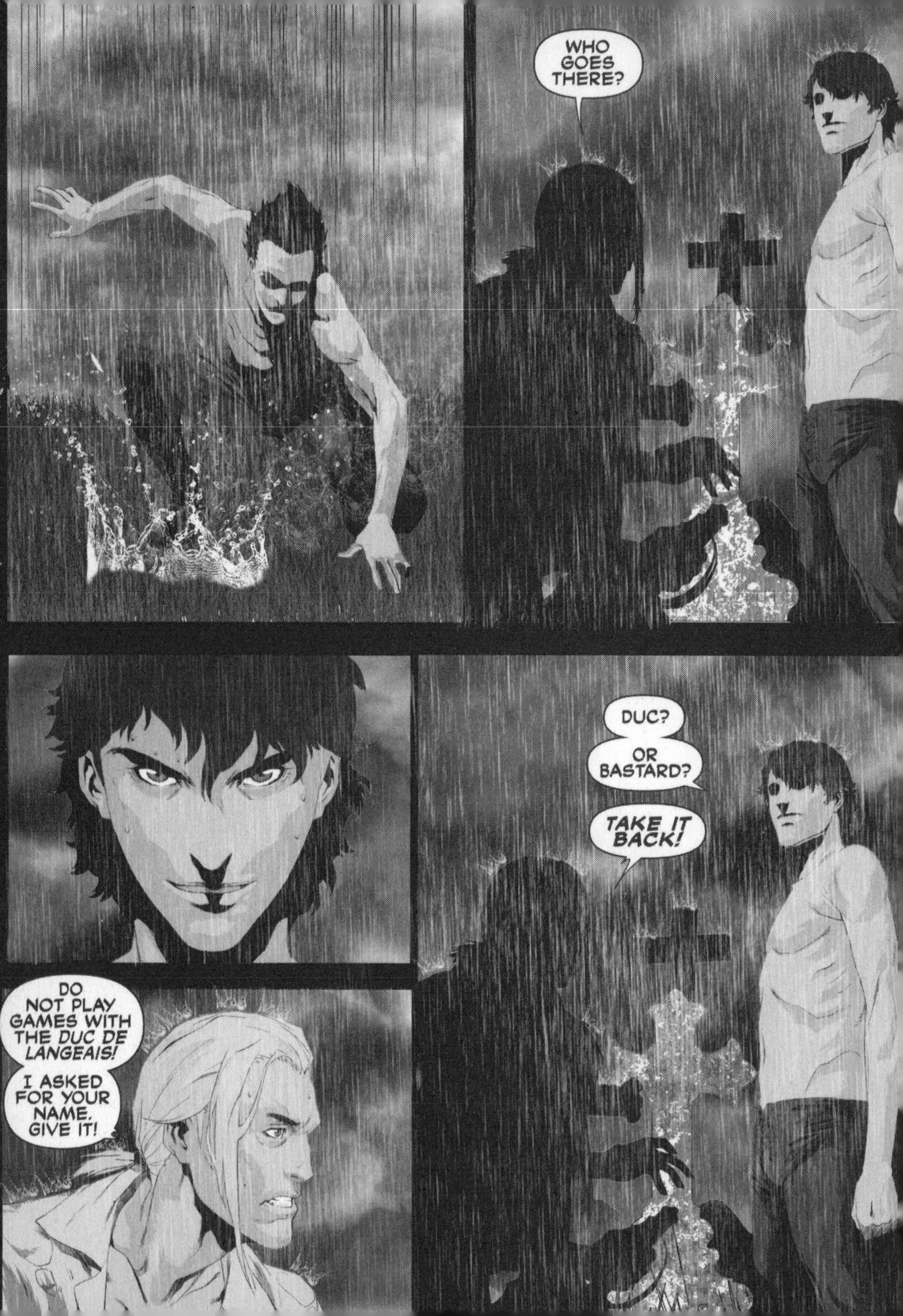
WHO GOES THERE?
DUC?
OR BASTARD?
TAKE IT BACK!
DO NOT PLAY GAMES WITH THE *DUC DE LANGEAIS!*
I ASKED FOR YOUR NAME. GIVE IT!

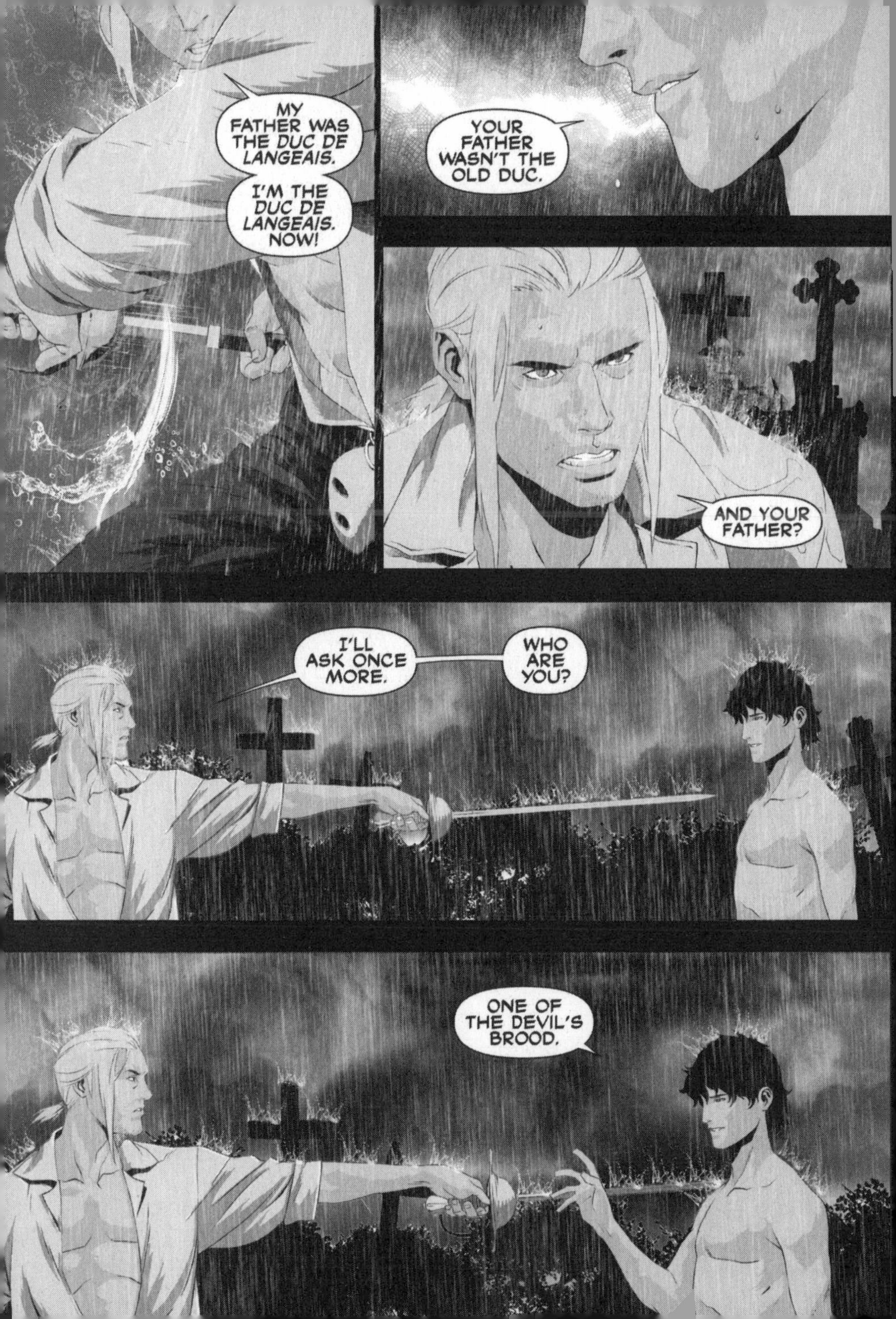
MY FATHER WAS THE DUC DE LANGEAIS.
I'M THE DUC DE LANGEAIS. NOW!
YOUR FATHER WASN'T THE OLD DUC.
AND YOUR FATHER?
I'LL ASK ONCE MORE.
WHO ARE YOU?
ONE OF THE DEVIL'S BROOD.

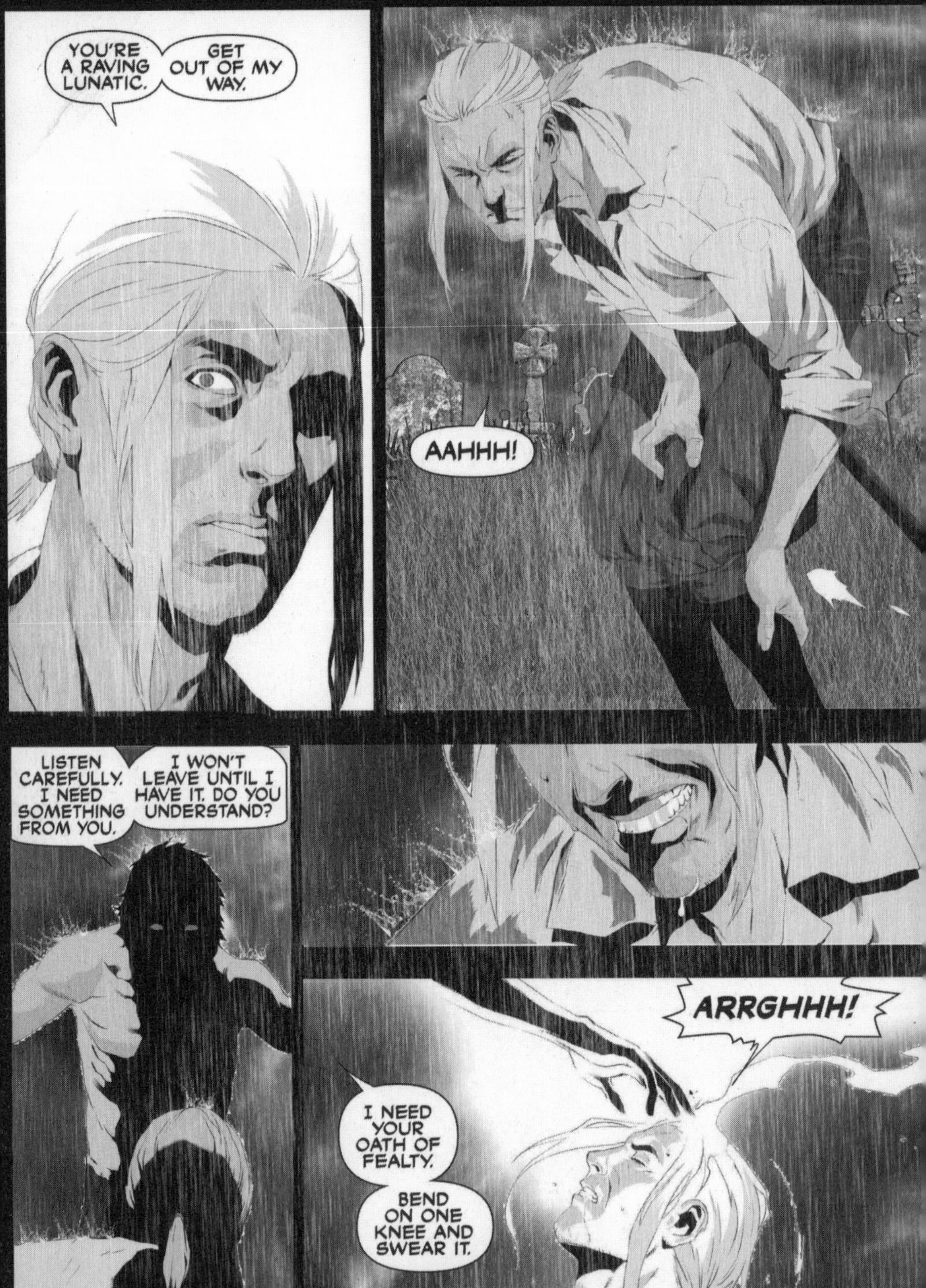
YOU'RE A RAVING LUNATIC.
GET OUT OF MY WAY.
AAHHH!
LISTEN CAREFULLY. I NEED SOMETHING FROM YOU.
I WON'T LEAVE UNTIL I HAVE IT. DO YOU UNDERSTAND?
ARRGHHH!
I NEED YOUR OATH OF FEALTY.
BEND ON ONE KNEE AND SWEAR IT.

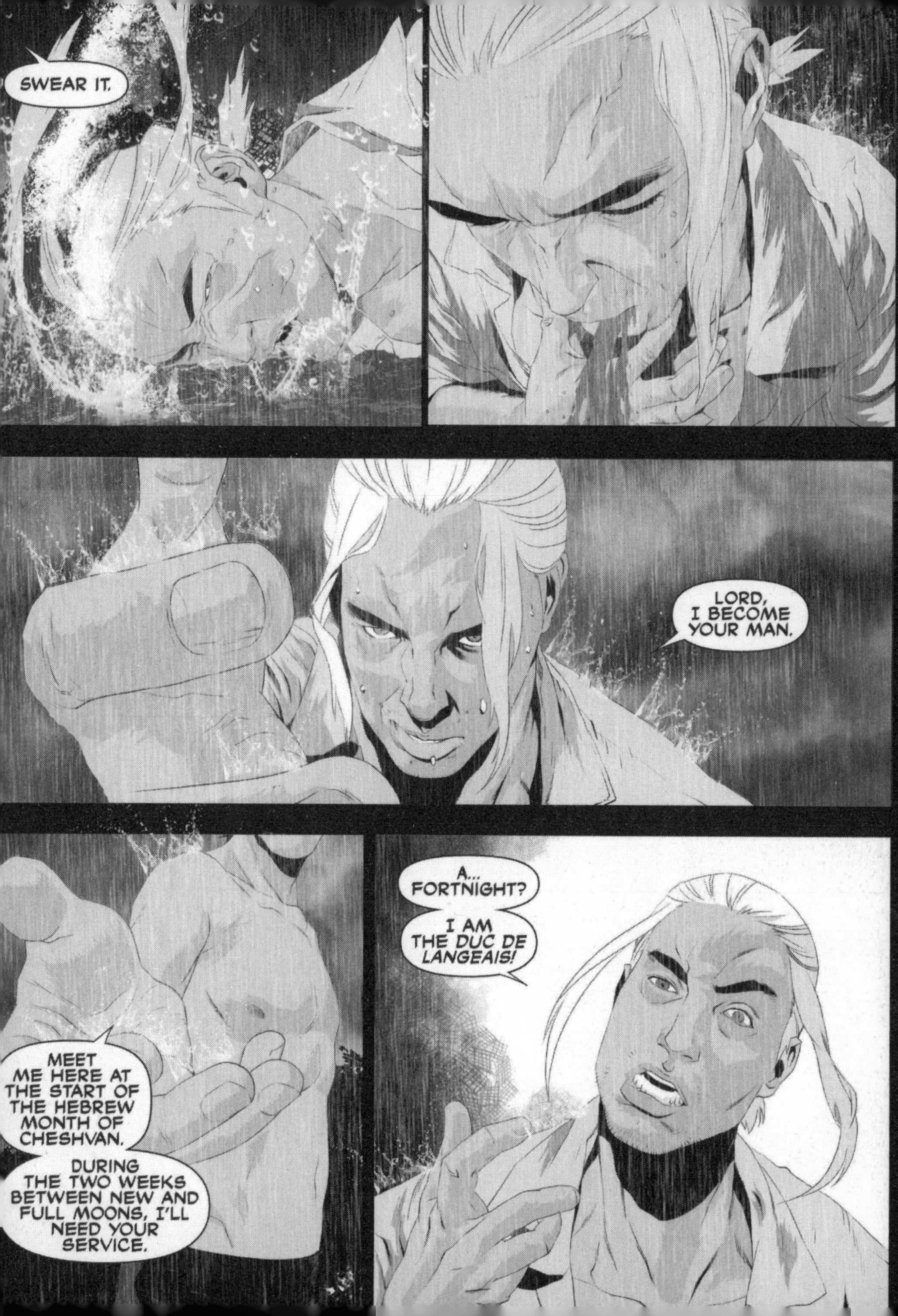
SWEAR IT.
LORD, I BECOME YOUR MAN.
MEET ME HERE AT THE START OF THE HEBREW MONTH OF CHESHVAN.
DURING THE TWO WEEKS BETWEEN NEW AND FULL MOONS, I'LL NEED YOUR SERVICE.
A... FORTNIGHT?
I AM THE *DUC DE LANGEAIS!*

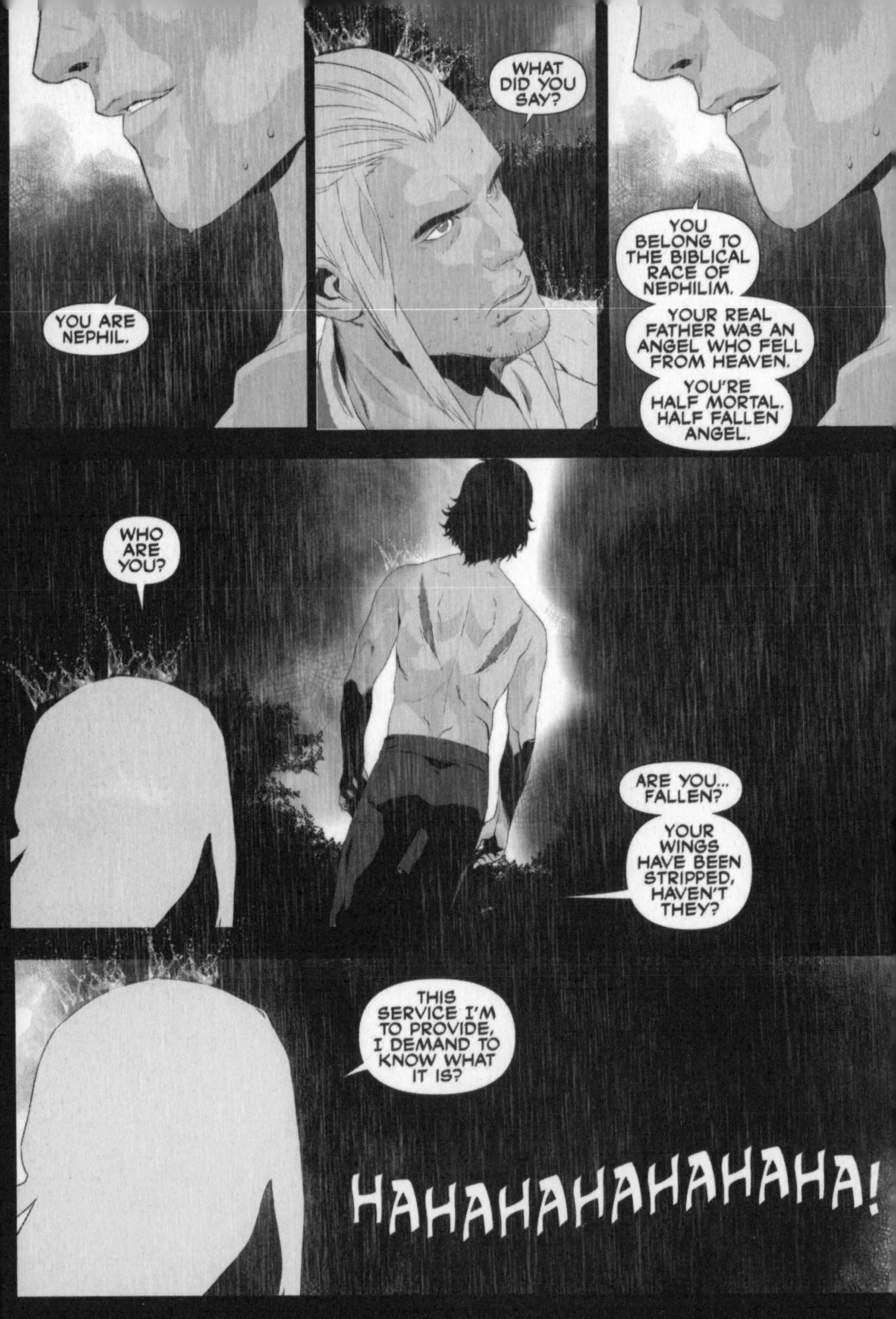
YOU ARE NEPHIL.
WHAT DID YOU SAY?
YOU BELONG TO THE BIBLICAL RACE OF NEPHILIM.
YOUR REAL FATHER WAS AN ANGEL WHO FELL FROM HEAVEN.
YOU'RE HALF MORTAL, HALF FALLEN ANGEL.
WHO ARE YOU?
ARE YOU... FALLEN?
YOUR WINGS HAVE BEEN STRIPPED, HAVEN'T THEY?
THIS SERVICE I'M TO PROVIDE, I DEMAND TO KNOW WHAT IT IS?
HAHAHAHAHAHAHAHA!

COLDWATER HIGH SCHOOL, MAINE.

PRESENT DAY.

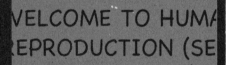

VELCOME TO HUMA
REPRODUCTION (SE

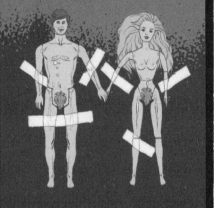

THIS IS EXACTLY WHY THE SCHOOL OUTLAWS CAMERA PHONES.

PICTURES OF THIS IN THE EZINE WOULD BE ALL THE EVIDENCE I NEED TO GET THE BOARD OF EDUCATION TO AX BIOLOGY.

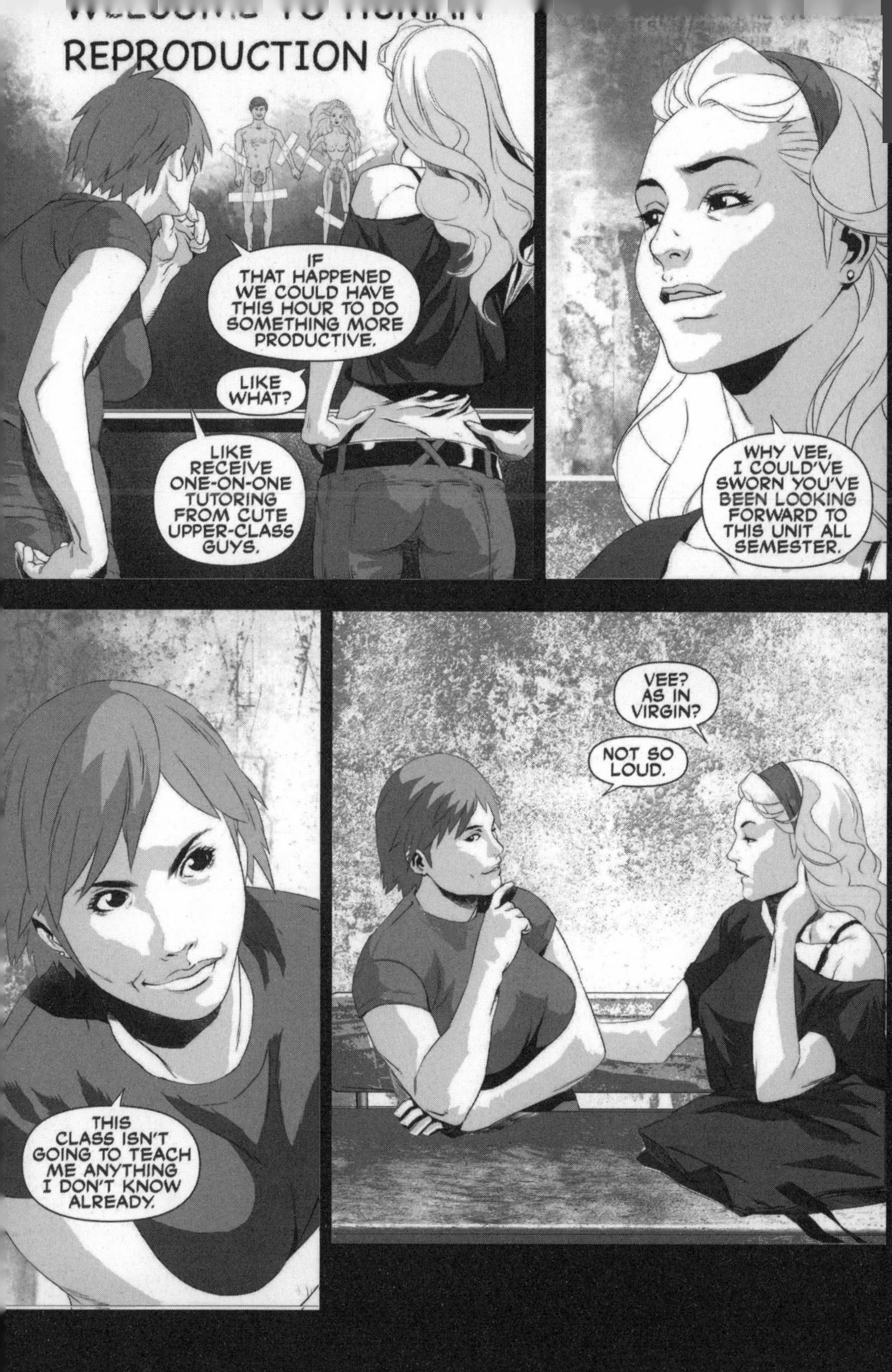
REPRODUCTION
IF THAT HAPPENED WE COULD HAVE THIS HOUR TO DO SOMETHING MORE PRODUCTIVE.
LIKE WHAT?
LIKE RECEIVE ONE-ON-ONE TUTORING FROM CUTE UPPER-CLASS GUYS.
WHY VEE, I COULD'VE SWORN YOU'VE BEEN LOOKING FORWARD TO THIS UNIT ALL SEMESTER.
THIS CLASS ISN'T GOING TO TEACH ME ANYTHING I DON'T KNOW ALREADY.
VEE? AS IN VIRGIN?
NOT SO LOUD.

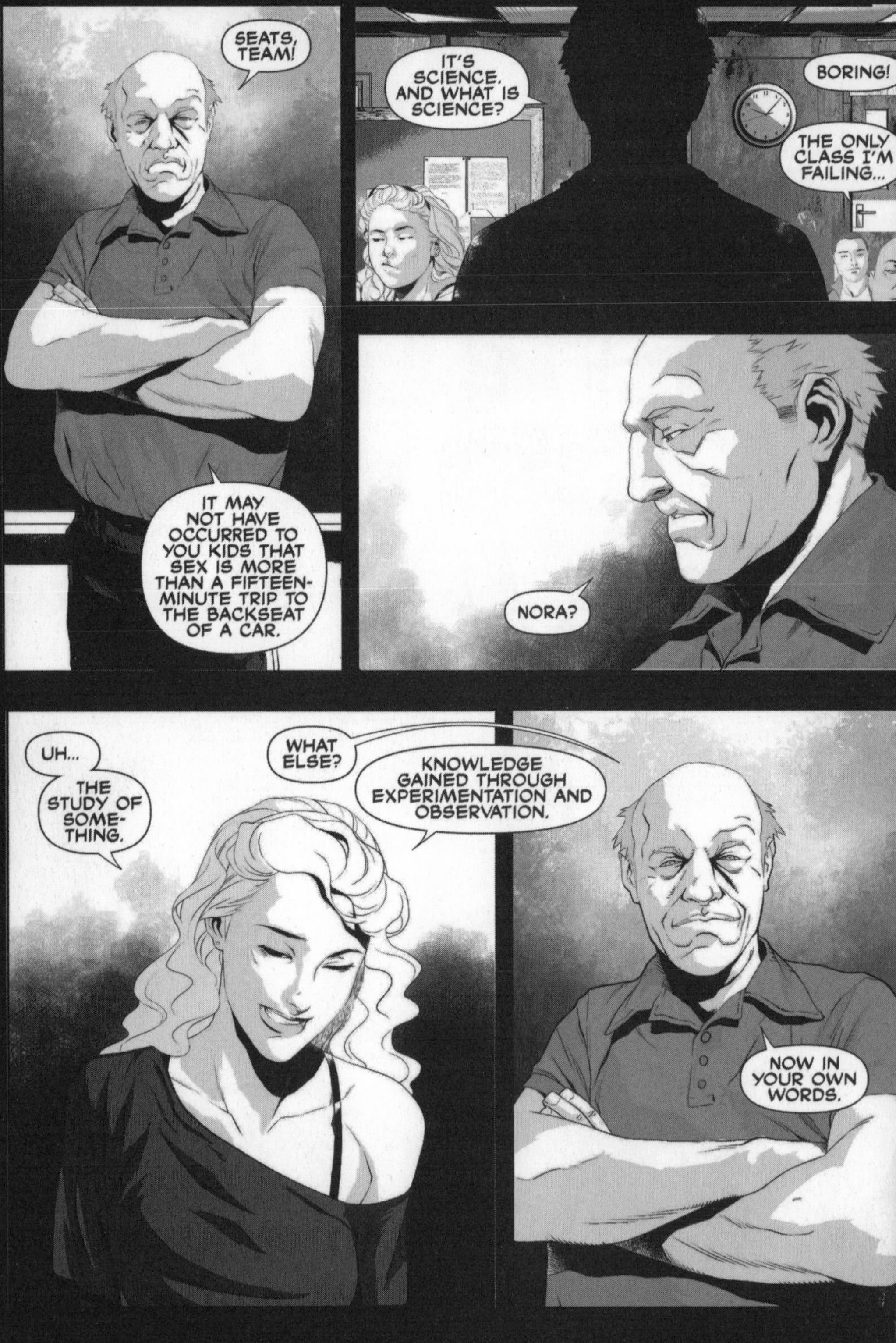
SEATS, TEAM!
IT'S SCIENCE. AND WHAT IS SCIENCE?
BORING!
THE ONLY CLASS I'M FAILING...
IT MAY NOT HAVE OCCURRED TO YOU KIDS THAT SEX IS MORE THAN A FIFTEEN-MINUTE TRIP TO THE BACKSEAT OF A CAR.
NORA?
UH...
THE STUDY OF SOME-THING.
WHAT ELSE?
KNOWLEDGE GAINED THROUGH EXPERIMENTATION AND OBSERVATION.
NOW IN YOUR OWN WORDS.

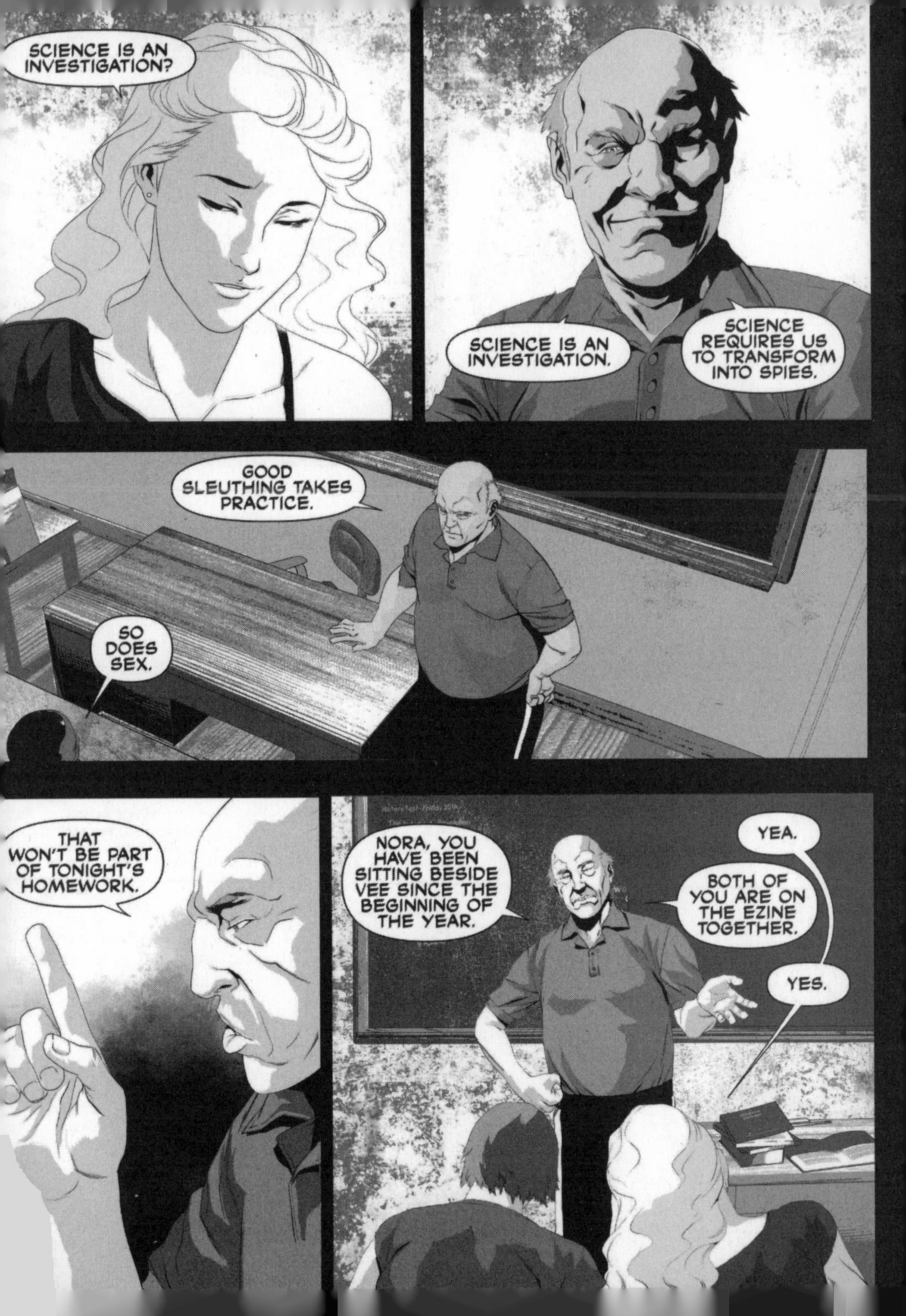
SCIENCE IS AN INVESTIGATION?
SCIENCE IS AN INVESTIGATION.
SCIENCE REQUIRES US TO TRANSFORM INTO SPIES.
GOOD SLEUTHING TAKES PRACTICE.
SO DOES SEX.
THAT WON'T BE PART OF TONIGHT'S HOMEWORK.
NORA, YOU HAVE BEEN SITTING BESIDE VEE SINCE THE BEGINNING OF THE YEAR.
YEA.
BOTH OF YOU ARE ON THE EZINE TOGETHER.
YES.

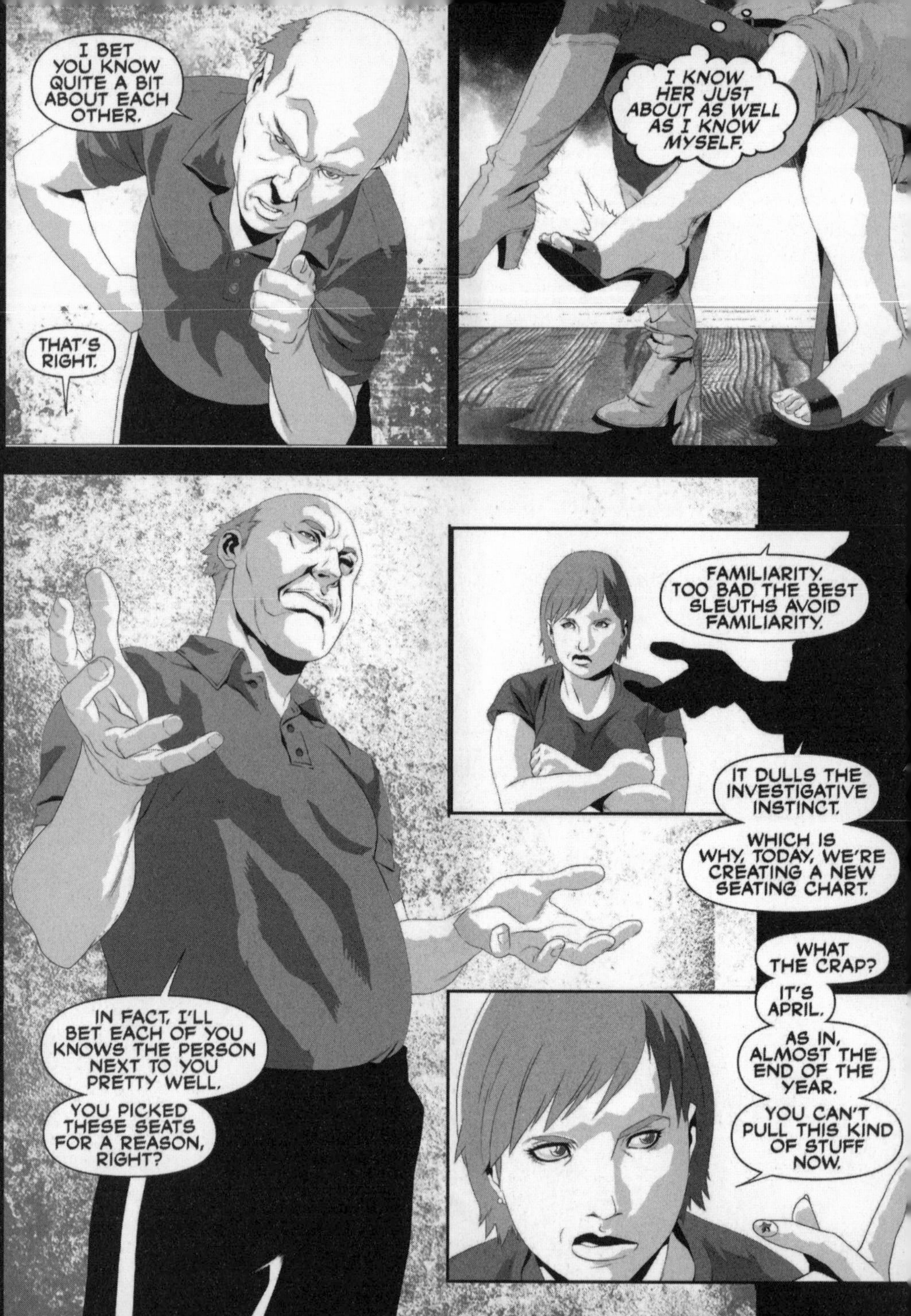
I BET YOU KNOW QUITE A BIT ABOUT EACH OTHER.
THAT'S RIGHT.
I KNOW HER JUST ABOUT AS WELL AS I KNOW MYSELF.
IN FACT, I'LL BET EACH OF YOU KNOWS THE PERSON NEXT TO YOU PRETTY WELL.
YOU PICKED THESE SEATS FOR A REASON, RIGHT?
FAMILIARITY. TOO BAD THE BEST SLEUTHS AVOID FAMILIARITY.
IT DULLS THE INVESTIGATIVE INSTINCT.
WHICH IS WHY, TODAY, WE'RE CREATING A NEW SEATING CHART.
WHAT THE CRAP?
IT'S APRIL.
AS IN, ALMOST THE END OF THE YEAR.
YOU CAN'T PULL THIS KIND OF STUFF NOW.

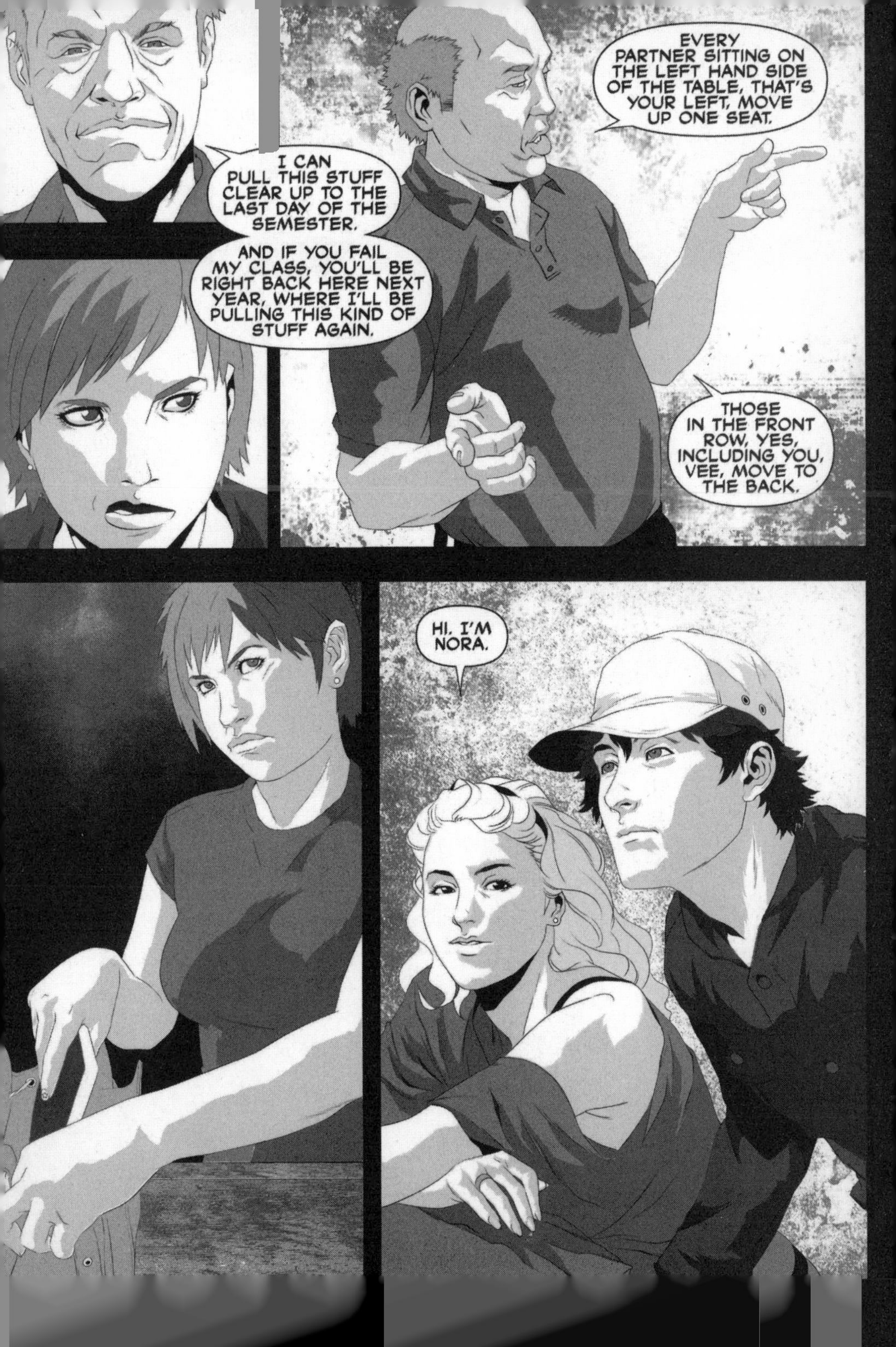

I CAN PULL THIS STUFF CLEAR UP TO THE LAST DAY OF THE SEMESTER.
AND IF YOU FAIL MY CLASS, YOU'LL BE RIGHT BACK HERE NEXT YEAR, WHERE I'LL BE PULLING THIS KIND OF STUFF AGAIN.
EVERY PARTNER SITTING ON THE LEFT HAND SIDE OF THE TABLE, THAT'S YOUR LEFT, MOVE UP ONE SEAT.
THOSE IN THE FRONT ROW, YES, INCLUDING YOU, VEE, MOVE TO THE BACK.
HI. I'M NORA.

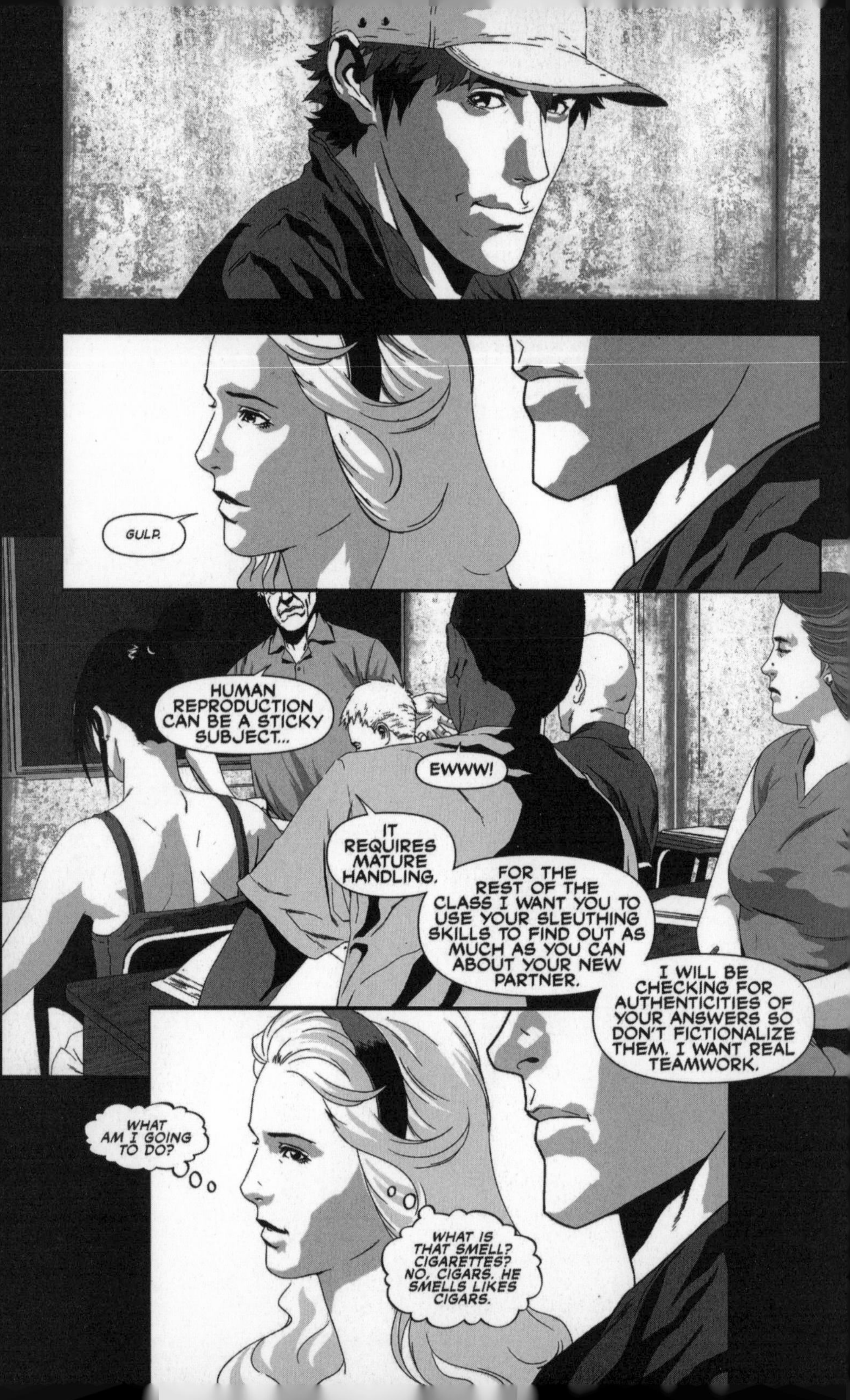
GULP.
HUMAN REPRODUCTION CAN BE A STICKY SUBJECT...
EWWW!
IT REQUIRES MATURE HANDLING.
FOR THE REST OF THE CLASS I WANT YOU TO USE YOUR SLEUTHING SKILLS TO FIND OUT AS MUCH AS YOU CAN ABOUT YOUR NEW PARTNER.
I WILL BE CHECKING FOR AUTHENTICITIES OF YOUR ANSWERS SO DON'T FICTIONALIZE THEM. I WANT REAL TEAMWORK.
WHAT AM I GOING TO DO?
WHAT IS THAT SMELL? CIGARETTES? NO, CIGARS. HE SMELLS LIKES CIGARS.

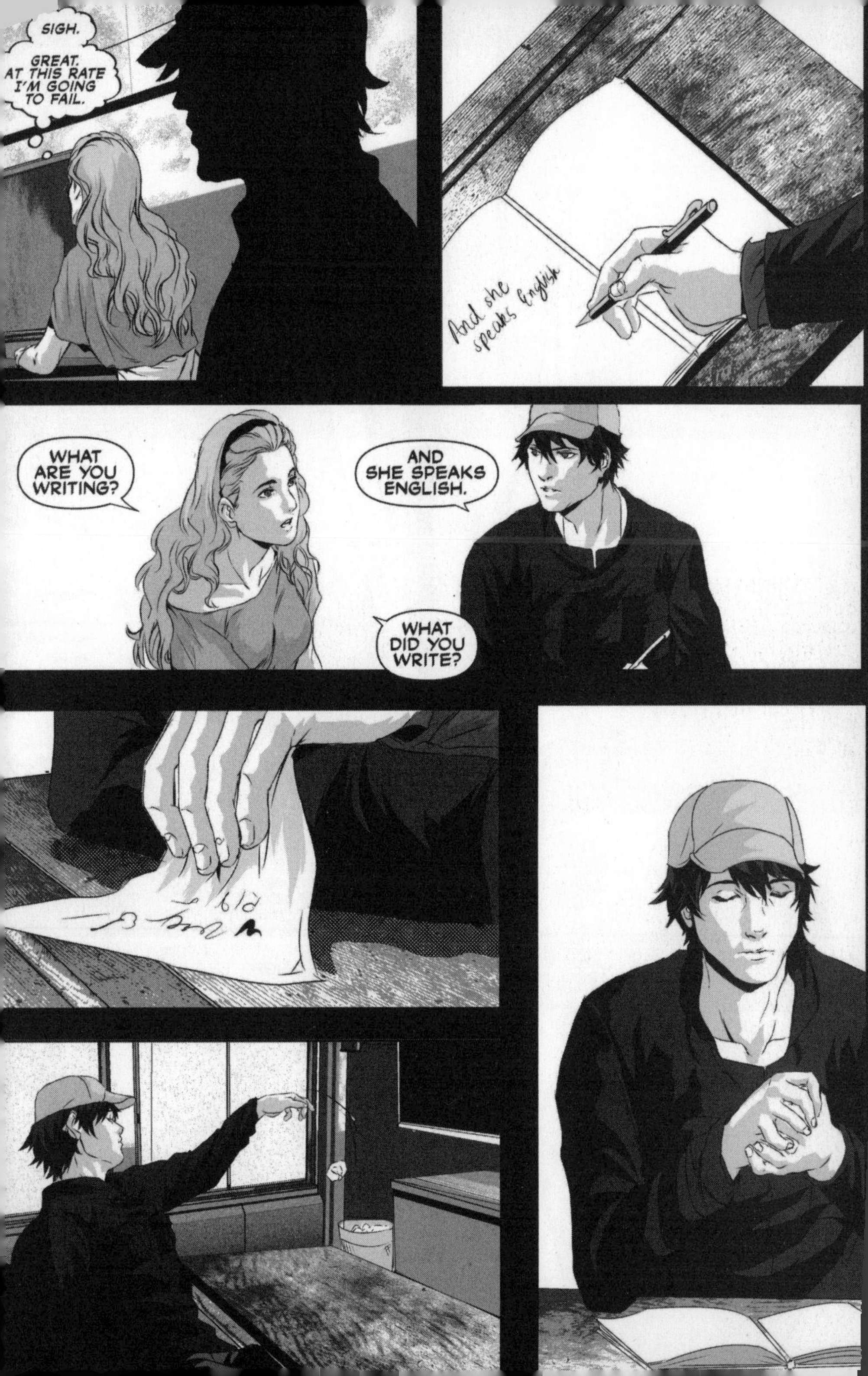
SIGH.
GREAT. AT THIS RATE I'M GOING TO FAIL.
And she speaks English
WHAT ARE YOU WRITING?
AND SHE SPEAKS ENGLISH.
WHAT DID YOU WRITE?

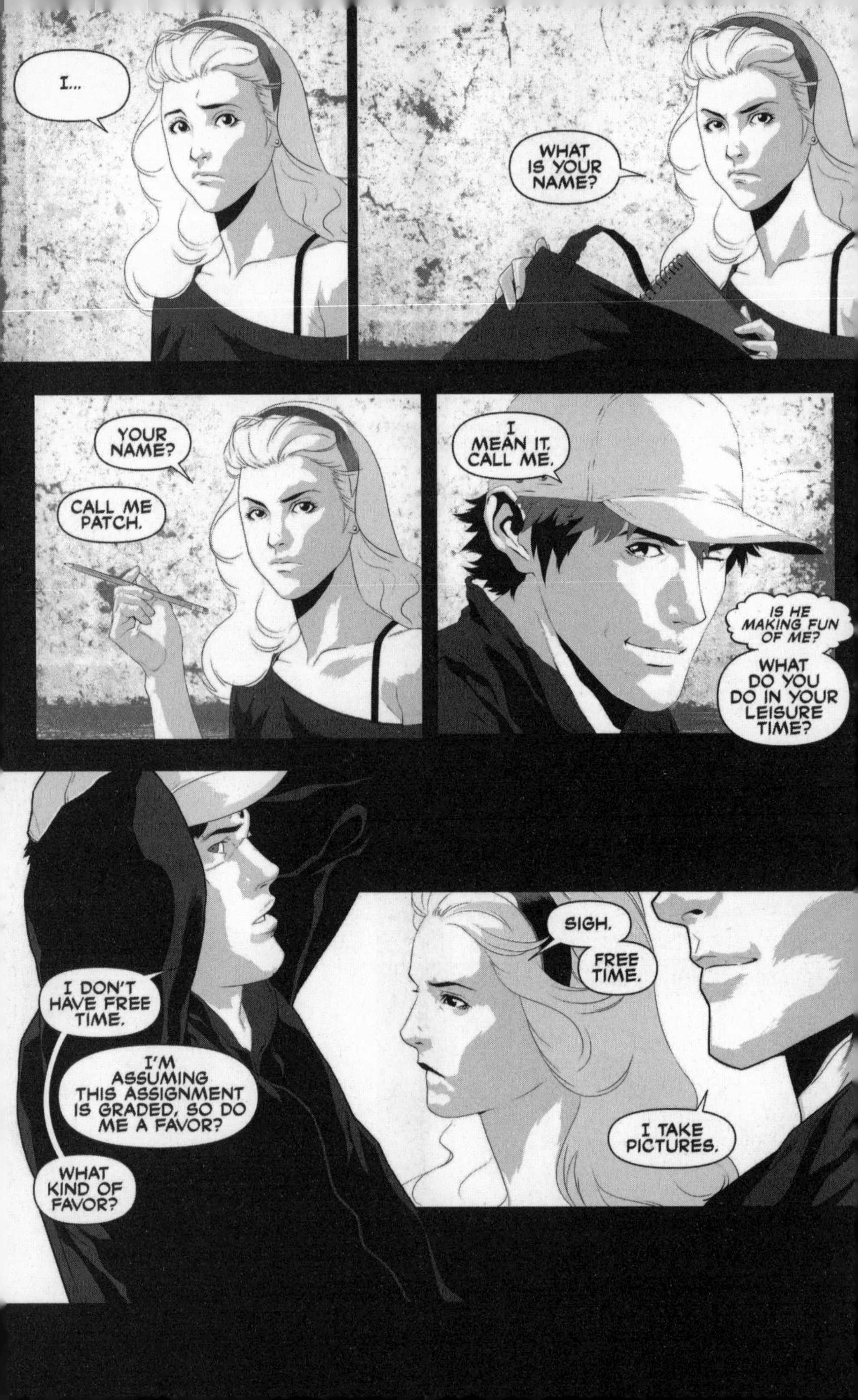
I...
WHAT IS YOUR NAME?
YOUR NAME?
CALL ME PATCH.
I MEAN IT. CALL ME.
IS HE MAKING FUN OF ME?
WHAT DO YOU DO IN YOUR LEISURE TIME?
SIGH.
FREE TIME.
I TAKE PICTURES.
I DON'T HAVE FREE TIME.
I'M ASSUMING THIS ASSIGNMENT IS GRADED, SO DO ME A FAVOR?
WHAT KIND OF FAVOR?

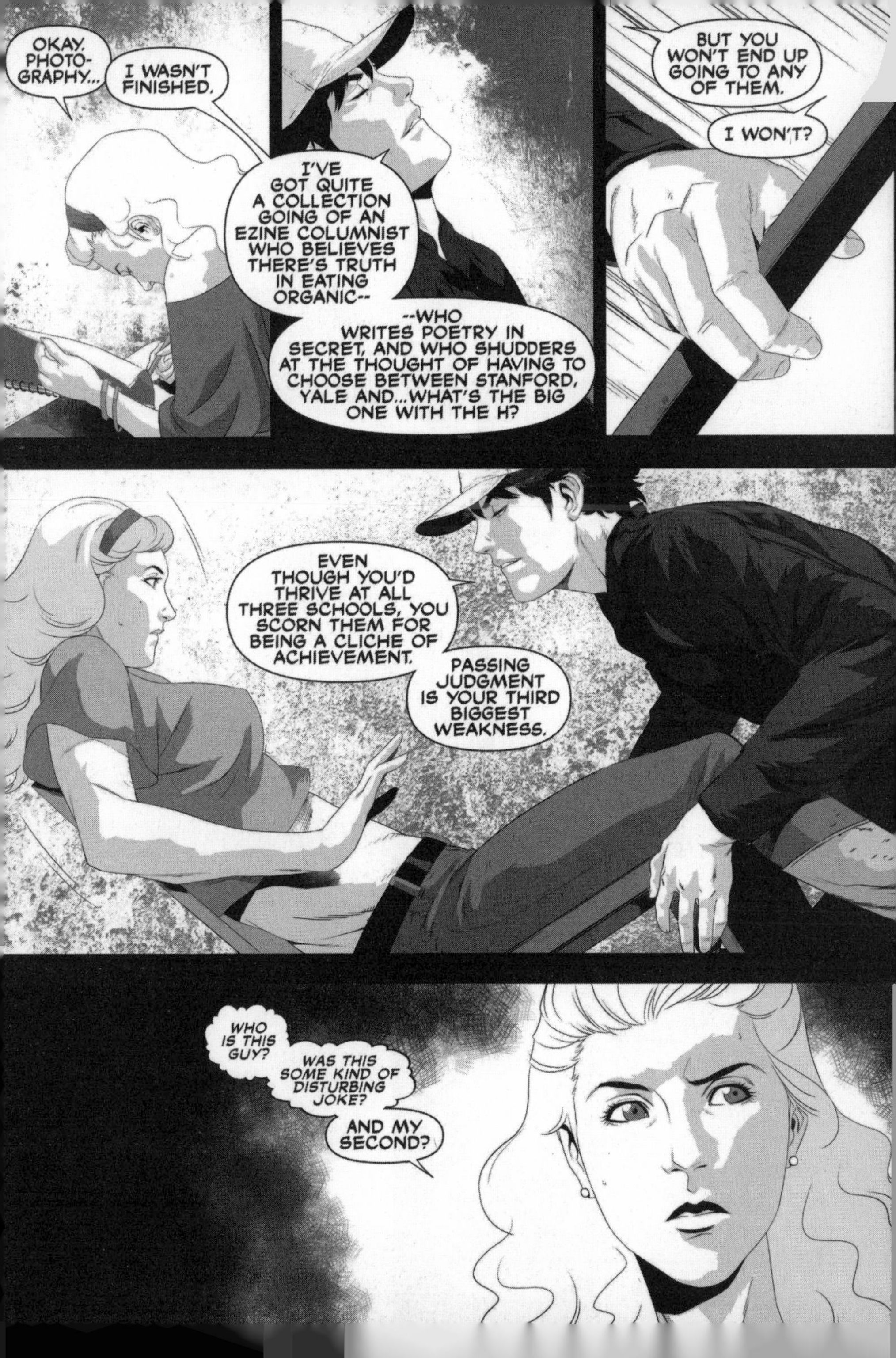
OKAY. PHOTOGRAPHY...
I WASN'T FINISHED.
I'VE GOT QUITE A COLLECTION GOING OF AN EZINE COLUMNIST WHO BELIEVES THERE'S TRUTH IN EATING ORGANIC--
--WHO WRITES POETRY IN SECRET, AND WHO SHUDDERS AT THE THOUGHT OF HAVING TO CHOOSE BETWEEN STANFORD, YALE AND...WHAT'S THE BIG ONE WITH THE H?
BUT YOU WON'T END UP GOING TO ANY OF THEM.
I WON'T?
EVEN THOUGH YOU'D THRIVE AT ALL THREE SCHOOLS, YOU SCORN THEM FOR BEING A CLICHE OF ACHIEVEMENT.
PASSING JUDGMENT IS YOUR THIRD BIGGEST WEAKNESS.
WHO IS THIS GUY?
WAS THIS SOME KIND OF DISTURBING JOKE?
AND MY SECOND?

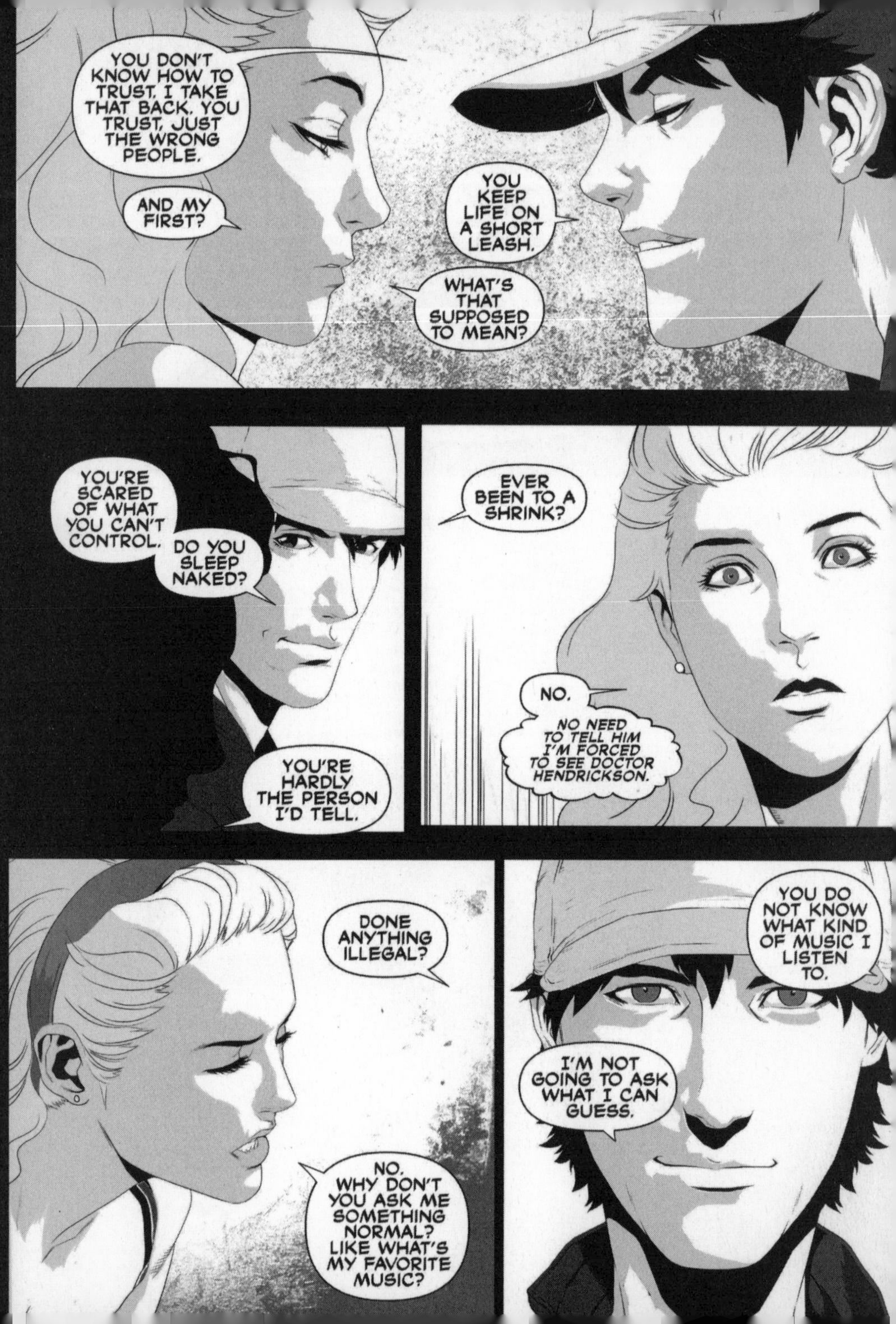
YOU DON'T KNOW HOW TO TRUST. I TAKE THAT BACK. YOU TRUST, JUST THE WRONG PEOPLE.
AND MY FIRST?
YOU KEEP LIFE ON A SHORT LEASH.
WHAT'S THAT SUPPOSED TO MEAN?
YOU'RE SCARED OF WHAT YOU CAN'T CONTROL.
DO YOU SLEEP NAKED?
YOU'RE HARDLY THE PERSON I'D TELL.
EVER BEEN TO A SHRINK?
NO.
NO NEED TO TELL HIM I'M FORCED TO SEE DOCTOR HENDRICKSON.
DONE ANYTHING ILLEGAL?
NO. WHY DON'T YOU ASK ME SOMETHING NORMAL? LIKE WHAT'S MY FAVORITE MUSIC?
YOU DO NOT KNOW WHAT KIND OF MUSIC I LISTEN TO.
I'M NOT GOING TO ASK WHAT I CAN GUESS.

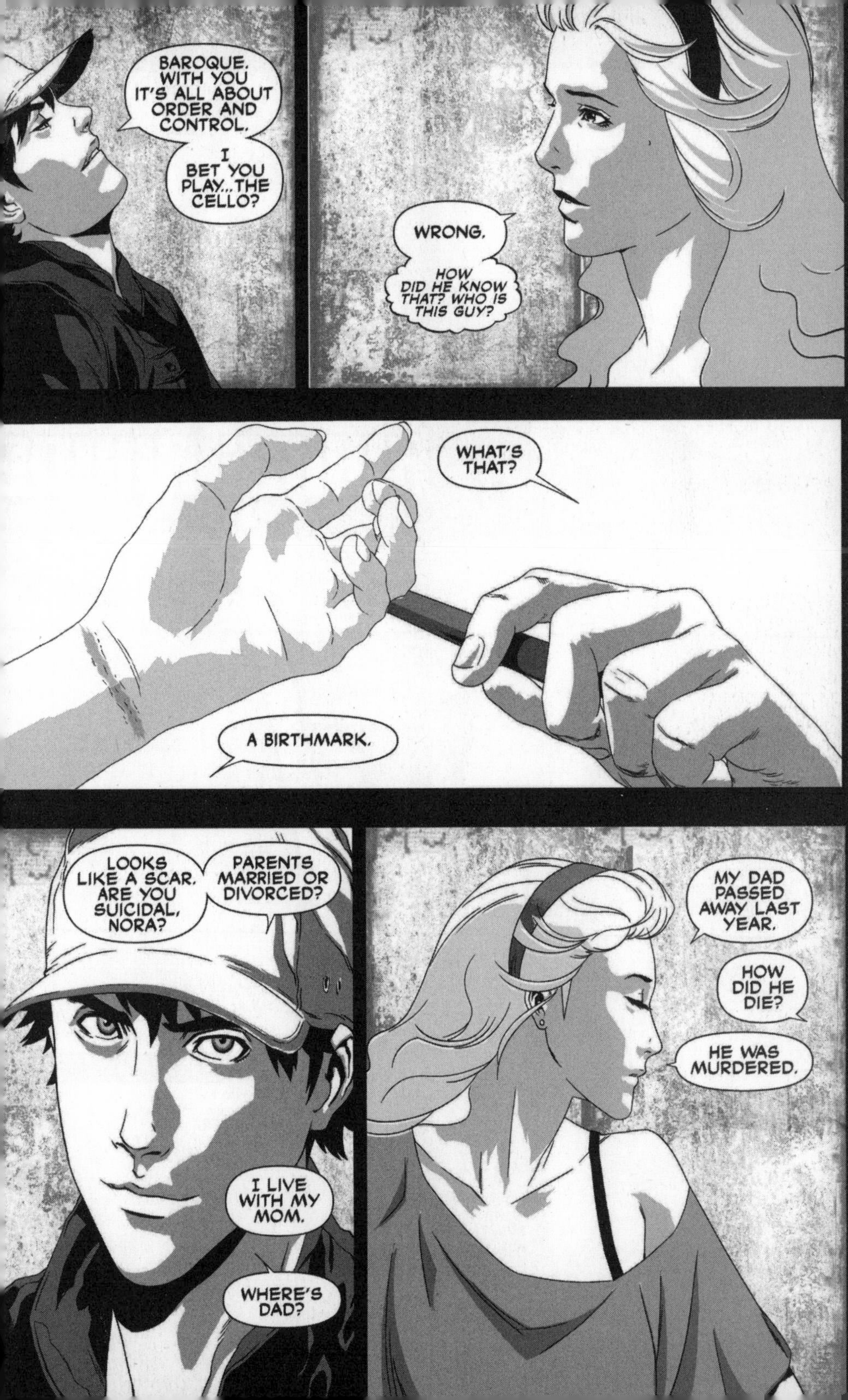
BAROQUE. WITH YOU IT'S ALL ABOUT ORDER AND CONTROL.
I BET YOU PLAY...THE CELLO?
WRONG.
HOW DID HE KNOW THAT? WHO IS THIS GUY?
WHAT'S THAT?
A BIRTHMARK.
LOOKS LIKE A SCAR. ARE YOU SUICIDAL, NORA?
PARENTS MARRIED OR DIVORCED?
I LIVE WITH MY MOM.
WHERE'S DAD?
MY DAD PASSED AWAY LAST YEAR.
HOW DID HE DIE?
HE WAS MURDERED.

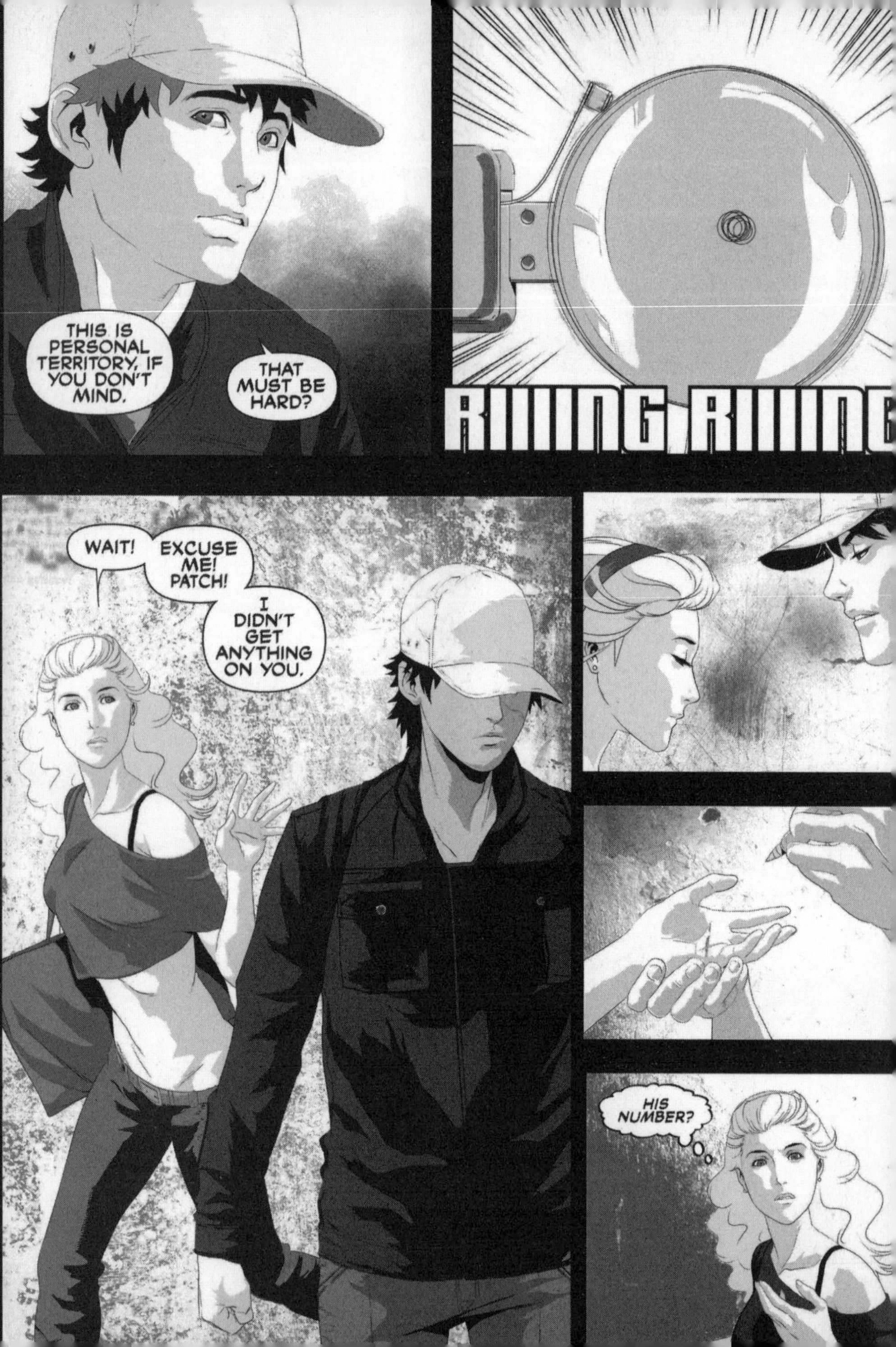
THIS IS PERSONAL TERRITORY, IF YOU DON'T MIND.
THAT MUST BE HARD?
RIIIING RIIIING
WAIT!
EXCUSE ME! PATCH!
I DIDN'T GET ANYTHING ON YOU.
HIS NUMBER?

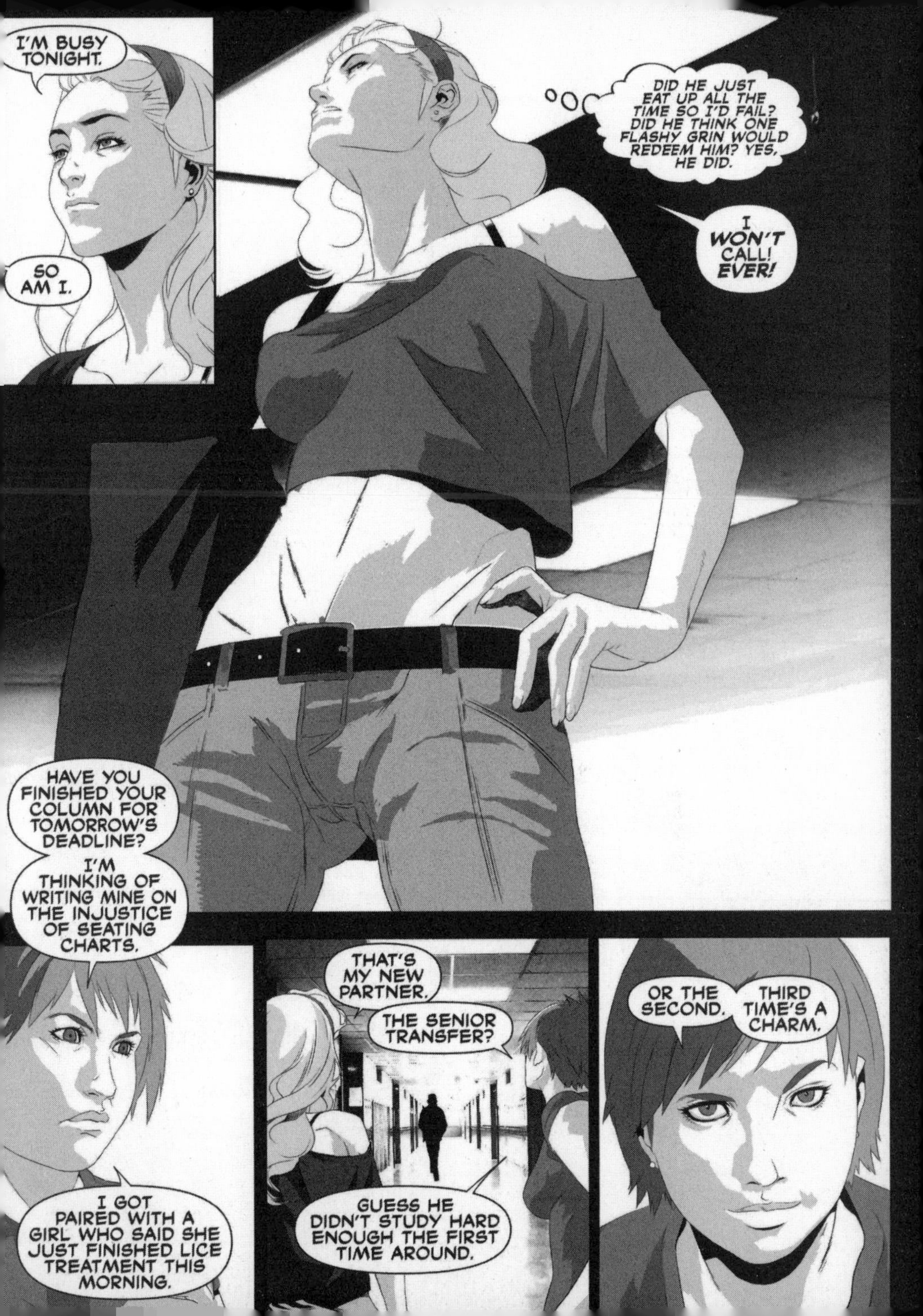
I'M BUSY TONIGHT.
SO AM I.
DID HE JUST EAT UP ALL THE TIME SO I'D FAIL? DID HE THINK ONE FLASHY GRIN WOULD REDEEM HIM? YES, HE DID.
I *WON'T* CALL! *EVER!*
HAVE YOU FINISHED YOUR COLUMN FOR TOMORROW'S DEADLINE?
I'M THINKING OF WRITING MINE ON THE INJUSTICE OF SEATING CHARTS.
I GOT PAIRED WITH A GIRL WHO SAID SHE JUST FINISHED LICE TREATMENT THIS MORNING.
THAT'S MY NEW PARTNER.
THE SENIOR TRANSFER?
GUESS HE DIDN'T STUDY HARD ENOUGH THE FIRST TIME AROUND.
OR THE SECOND.
THIRD TIME'S A CHARM.

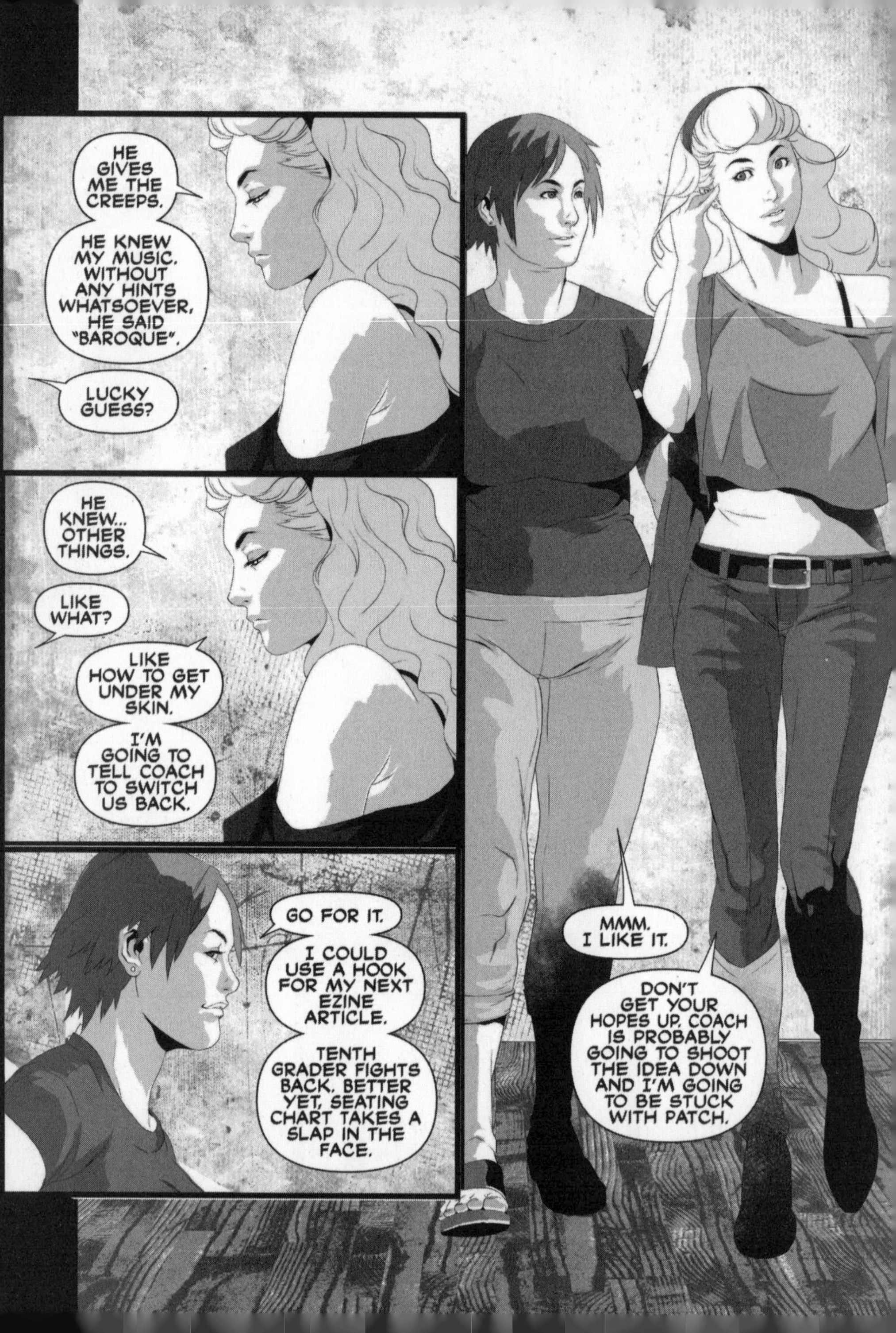
HE GIVES ME THE CREEPS.
HE KNEW MY MUSIC. WITHOUT ANY HINTS WHATSOEVER. HE SAID "BAROQUE".
LUCKY GUESS?
HE KNEW... OTHER THINGS.
LIKE WHAT?
LIKE HOW TO GET UNDER MY SKIN.
I'M GOING TO TELL COACH TO SWITCH US BACK.
GO FOR IT.
I COULD USE A HOOK FOR MY NEXT EZINE ARTICLE.
TENTH GRADER FIGHTS BACK. BETTER YET, SEATING CHART TAKES A SLAP IN THE FACE.
MMM. I LIKE IT.
DON'T GET YOUR HOPES UP. COACH IS PROBABLY GOING TO SHOOT THE IDEA DOWN AND I'M GOING TO BE STUCK WITH PATCH.

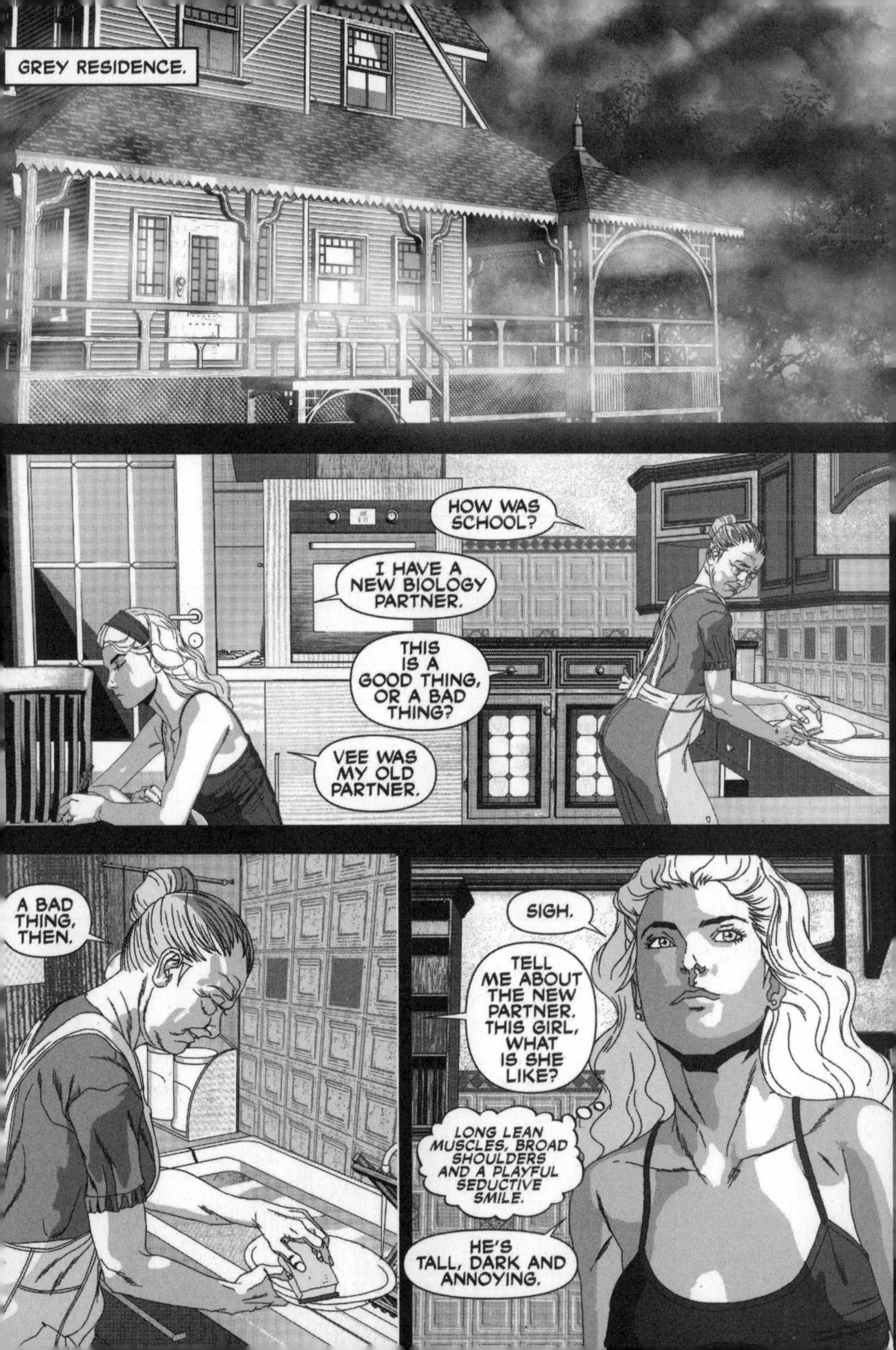

GREY RESIDENCE.
HOW WAS SCHOOL?
I HAVE A NEW BIOLOGY PARTNER.
THIS IS A GOOD THING, OR A BAD THING?
VEE WAS MY OLD PARTNER.
A BAD THING, THEN.
SIGH.
TELL ME ABOUT THE NEW PARTNER. THIS GIRL, WHAT IS SHE LIKE?
LONG LEAN MUSCLES, BROAD SHOULDERS AND A PLAYFUL SEDUCTIVE SMILE.
HE'S TALL, DARK AND ANNOYING.

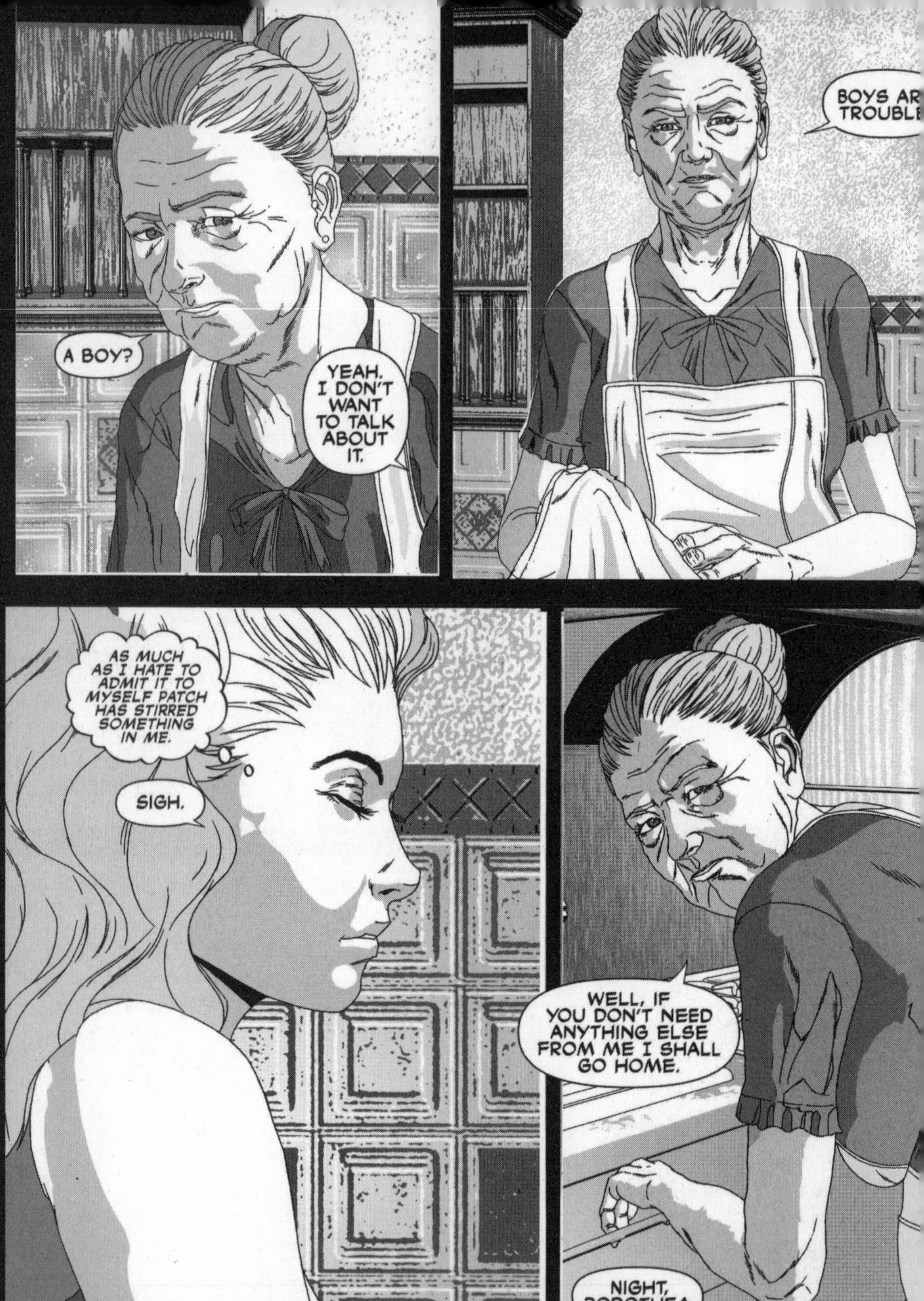
A BOY?
YEAH. I DON'T WANT TO TALK ABOUT IT.
BOYS AR
TROUBLE
AS MUCH AS I HATE TO ADMIT IT TO MYSELF PATCH HAS STIRRED SOMETHING IN ME.
SIGH.
WELL, IF YOU DON'T NEED ANYTHING ELSE FROM ME I SHALL GO HOME.
NIGHT, DOROTHEA.

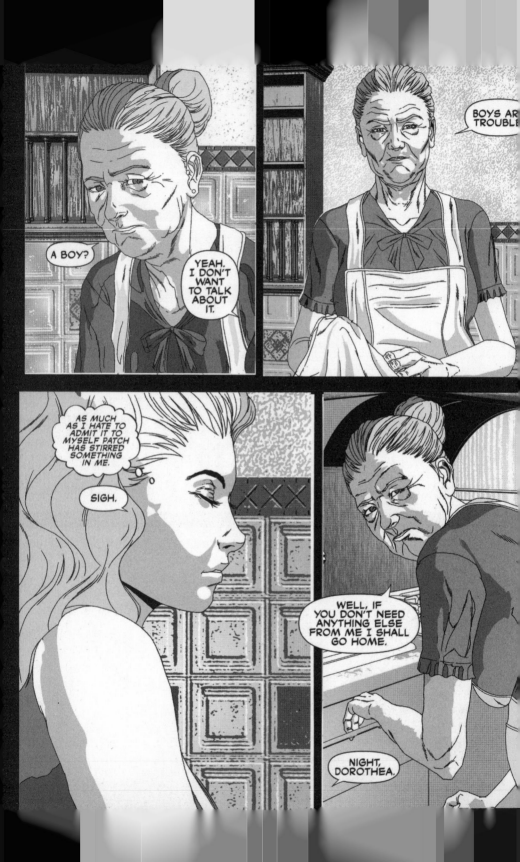

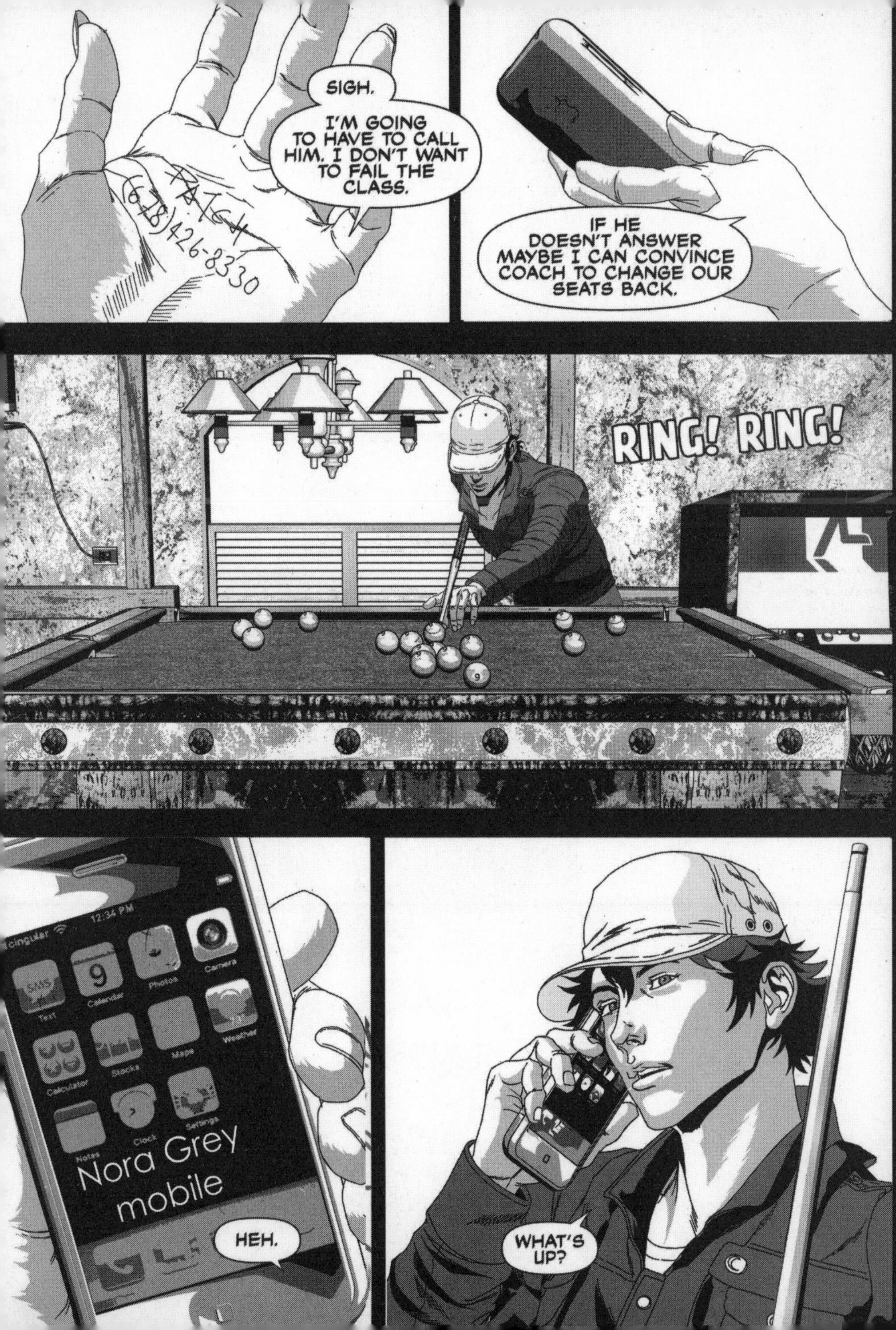
PATCH
(678)426-8330
SIGH.
I'M GOING TO HAVE TO CALL HIM. I DON'T WANT TO FAIL THE CLASS.
IF HE DOESN'T ANSWER MAYBE I CAN CONVINCE COACH TO CHANGE OUR SEATS BACK.
RING! RING!
12:34 PM
Cingular
Text
Calendar
Photos
Camera
Calculator
Stocks
Maps
Weather
Notes
Clock
Settings
Nora Grey
mobile
HEH.
WHAT'S UP?

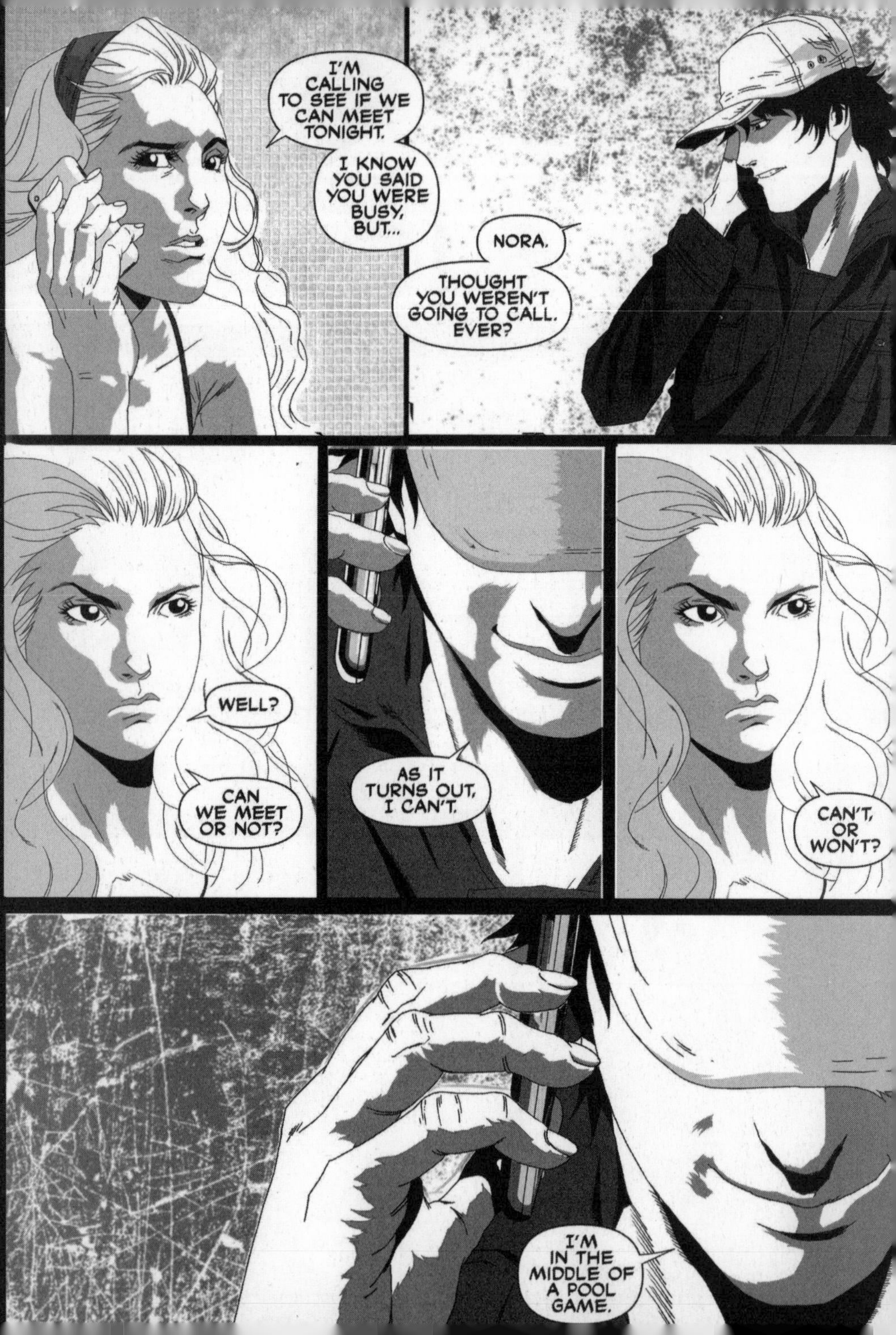
I'M CALLING TO SEE IF WE CAN MEET TONIGHT.
I KNOW YOU SAID YOU WERE BUSY, BUT...
NORA.
THOUGHT YOU WEREN'T GOING TO CALL. EVER?
WELL?
CAN WE MEET OR NOT?
AS IT TURNS OUT, I CAN'T.
CAN'T, OR WON'T?
I'M IN THE MIDDLE OF A POOL GAME.

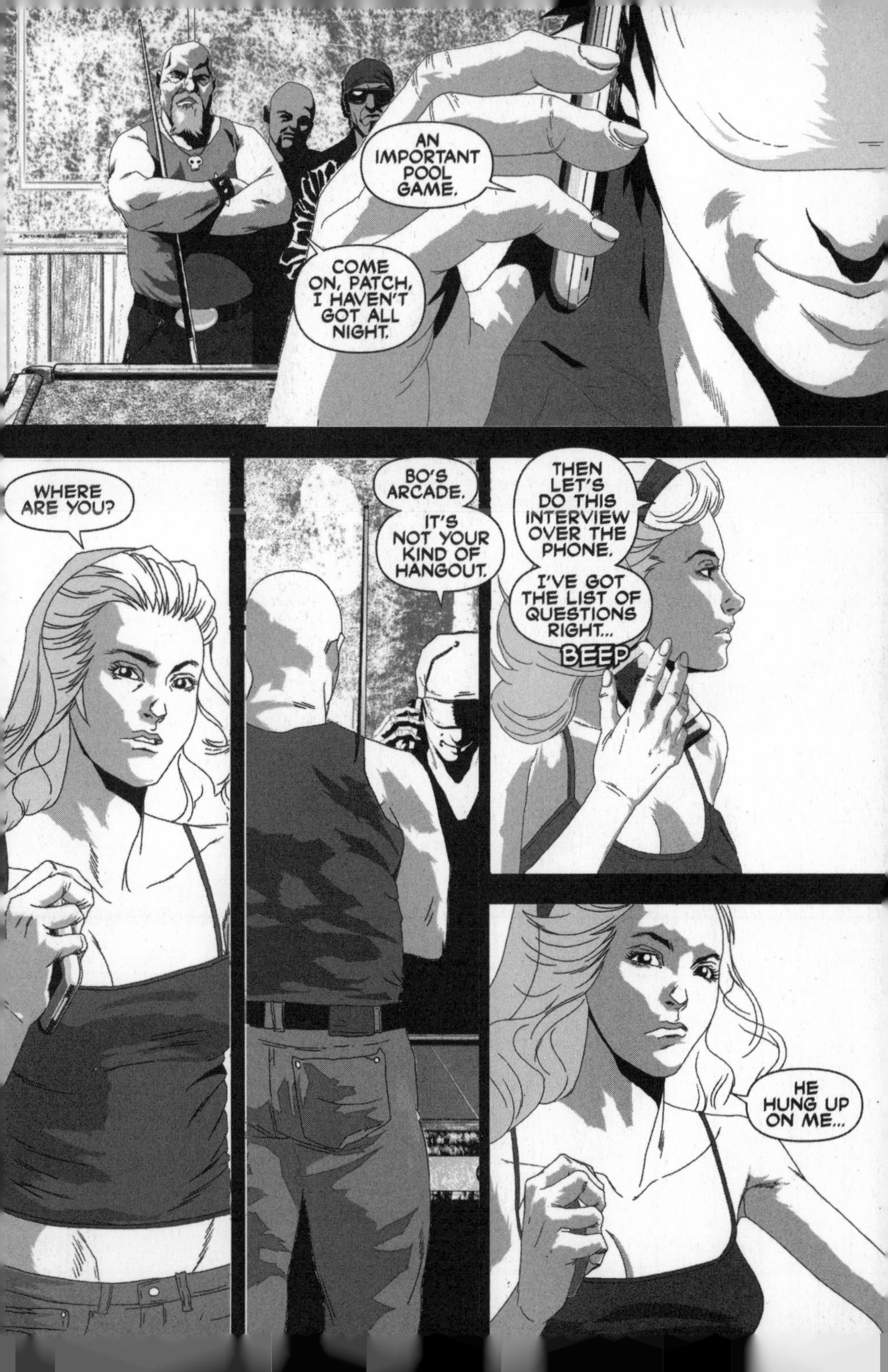
AN IMPORTANT POOL GAME.
COME ON, PATCH, I HAVEN'T GOT ALL NIGHT.
WHERE ARE YOU?
BO'S ARCADE.
IT'S NOT YOUR KIND OF HANGOUT.
THEN LET'S DO THIS INTERVIEW OVER THE PHONE.
I'VE GOT THE LIST OF QUESTIONS RIGHT...
BEEP
HE HUNG UP ON ME...

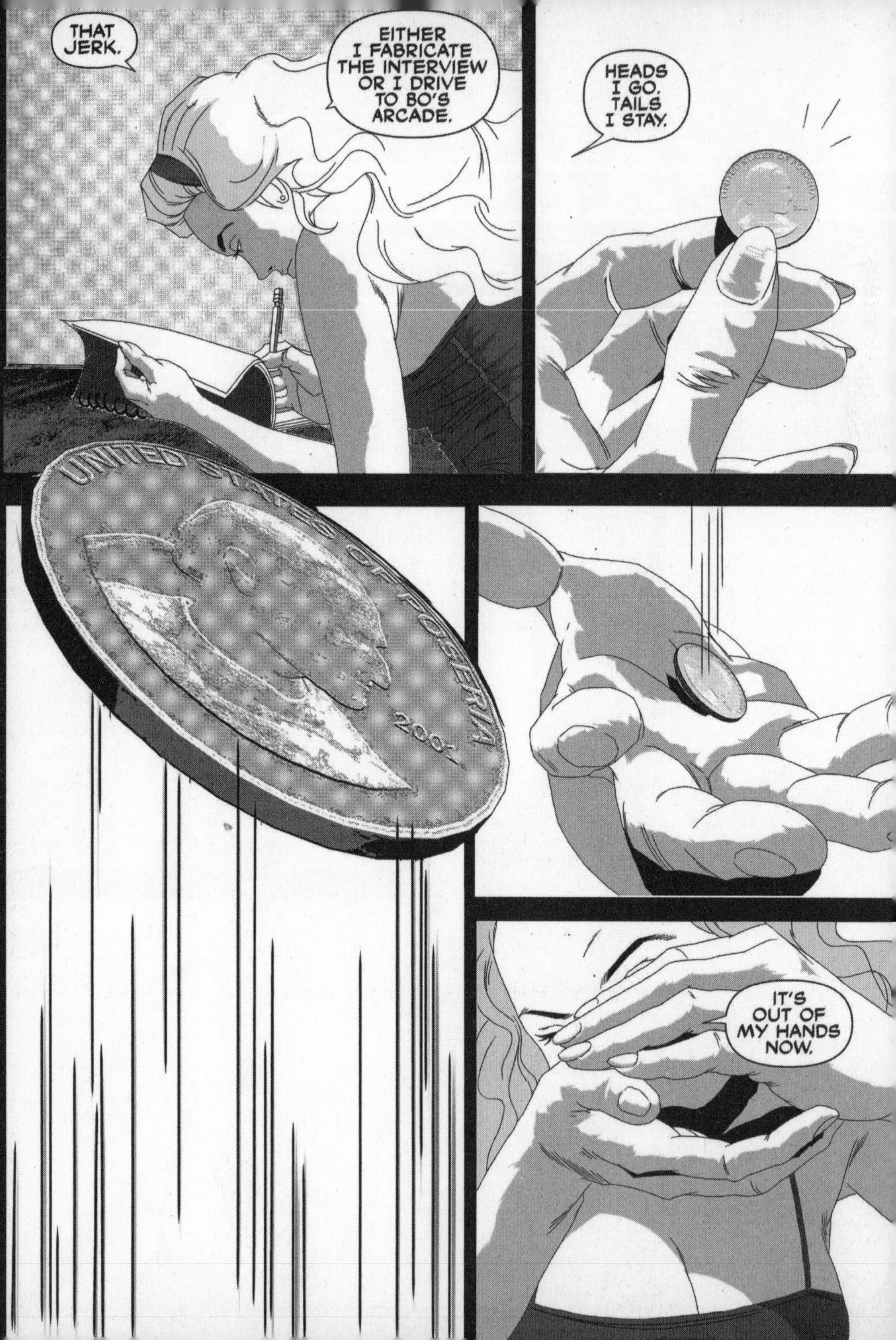
THAT JERK.
EITHER I FABRICATE THE INTERVIEW OR I DRIVE TO BO'S ARCADE.
HEADS I GO. TAILS I STAY.
UNITED STATES OF POSERIA
2001
IT'S OUT OF MY HANDS NOW.

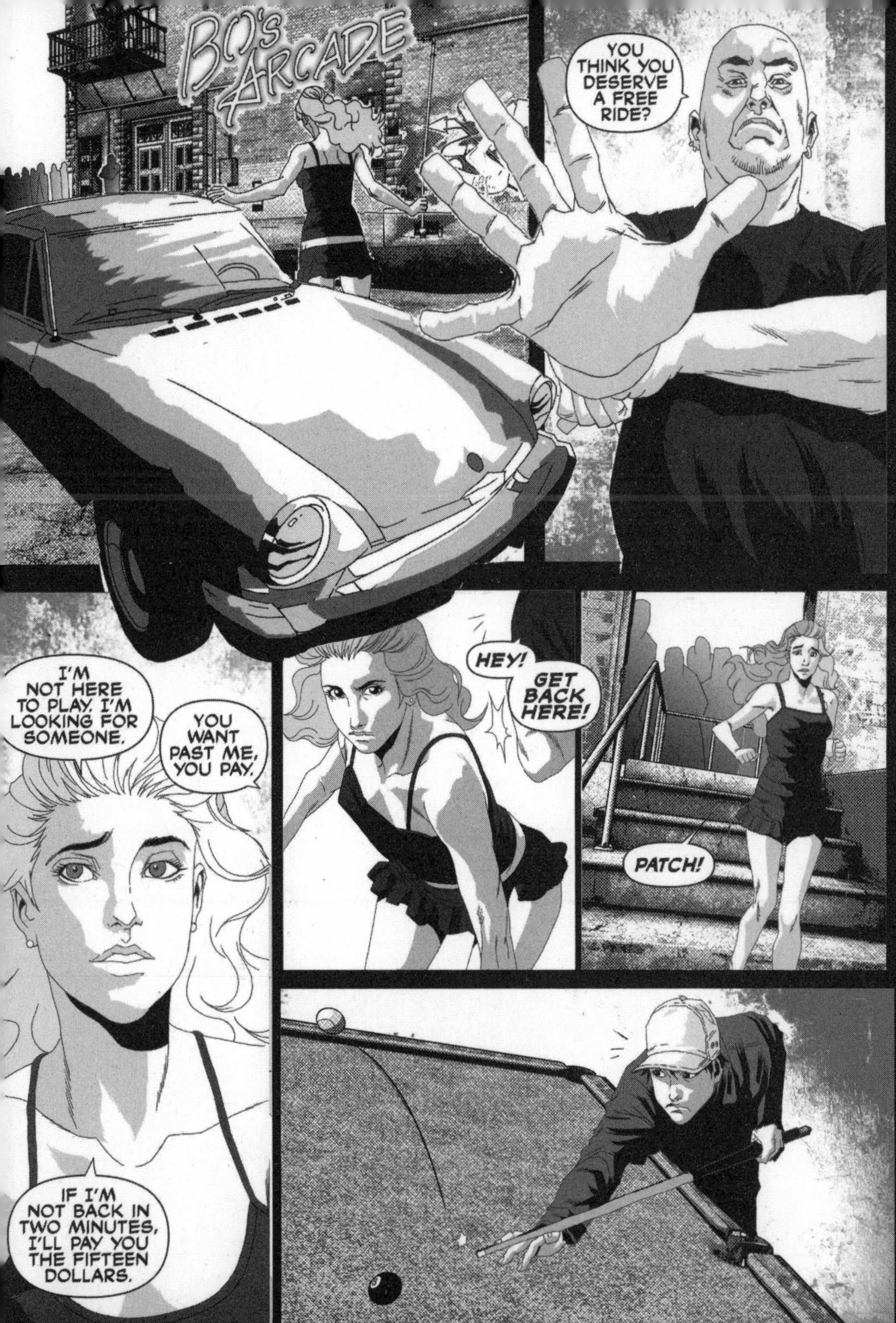
BO'S ARCADE
YOU THINK YOU DESERVE A FREE RIDE?
I'M NOT HERE TO PLAY. I'M LOOKING FOR SOMEONE.
YOU WANT PAST ME, YOU PAY.
IF I'M NOT BACK IN TWO MINUTES, I'LL PAY YOU THE FIFTEEN DOLLARS.
HEY!
GET BACK HERE!
PATCH!

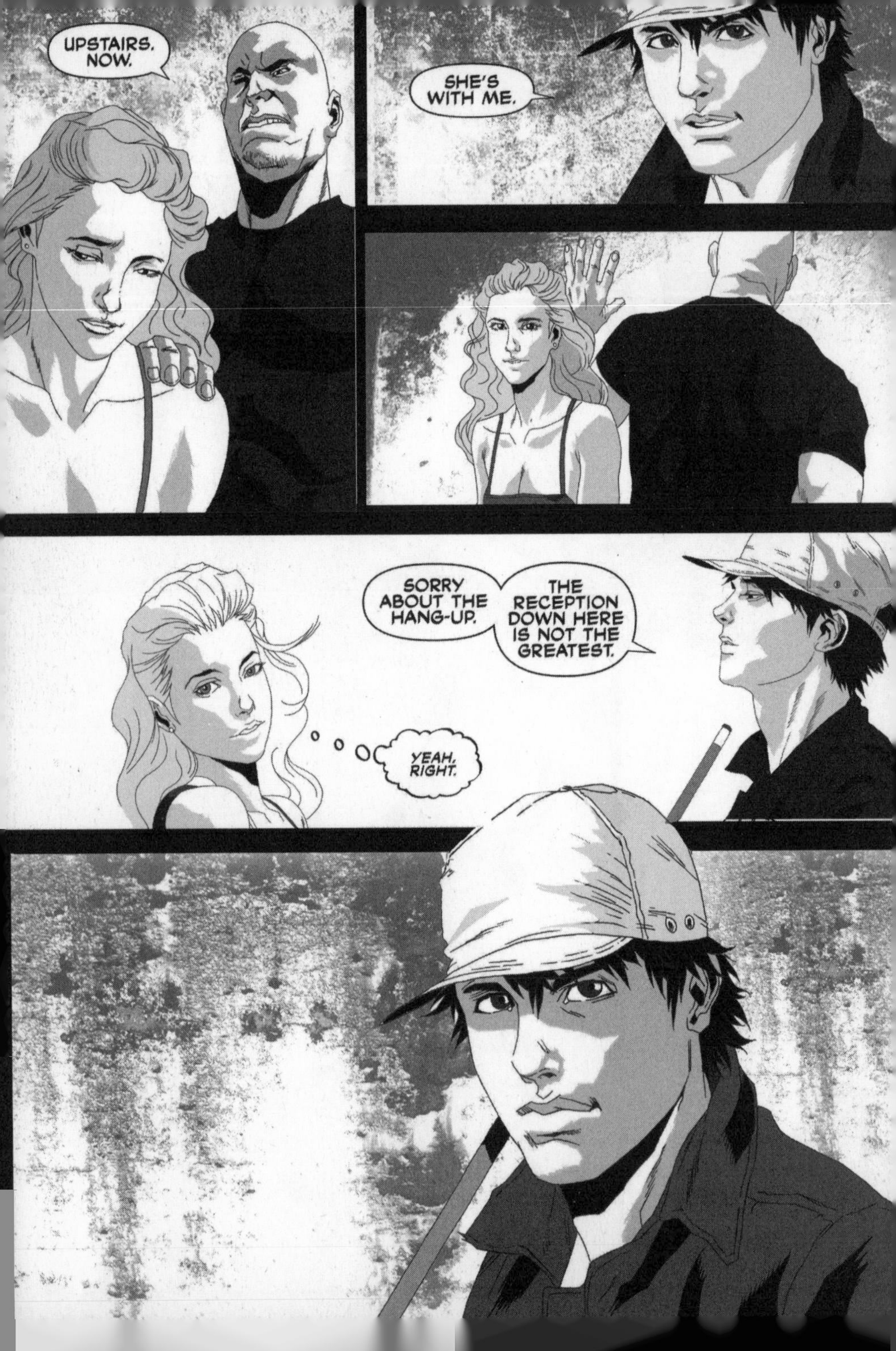
UPSTAIRS. NOW.
SHE'S WITH ME.
SORRY ABOUT THE HANG-UP.
THE RECEPTION DOWN HERE IS NOT THE GREATEST.
YEAH, RIGHT.

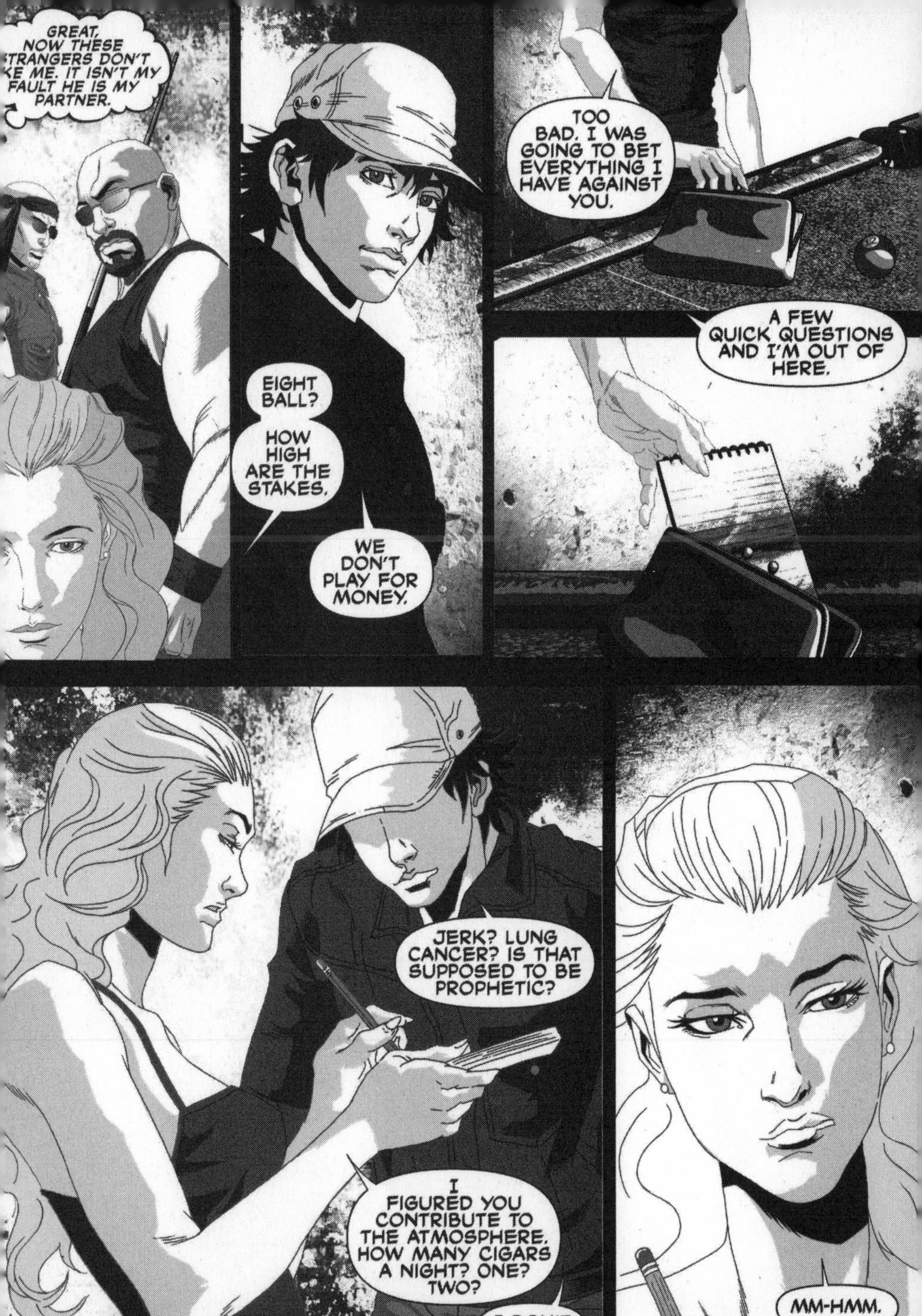
GREAT, NOW THESE STRANGERS DON'T LIKE ME. IT ISN'T MY FAULT HE IS MY PARTNER.
EIGHT BALL?
HOW HIGH ARE THE STAKES.
WE DON'T PLAY FOR MONEY.
TOO BAD. I WAS GOING TO BET EVERYTHING I HAVE AGAINST YOU.
A FEW QUICK QUESTIONS AND I'M OUT OF HERE.
JERK? LUNG CANCER? IS THAT SUPPOSED TO BE PROPHETIC?
I FIGURED YOU CONTRIBUTE TO THE ATMOSPHERE. HOW MANY CIGARS A NIGHT? ONE? TWO?
I DON'T SMOKE.
MM-HMM.

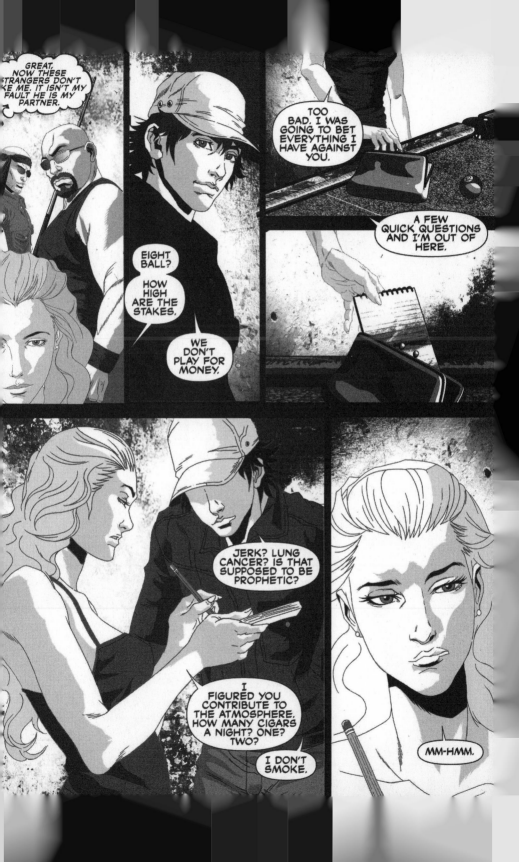

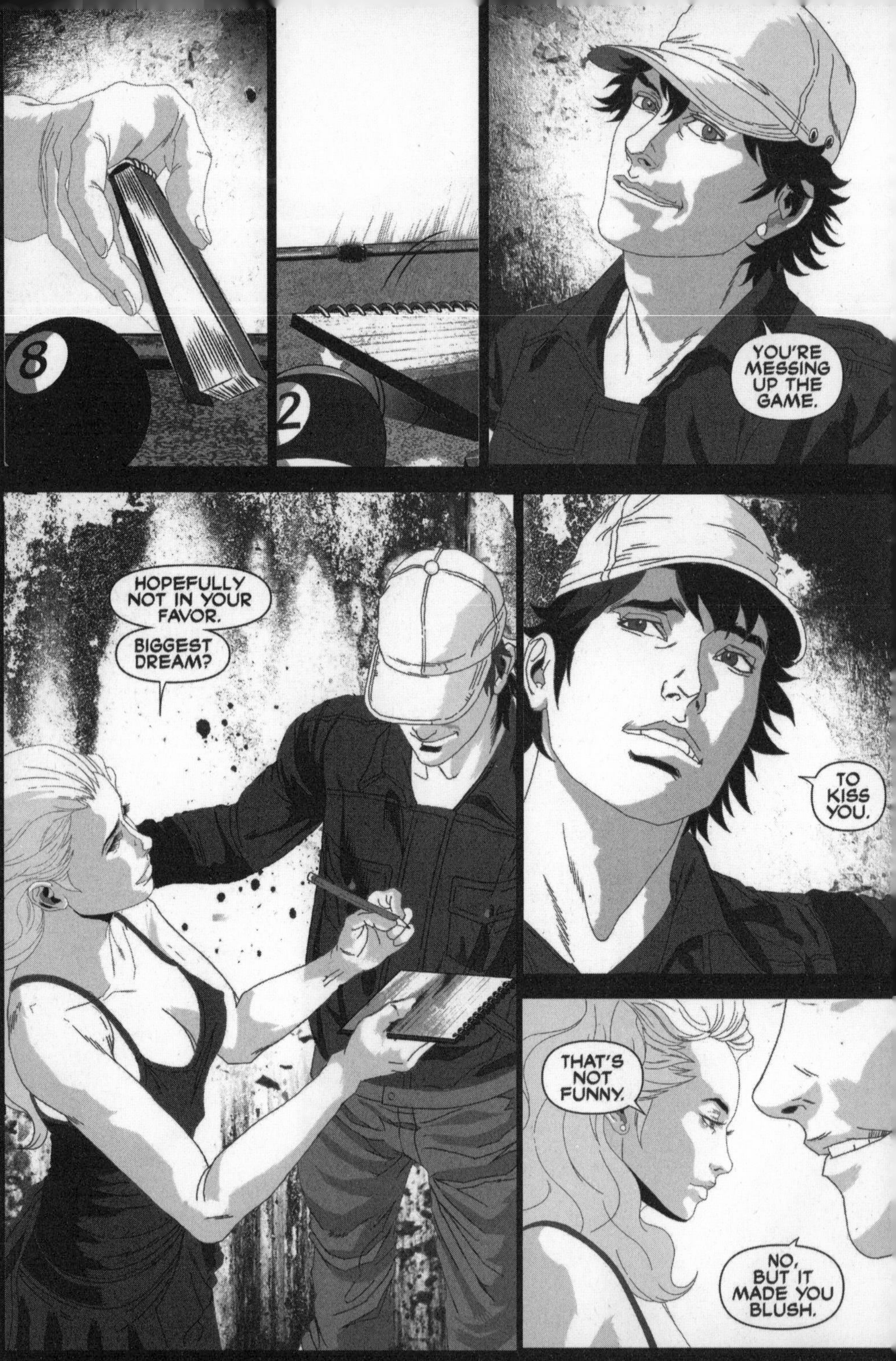
YOU'RE MESSING UP THE GAME.
HOPEFULLY NOT IN YOUR FAVOR.
BIGGEST DREAM?
TO KISS YOU.
THAT'S NOT FUNNY.
NO, BUT IT MADE YOU BLUSH.

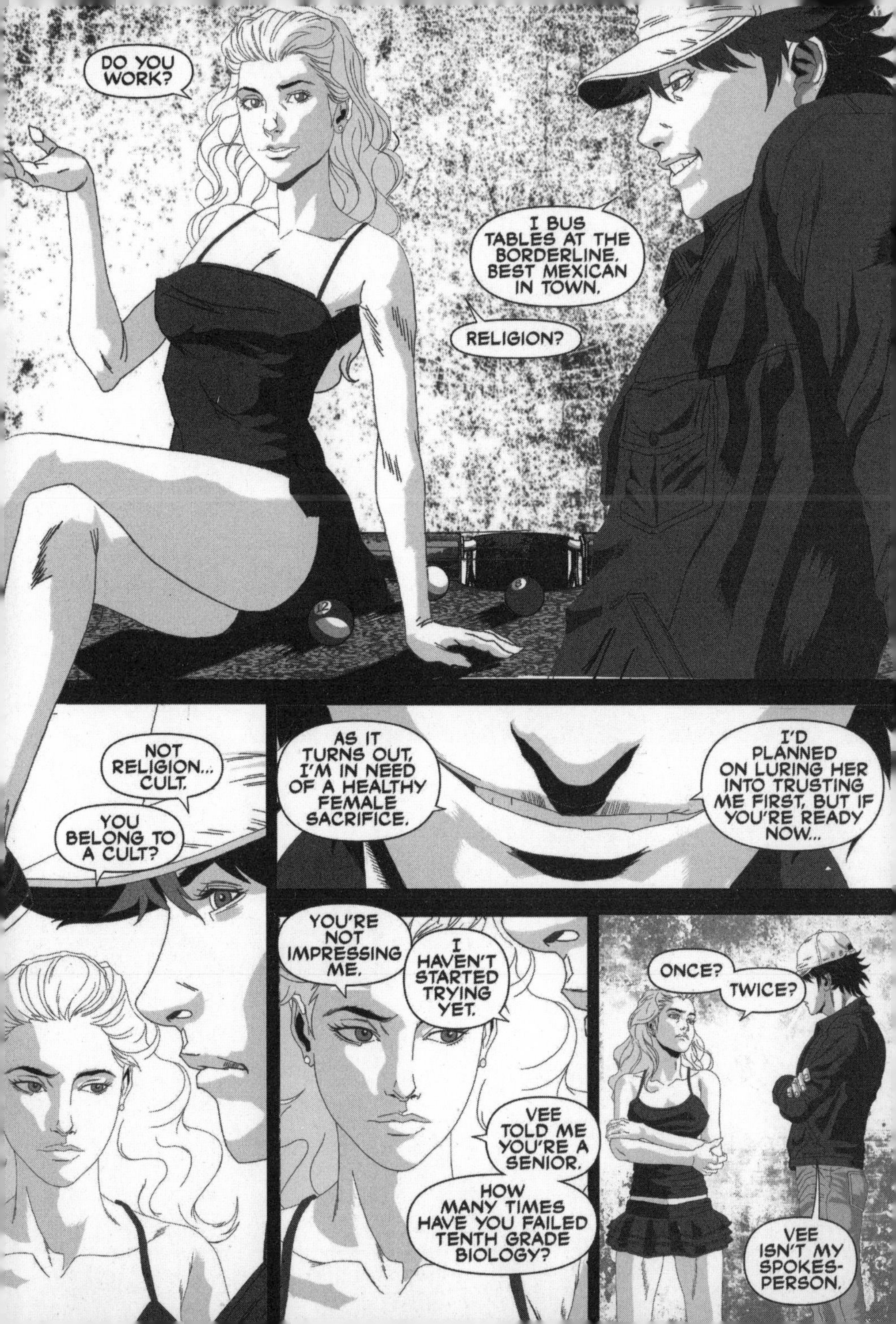
DO YOU WORK?
I BUS TABLES AT THE BORDERLINE. BEST MEXICAN IN TOWN.
RELIGION?
NOT RELIGION... CULT.
YOU BELONG TO A CULT?
AS IT TURNS OUT, I'M IN NEED OF A HEALTHY FEMALE SACRIFICE.
I'D PLANNED ON LURING HER INTO TRUSTING ME FIRST, BUT IF YOU'RE READY NOW...
YOU'RE NOT IMPRESSING ME.
I HAVEN'T STARTED TRYING YET.
VEE TOLD ME YOU'RE A SENIOR.
HOW MANY TIMES HAVE YOU FAILED TENTH GRADE BIOLOGY?
ONCE?
TWICE?
VEE ISN'T MY SPOKES-PERSON.

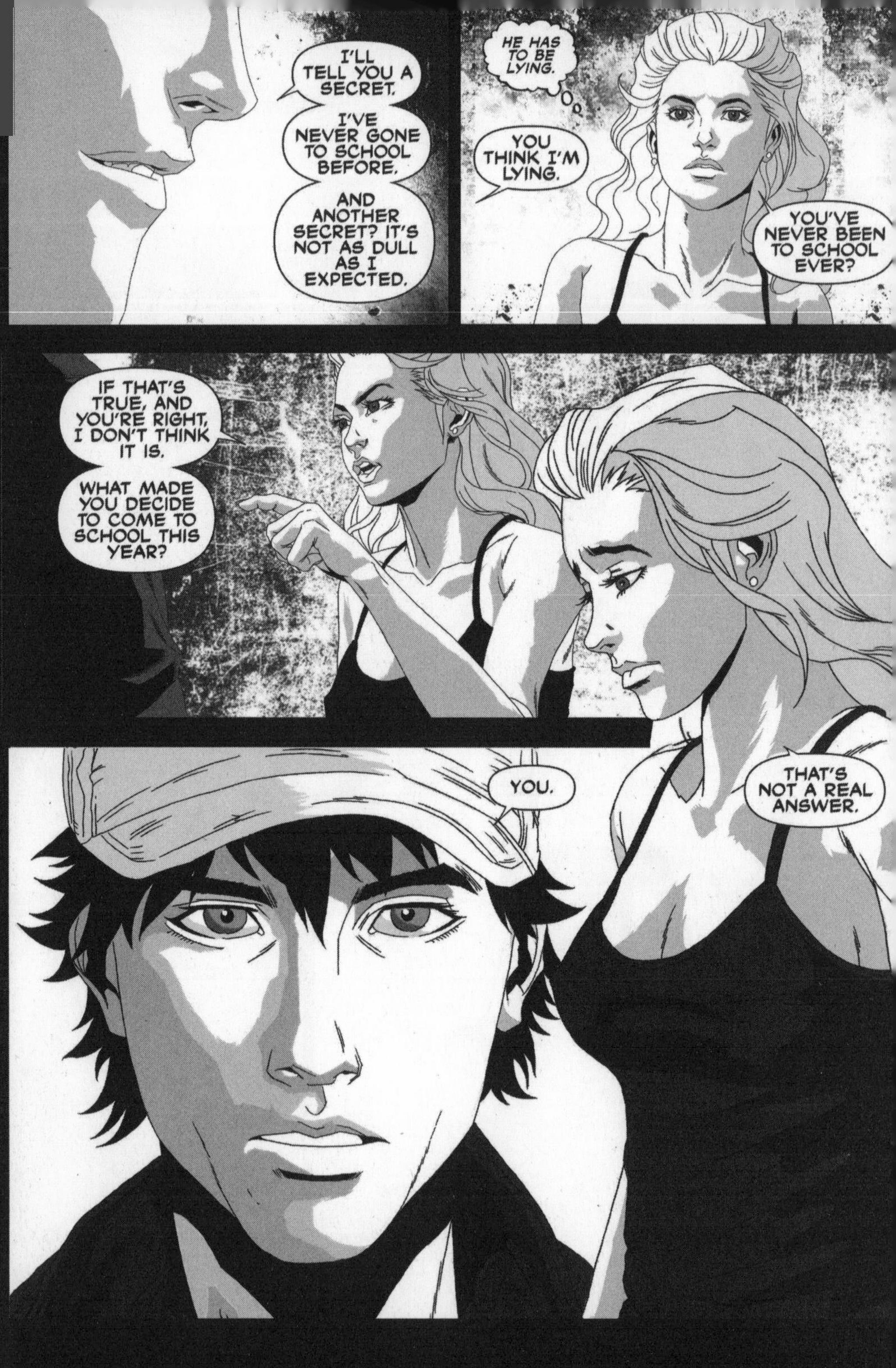
I'LL TELL YOU A SECRET.
I'VE NEVER GONE TO SCHOOL BEFORE.
AND ANOTHER SECRET? IT'S NOT AS DULL AS I EXPECTED.
HE HAS TO BE LYING.
YOU THINK I'M LYING.
YOU'VE NEVER BEEN TO SCHOOL EVER?
IF THAT'S TRUE, AND YOU'RE RIGHT, I DON'T THINK IT IS.
WHAT MADE YOU DECIDE TO COME TO SCHOOL THIS YEAR?
YOU.
THAT'S NOT A REAL ANSWER.

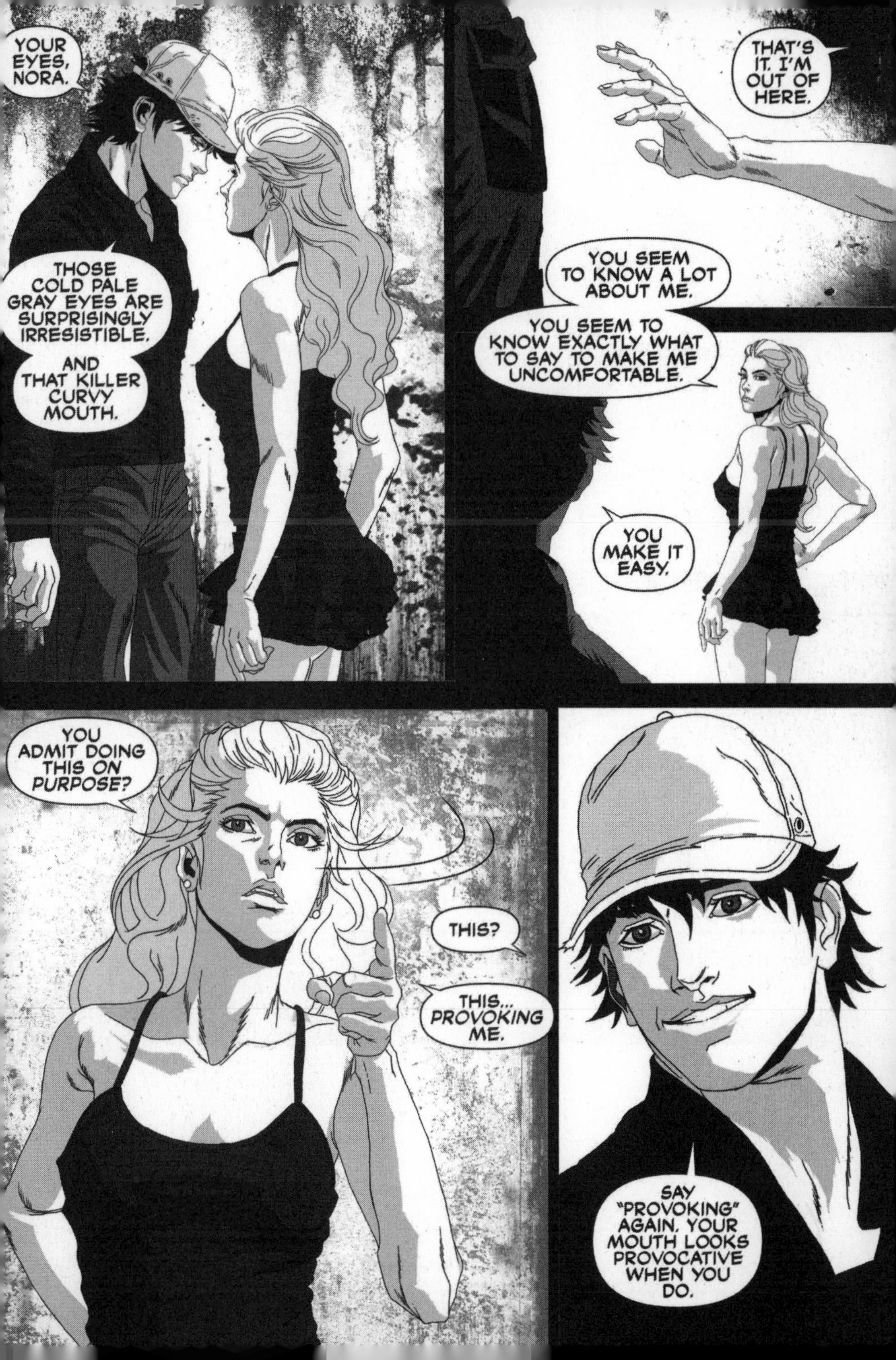
YOUR EYES, NORA.
THOSE COLD PALE GRAY EYES ARE SURPRISINGLY IRRESISTIBLE.
AND THAT KILLER CURVY MOUTH.
THAT'S IT. I'M OUT OF HERE.
YOU SEEM TO KNOW A LOT ABOUT ME.
YOU SEEM TO KNOW EXACTLY WHAT TO SAY TO MAKE ME UNCOMFORTABLE.
YOU MAKE IT EASY.
YOU ADMIT DOING THIS ON PURPOSE?
THIS?
THIS... PROVOKING ME.
SAY "PROVOKING" AGAIN. YOUR MOUTH LOOKS PROVOCATIVE WHEN YOU DO.

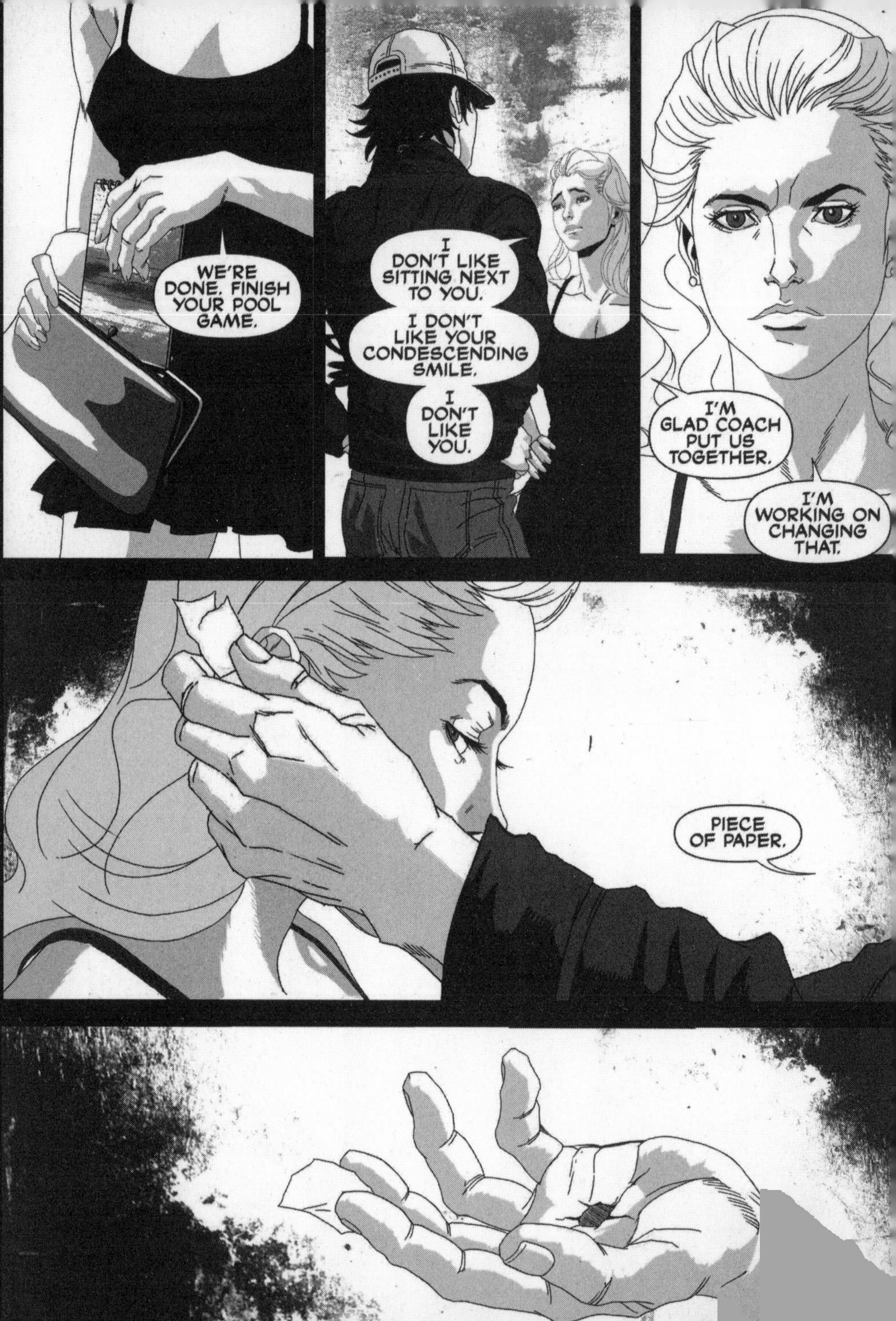
WE'RE DONE. FINISH YOUR POOL GAME.
I DON'T LIKE SITTING NEXT TO YOU.
I DON'T LIKE YOUR CONDESCENDING SMILE.
I DON'T LIKE YOU.
I'M GLAD COACH PUT US TOGETHER.
I'M WORKING ON CHANGING THAT.
PIECE OF PAPER.

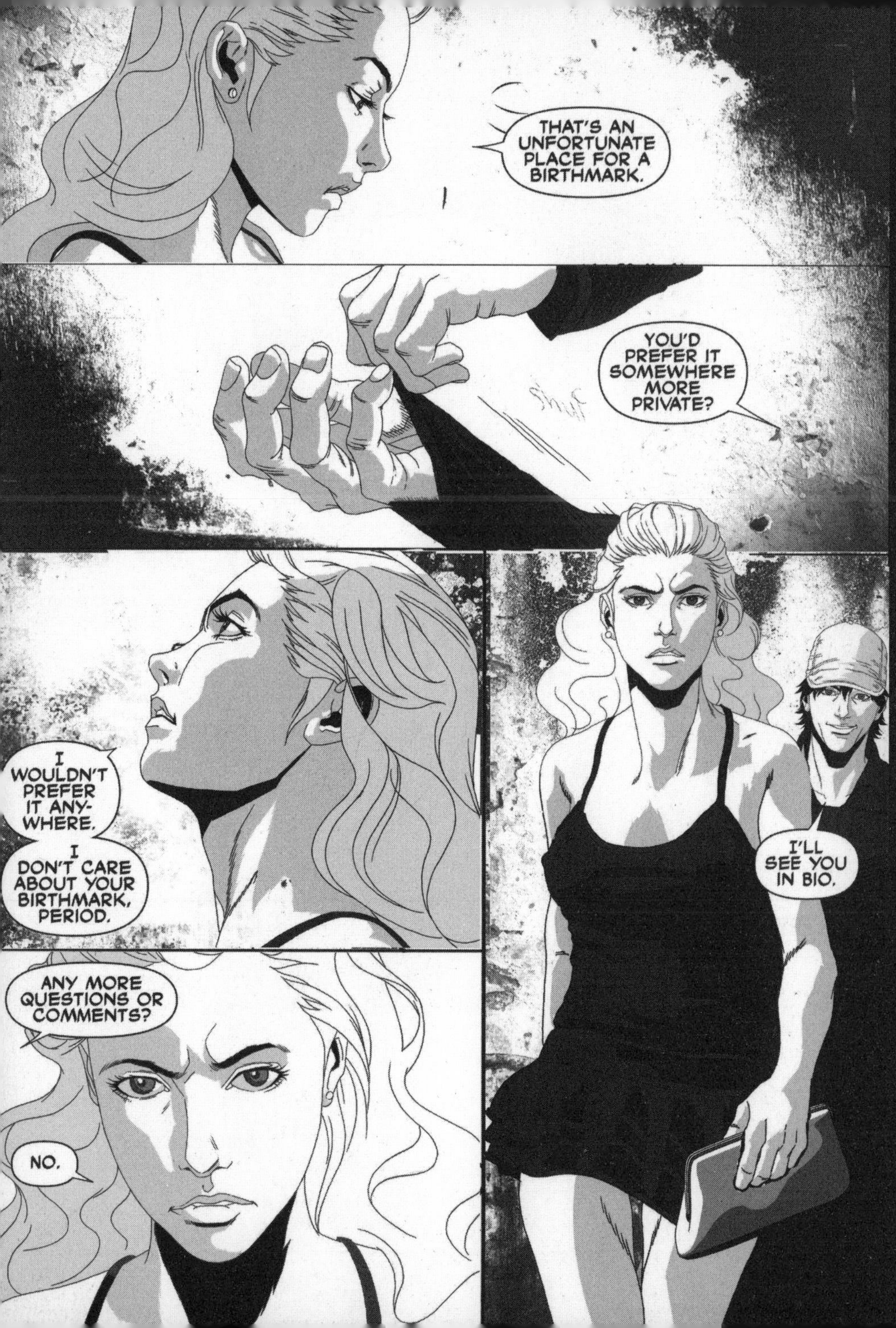
THAT'S AN UNFORTUNATE PLACE FOR A BIRTHMARK.
YOU'D PREFER IT SOMEWHERE MORE PRIVATE?
I WOULDN'T PREFER IT ANY-WHERE.
I DON'T CARE ABOUT YOUR BIRTHMARK, PERIOD.
ANY MORE QUESTIONS OR COMMENTS?
NO.
I'LL SEE YOU IN BIO.

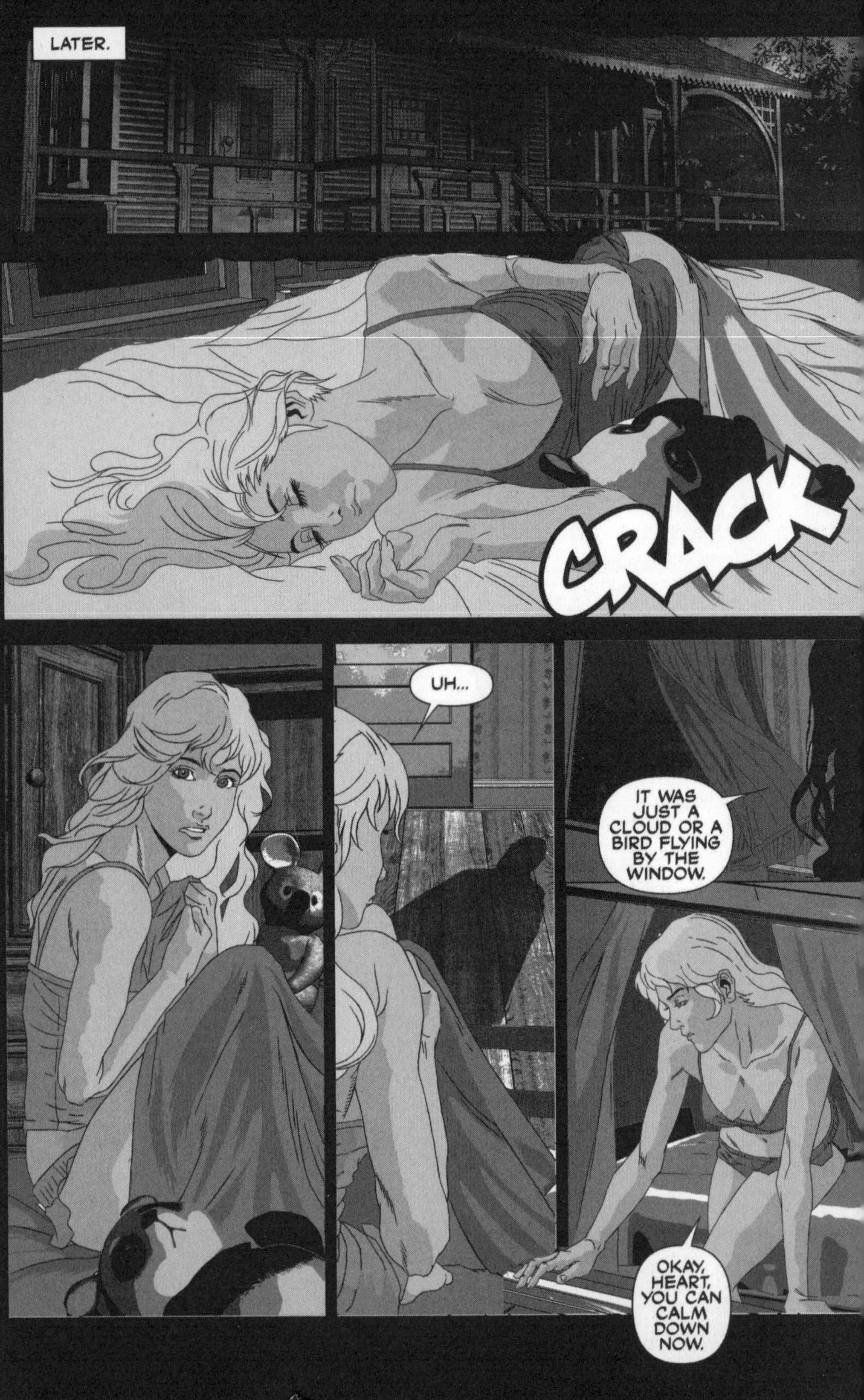
LATER.
CRACK
UH...
IT WAS JUST A CLOUD OR A BIRD FLYING BY THE WINDOW.
OKAY, HEART, YOU CAN CALM DOWN NOW.

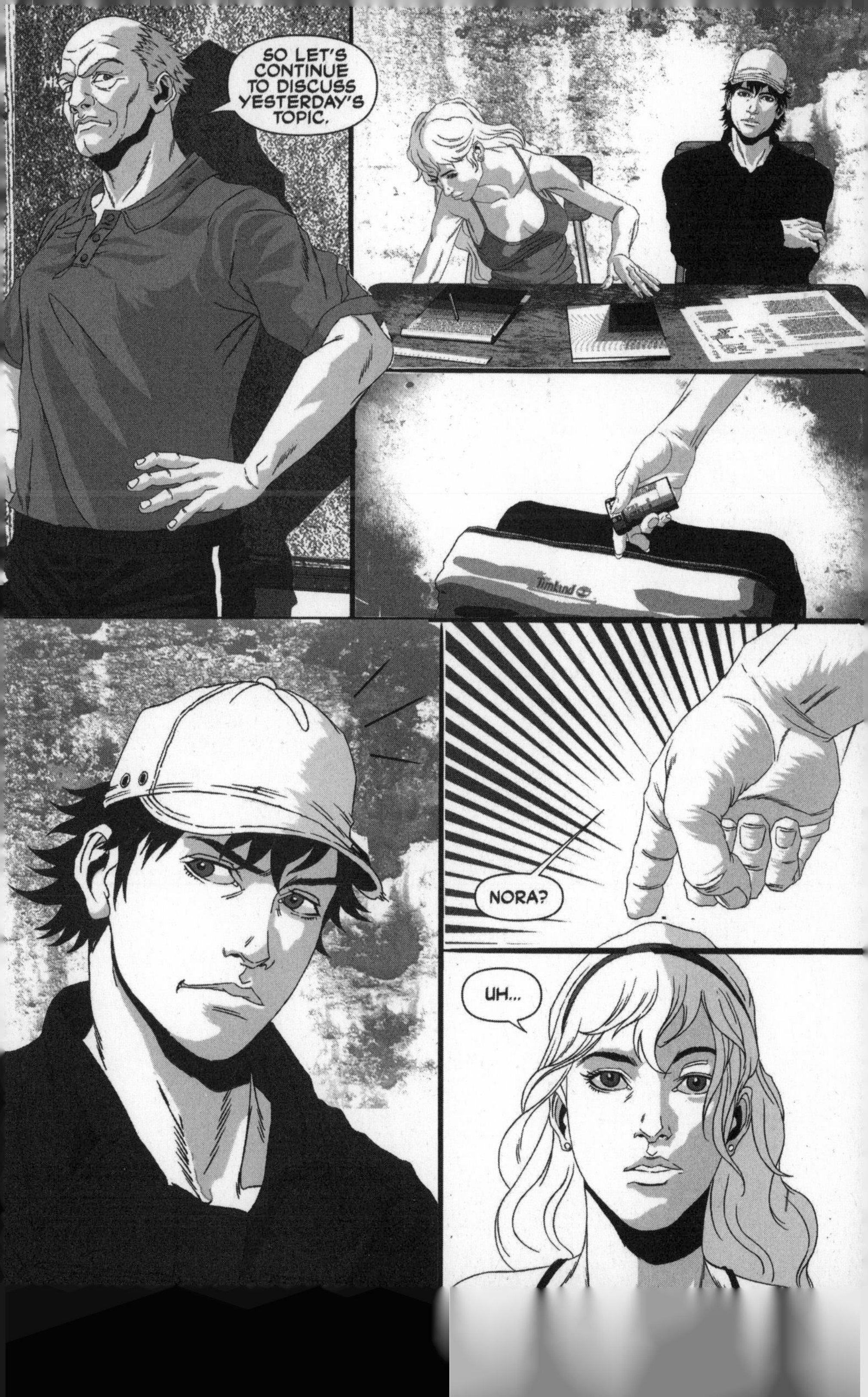
SO LET'S CONTINUE TO DISCUSS YESTERDAY'S TOPIC.
Timland
NORA?
UH...

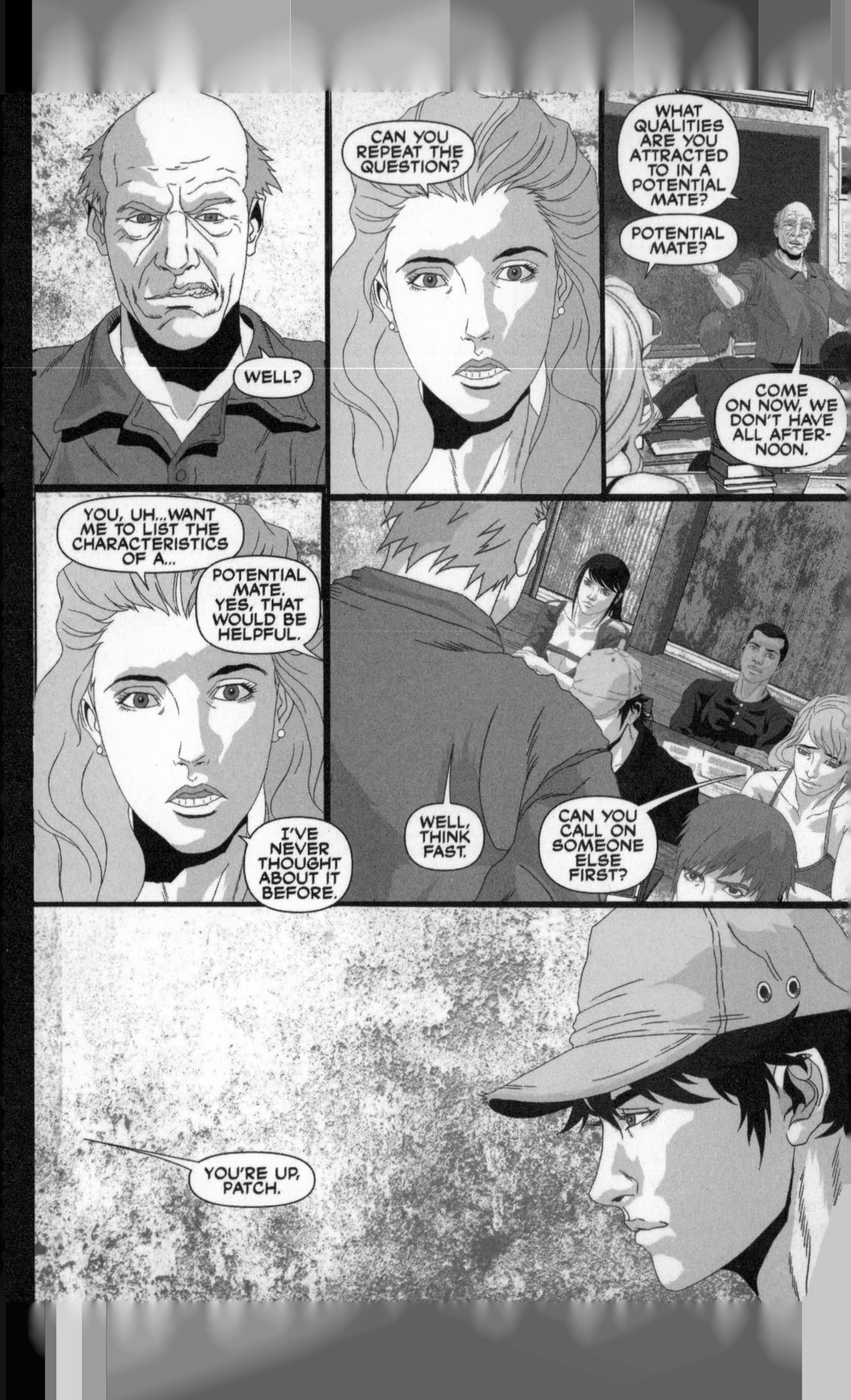
WELL?
CAN YOU REPEAT THE QUESTION?
WHAT QUALITIES ARE YOU ATTRACTED TO IN A POTENTIAL MATE?
POTENTIAL MATE?
COME ON NOW, WE DON'T HAVE ALL AFTER-NOON.
YOU, UH...WANT ME TO LIST THE CHARACTERISTICS OF A...
POTENTIAL MATE. YES, THAT WOULD BE HELPFUL.
I'VE NEVER THOUGHT ABOUT IT BEFORE.
WELL, THINK FAST.
CAN YOU CALL ON SOMEONE ELSE FIRST?
YOU'RE UP, PATCH.

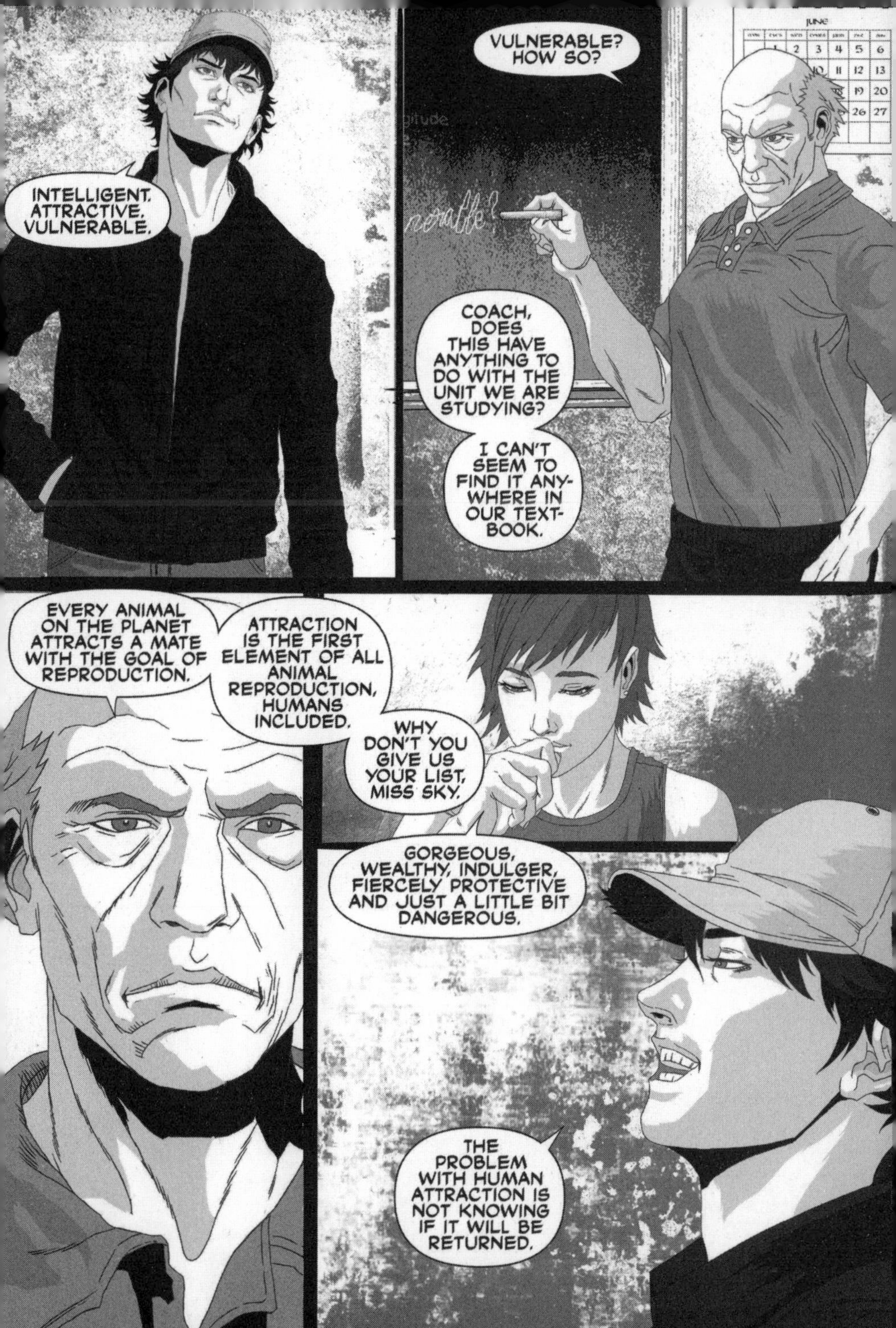

INTELLIGENT. ATTRACTIVE. VULNERABLE.
VULNERABLE? HOW SO?
COACH, DOES THIS HAVE ANYTHING TO DO WITH THE UNIT WE ARE STUDYING?
I CAN'T SEEM TO FIND IT ANY-WHERE IN OUR TEXT-BOOK.
EVERY ANIMAL ON THE PLANET ATTRACTS A MATE WITH THE GOAL OF REPRODUCTION.
ATTRACTION IS THE FIRST ELEMENT OF ALL ANIMAL REPRODUCTION, HUMANS INCLUDED.
WHY DON'T YOU GIVE US YOUR LIST, MISS SKY.
GORGEOUS, WEALTHY, INDULGER, FIERCELY PROTECTIVE AND JUST A LITTLE BIT DANGEROUS.
THE PROBLEM WITH HUMAN ATTRACTION IS NOT KNOWING IF IT WILL BE RETURNED.

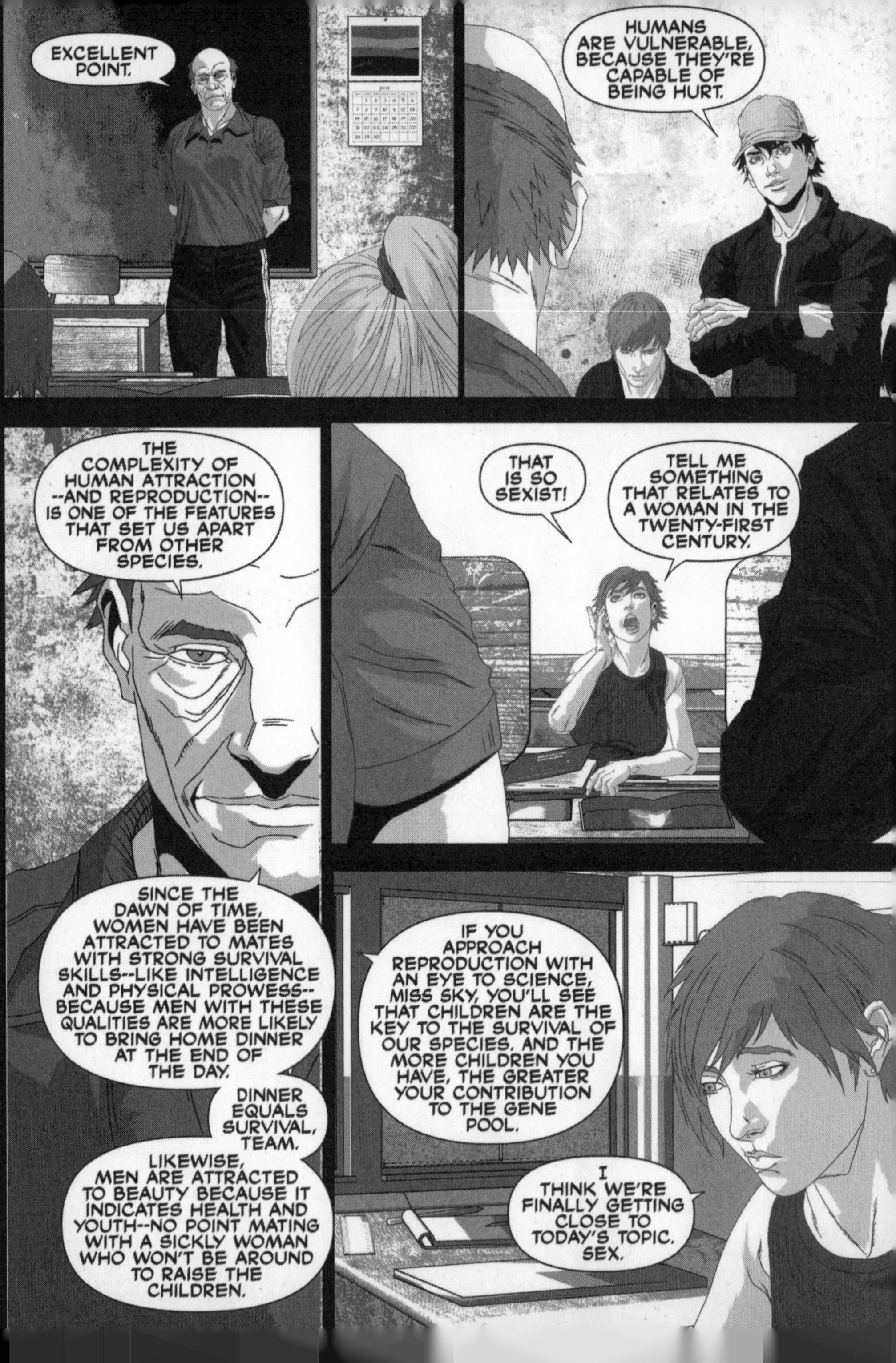
EXCELLENT POINT.
HUMANS ARE VULNERABLE, BECAUSE THEY'RE CAPABLE OF BEING HURT.
THE COMPLEXITY OF HUMAN ATTRACTION --AND REPRODUCTION-- IS ONE OF THE FEATURES THAT SET US APART FROM OTHER SPECIES.
THAT IS SO SEXIST!
TELL ME SOMETHING THAT RELATES TO A WOMAN IN THE TWENTY-FIRST CENTURY.
SINCE THE DAWN OF TIME, WOMEN HAVE BEEN ATTRACTED TO MATES WITH STRONG SURVIVAL SKILLS--LIKE INTELLIGENCE AND PHYSICAL PROWESS--BECAUSE MEN WITH THESE QUALITIES ARE MORE LIKELY TO BRING HOME DINNER AT THE END OF THE DAY.
DINNER EQUALS SURVIVAL, TEAM.
LIKEWISE, MEN ARE ATTRACTED TO BEAUTY BECAUSE IT INDICATES HEALTH AND YOUTH--NO POINT MATING WITH A SICKLY WOMAN WHO WON'T BE AROUND TO RAISE THE CHILDREN.
IF YOU APPROACH REPRODUCTION WITH AN EYE TO SCIENCE, MISS SKY, YOU'LL SEE THAT CHILDREN ARE THE KEY TO THE SURVIVAL OF OUR SPECIES. AND THE MORE CHILDREN YOU HAVE, THE GREATER YOUR CONTRIBUTION TO THE GENE POOL.
I THINK WE'RE FINALLY GETTING CLOSE TO TODAY'S TOPIC. SEX.

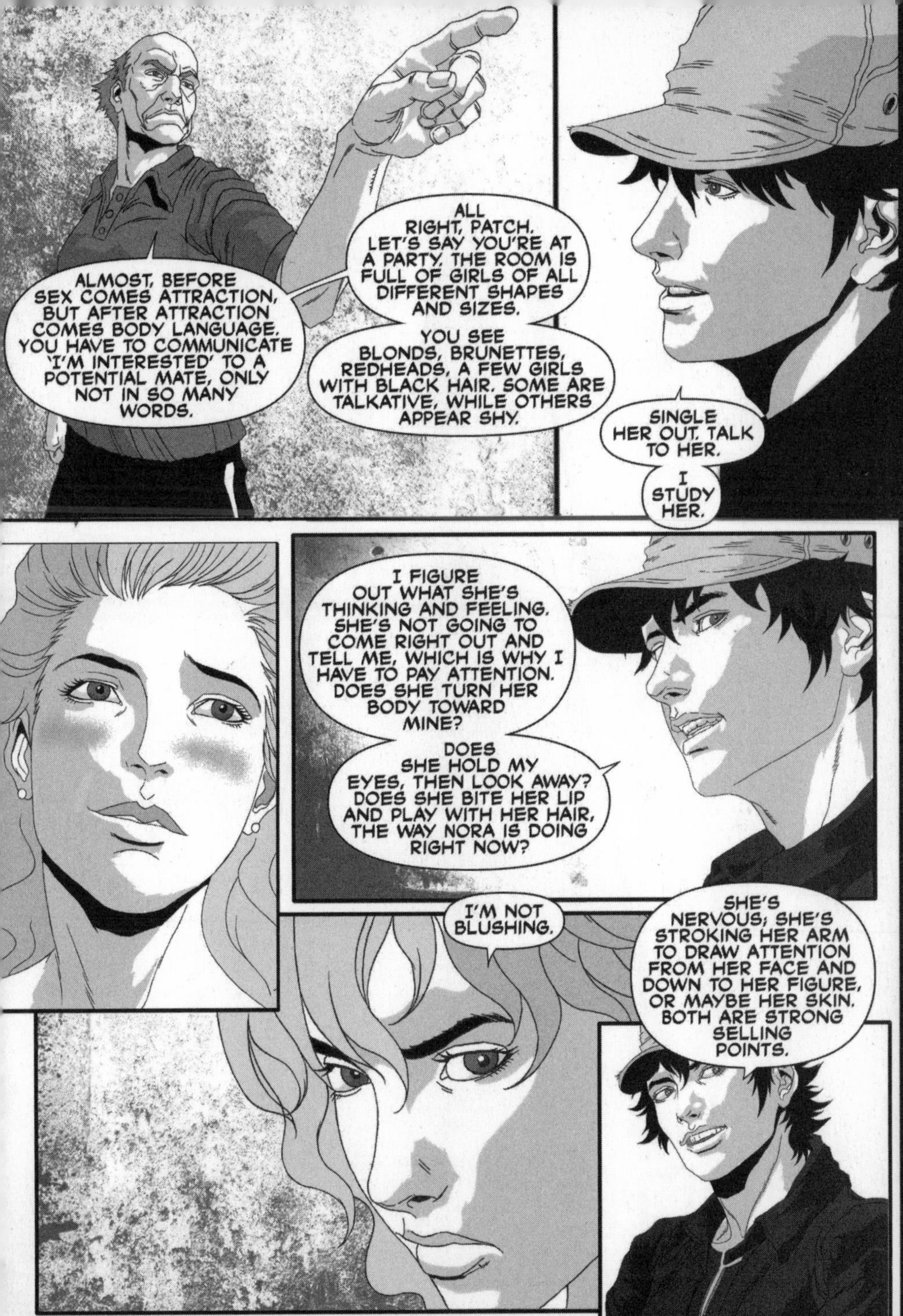
ALMOST, BEFORE SEX COMES ATTRACTION, BUT AFTER ATTRACTION COMES BODY LANGUAGE. YOU HAVE TO COMMUNICATE 'I'M INTERESTED' TO A POTENTIAL MATE, ONLY NOT IN SO MANY WORDS.
ALL RIGHT, PATCH. LET'S SAY YOU'RE AT A PARTY. THE ROOM IS FULL OF GIRLS OF ALL DIFFERENT SHAPES AND SIZES.
YOU SEE BLONDS, BRUNETTES, REDHEADS, A FEW GIRLS WITH BLACK HAIR. SOME ARE TALKATIVE, WHILE OTHERS APPEAR SHY.
SINGLE HER OUT. TALK TO HER.
I STUDY HER.
I FIGURE OUT WHAT SHE'S THINKING AND FEELING. SHE'S NOT GOING TO COME RIGHT OUT AND TELL ME, WHICH IS WHY I HAVE TO PAY ATTENTION. DOES SHE TURN HER BODY TOWARD MINE?
DOES SHE HOLD MY EYES, THEN LOOK AWAY? DOES SHE BITE HER LIP AND PLAY WITH HER HAIR, THE WAY NORA IS DOING RIGHT NOW?
I'M NOT BLUSHING.
SHE'S NERVOUS; SHE'S STROKING HER ARM TO DRAW ATTENTION FROM HER FACE AND DOWN TO HER FIGURE, OR MAYBE HER SKIN. BOTH ARE STRONG SELLING POINTS.

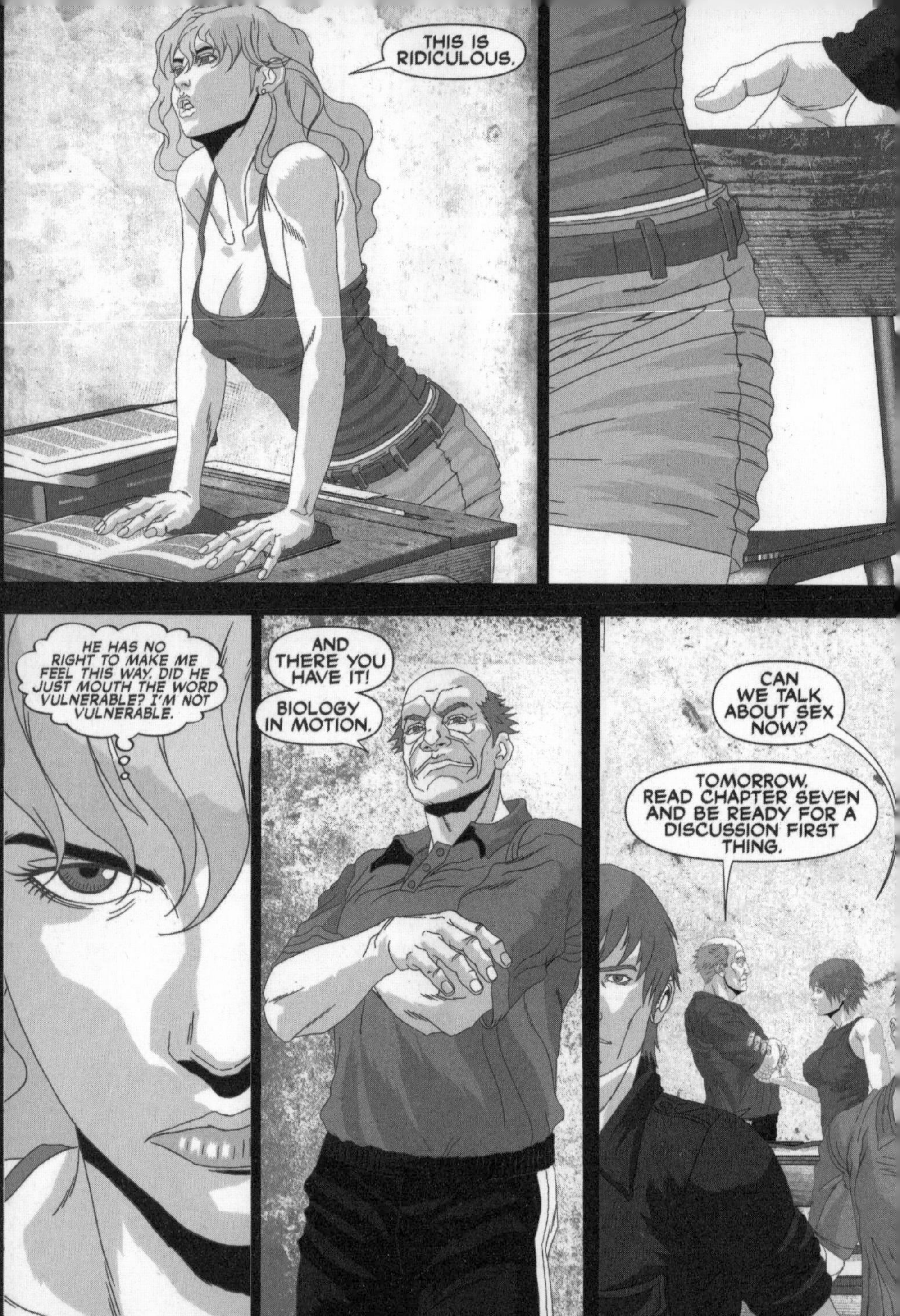
THIS IS RIDICULOUS.
HE HAS NO RIGHT TO MAKE ME FEEL THIS WAY. DID HE JUST MOUTH THE WORD VULNERABLE? I'M NOT VULNERABLE.
AND THERE YOU HAVE IT!
BIOLOGY IN MOTION.
CAN WE TALK ABOUT SEX NOW?
TOMORROW. READ CHAPTER SEVEN AND BE READY FOR A DISCUSSION FIRST THING.

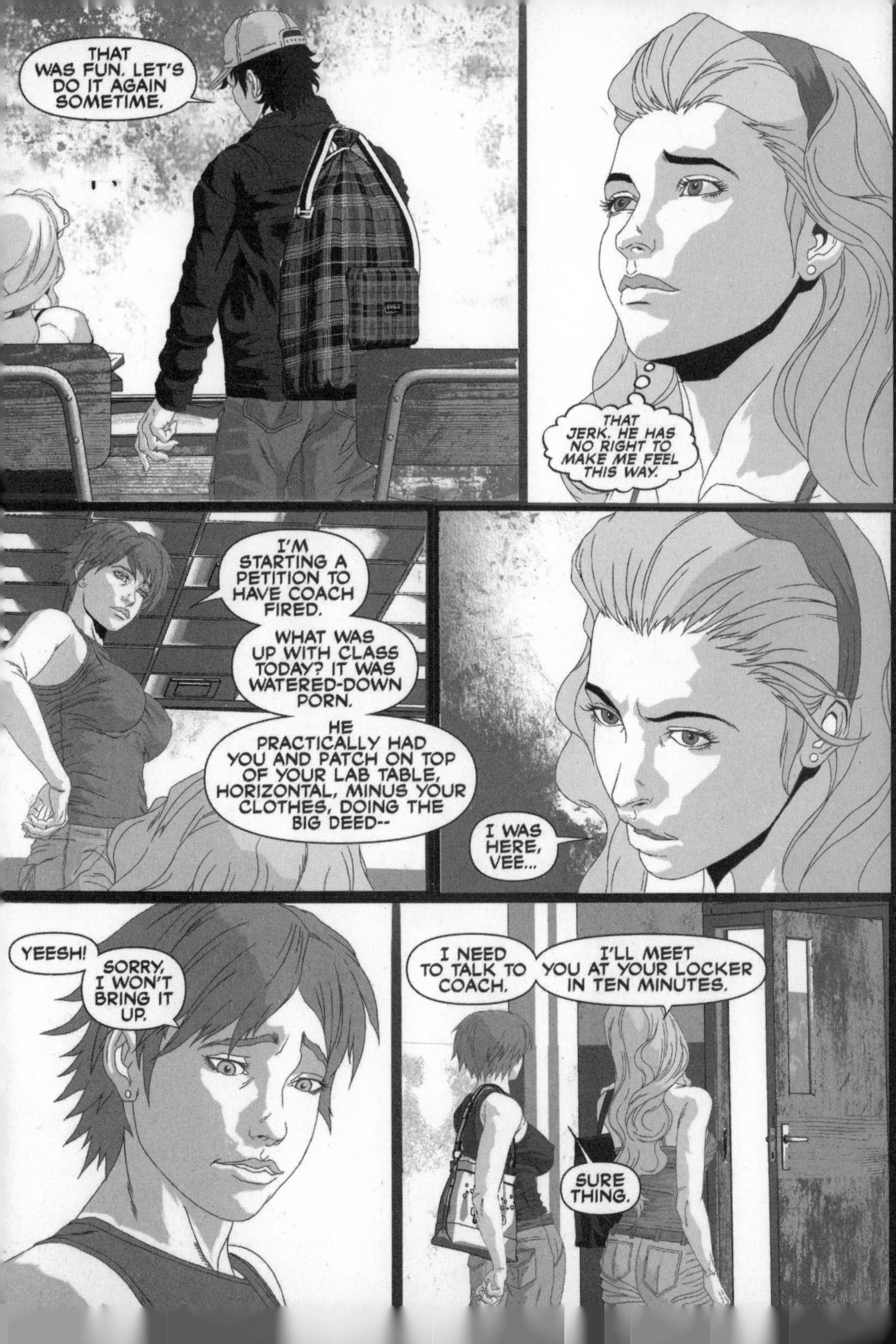
THAT WAS FUN. LET'S DO IT AGAIN SOMETIME.
THAT JERK. HE HAS NO RIGHT TO MAKE ME FEEL THIS WAY.
I'M STARTING A PETITION TO HAVE COACH FIRED.
WHAT WAS UP WITH CLASS TODAY? IT WAS WATERED-DOWN PORN.
HE PRACTICALLY HAD YOU AND PATCH ON TOP OF YOUR LAB TABLE, HORIZONTAL, MINUS YOUR CLOTHES, DOING THE BIG DEED--
I WAS HERE, VEE...
YEESH!
SORRY, I WON'T BRING IT UP.
I NEED TO TALK TO COACH.
I'LL MEET YOU AT YOUR LOCKER IN TEN MINUTES.
SURE THING.

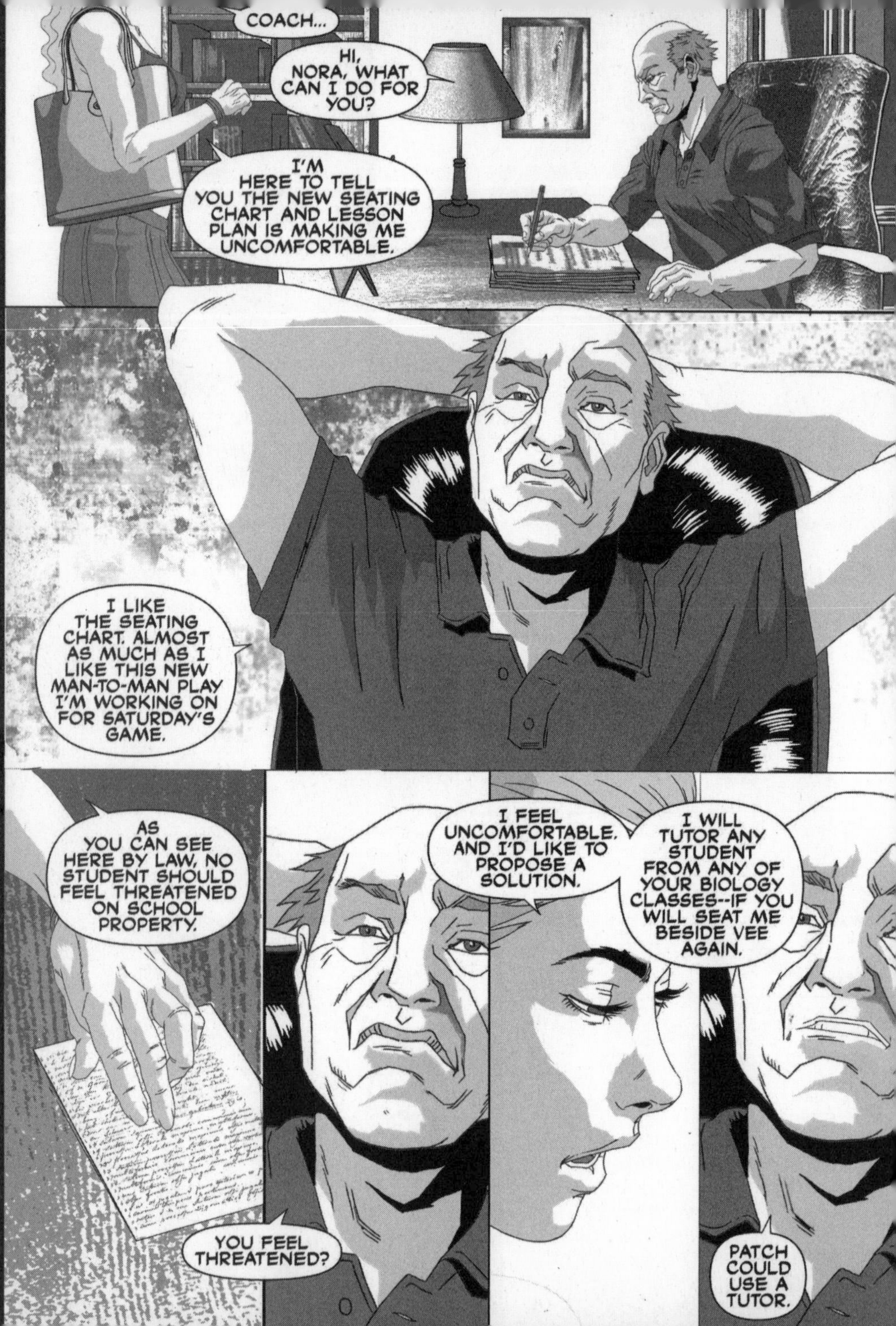
COACH...
HI, NORA, WHAT CAN I DO FOR YOU?
I'M HERE TO TELL YOU THE NEW SEATING CHART AND LESSON PLAN IS MAKING ME UNCOMFORTABLE.
I LIKE THE SEATING CHART. ALMOST AS MUCH AS I LIKE THIS NEW MAN-TO-MAN PLAY I'M WORKING ON FOR SATURDAY'S GAME.
AS YOU CAN SEE HERE BY LAW, NO STUDENT SHOULD FEEL THREATENED ON SCHOOL PROPERTY.
YOU FEEL THREATENED?
I FEEL UNCOMFORTABLE. AND I'D LIKE TO PROPOSE A SOLUTION.
I WILL TUTOR ANY STUDENT FROM ANY OF YOUR BIOLOGY CLASSES--IF YOU WILL SEAT ME BESIDE VEE AGAIN.
PATCH COULD USE A TUTOR.

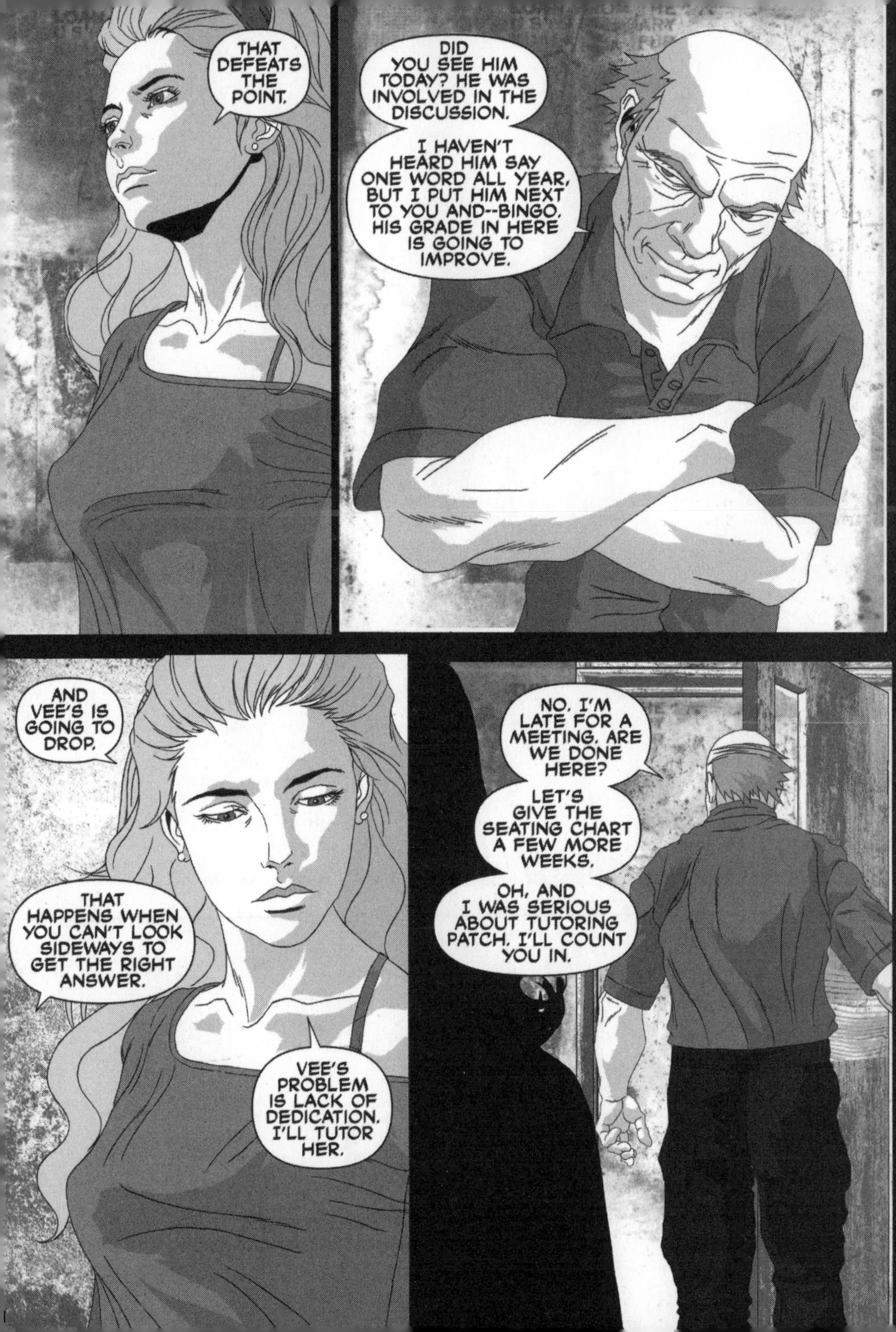

THAT DEFEATS THE POINT.
DID YOU SEE HIM TODAY? HE WAS INVOLVED IN THE DISCUSSION.
I HAVEN'T HEARD HIM SAY ONE WORD ALL YEAR, BUT I PUT HIM NEXT TO YOU AND--BINGO, HIS GRADE IN HERE IS GOING TO IMPROVE.
AND VEE'S IS GOING TO DROP.
THAT HAPPENS WHEN YOU CAN'T LOOK SIDEWAYS TO GET THE RIGHT ANSWER.
VEE'S PROBLEM IS LACK OF DEDICATION. I'LL TUTOR HER.
NO. I'M LATE FOR A MEETING. ARE WE DONE HERE?
LET'S GIVE THE SEATING CHART A FEW MORE WEEKS.
OH, AND I WAS SERIOUS ABOUT TUTORING PATCH. I'LL COUNT YOU IN.

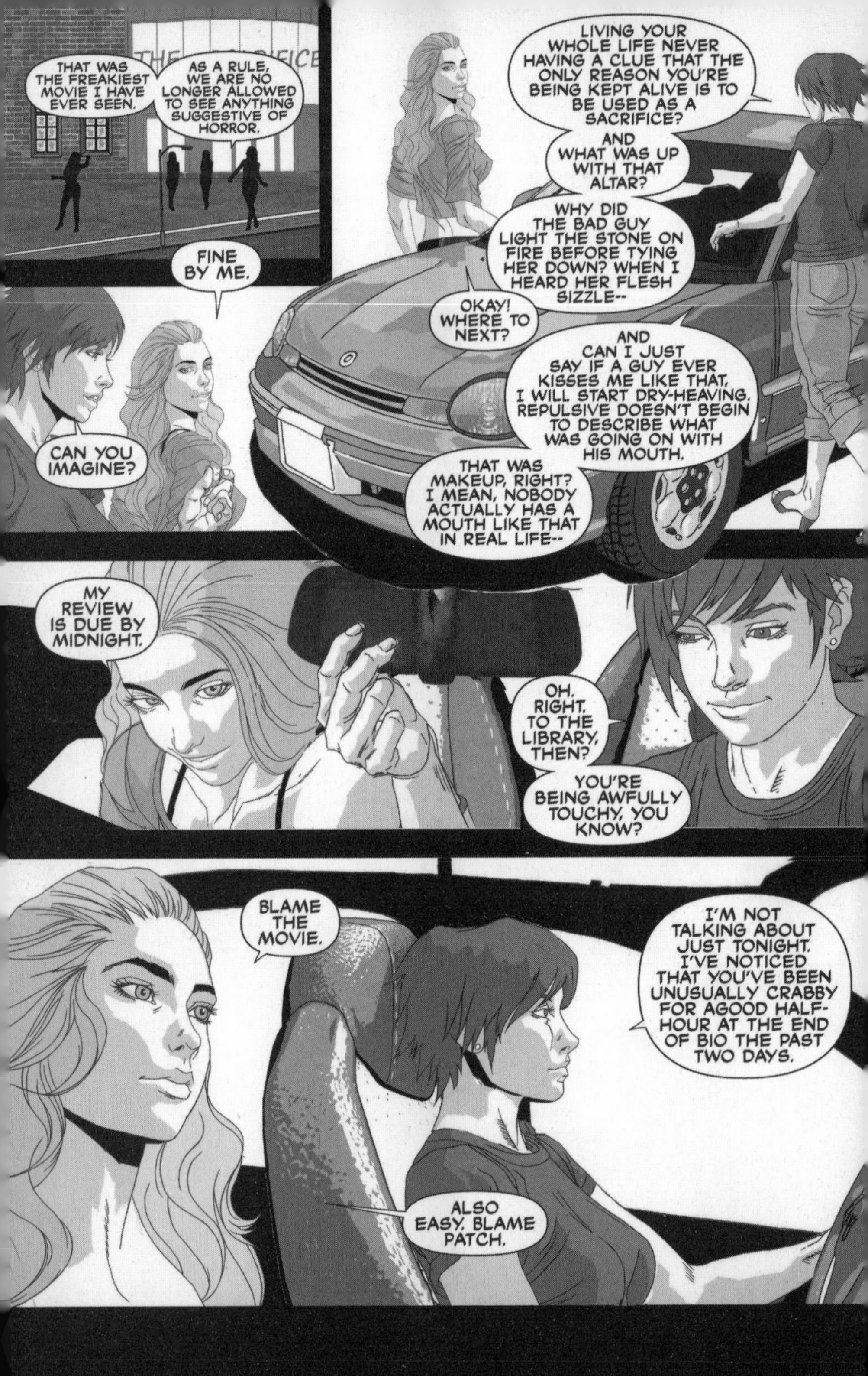
THAT WAS THE FREAKIEST MOVIE I HAVE EVER SEEN.
AS A RULE, WE ARE NO LONGER ALLOWED TO SEE ANYTHING SUGGESTIVE OF HORROR.
FINE BY ME.
CAN YOU IMAGINE?
LIVING YOUR WHOLE LIFE NEVER HAVING A CLUE THAT THE ONLY REASON YOU'RE BEING KEPT ALIVE IS TO BE USED AS A SACRIFICE?
AND WHAT WAS UP WITH THAT ALTAR?
WHY DID THE BAD GUY LIGHT THE STONE ON FIRE BEFORE TYING HER DOWN? WHEN I HEARD HER FLESH SIZZLE--
OKAY! WHERE TO NEXT?
AND CAN I JUST SAY IF A GUY EVER KISSES ME LIKE THAT, I WILL START DRY-HEAVING. REPULSIVE DOESN'T BEGIN TO DESCRIBE WHAT WAS GOING ON WITH HIS MOUTH.
THAT WAS MAKEUP, RIGHT? I MEAN, NOBODY ACTUALLY HAS A MOUTH LIKE THAT IN REAL LIFE--
MY REVIEW IS DUE BY MIDNIGHT.
OH, RIGHT. TO THE LIBRARY, THEN?
YOU'RE BEING AWFULLY TOUCHY, YOU KNOW?
BLAME THE MOVIE.
I'M NOT TALKING ABOUT JUST TONIGHT. I'VE NOTICED THAT YOU'VE BEEN UNUSUALLY CRABBY FOR AGOOD HALF-HOUR AT THE END OF BIO THE PAST TWO DAYS.
ALSO EASY. BLAME PATCH.

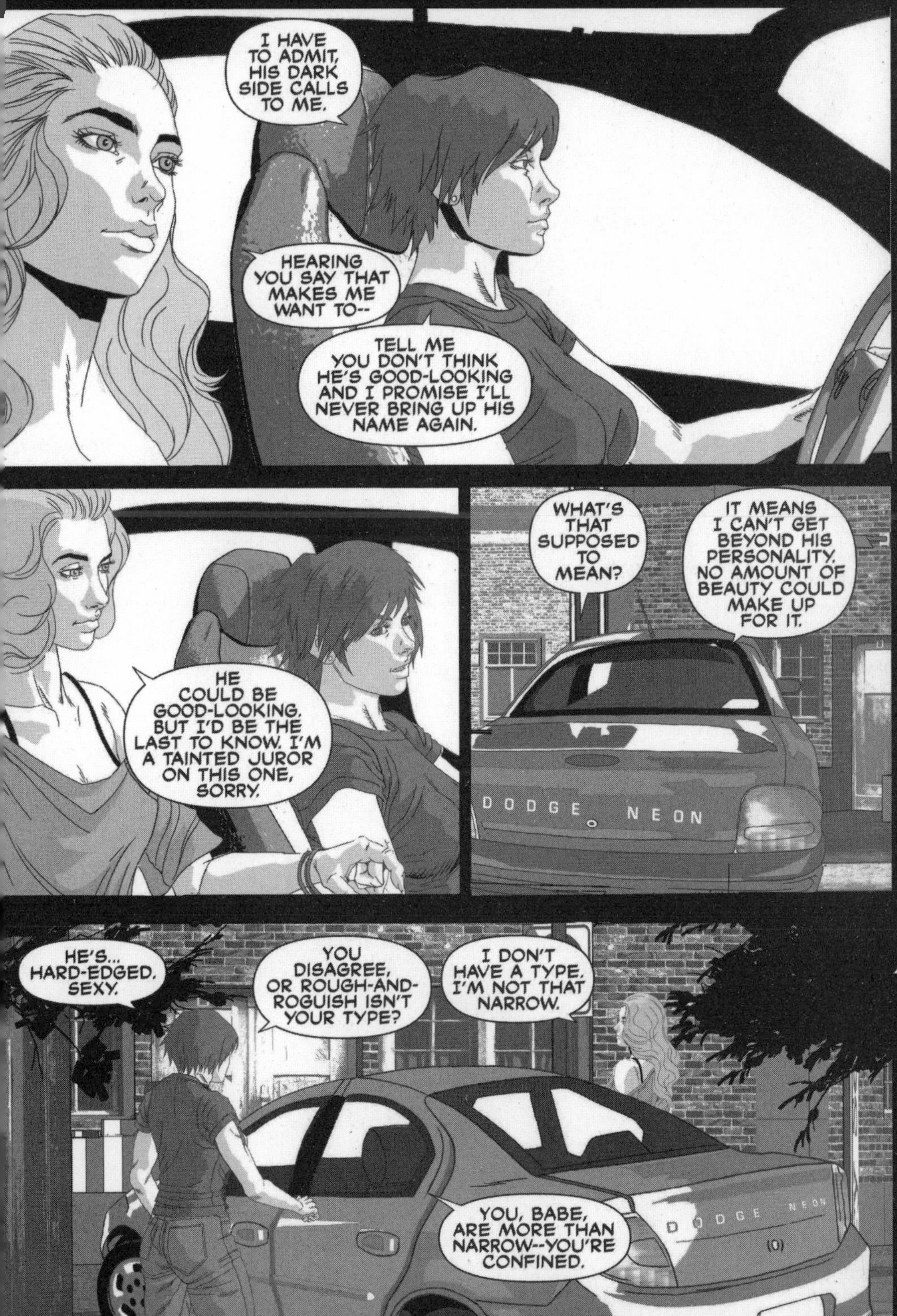
I HAVE TO ADMIT, HIS DARK SIDE CALLS TO ME.
HEARING YOU SAY THAT MAKES ME WANT TO--
TELL ME YOU DON'T THINK HE'S GOOD-LOOKING AND I PROMISE I'LL NEVER BRING UP HIS NAME AGAIN.
HE COULD BE GOOD-LOOKING. BUT I'D BE THE LAST TO KNOW. I'M A TAINTED JUROR ON THIS ONE, SORRY.
WHAT'S THAT SUPPOSED TO MEAN?
IT MEANS I CAN'T GET BEYOND HIS PERSONALITY. NO AMOUNT OF BEAUTY COULD MAKE UP FOR IT.
DODGE NEON
HE'S... HARD-EDGED. SEXY.
YOU DISAGREE, OR ROUGH-AND-ROGUISH ISN'T YOUR TYPE?
I DON'T HAVE A TYPE. I'M NOT THAT NARROW.
YOU, BABE, ARE MORE THAN NARROW--YOU'RE CONFINED.
DODGE NEON

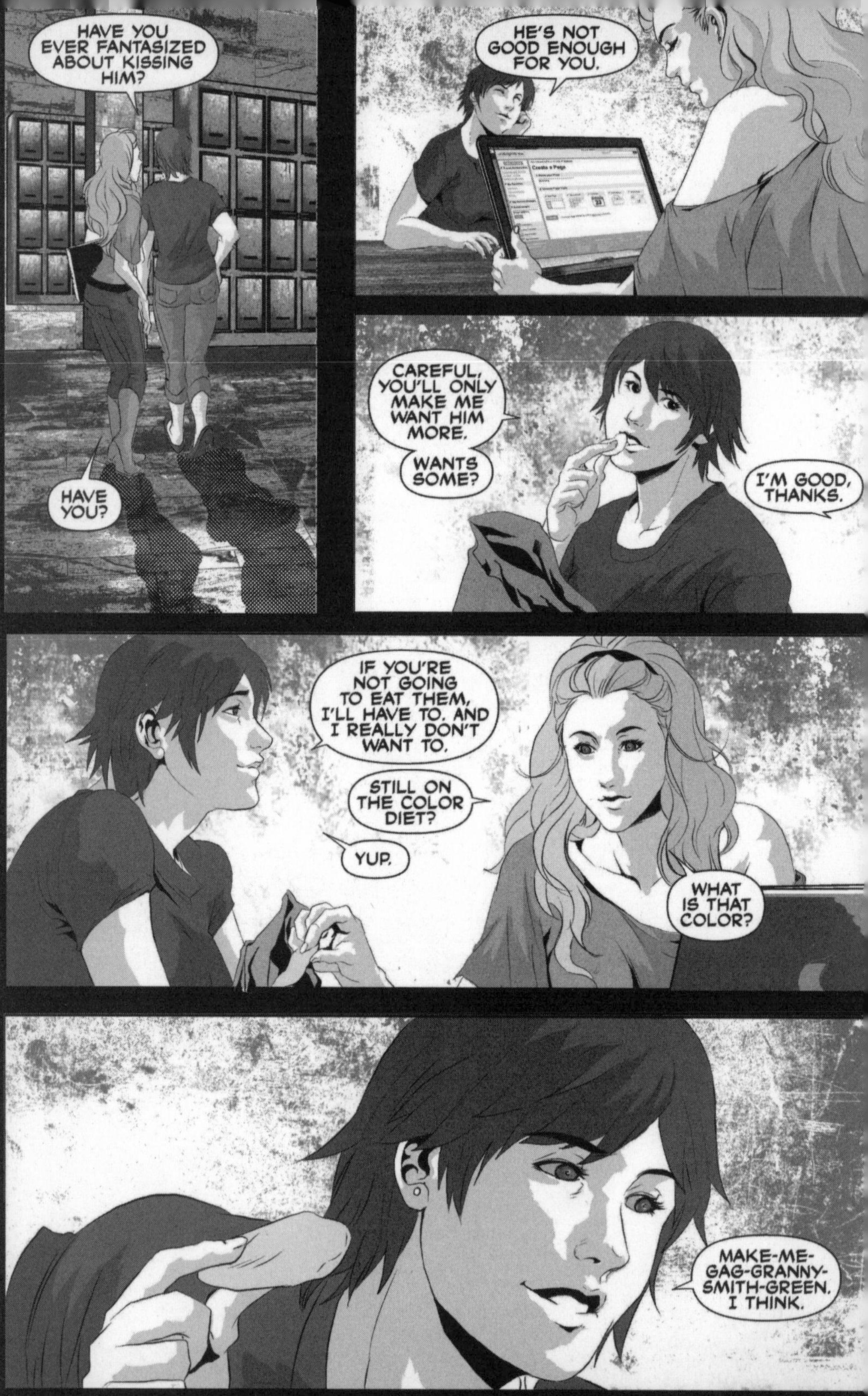
HAVE YOU EVER FANTASIZED ABOUT KISSING HIM?
HAVE YOU?
HE'S NOT GOOD ENOUGH FOR YOU.
CAREFUL, YOU'LL ONLY MAKE ME WANT HIM MORE.
WANTS SOME?
I'M GOOD, THANKS.
IF YOU'RE NOT GOING TO EAT THEM, I'LL HAVE TO. AND I REALLY DON'T WANT TO.
STILL ON THE COLOR DIET?
YUP.
WHAT IS THAT COLOR?
MAKE-ME-GAG-GRANNY-SMITH-GREEN, I THINK.

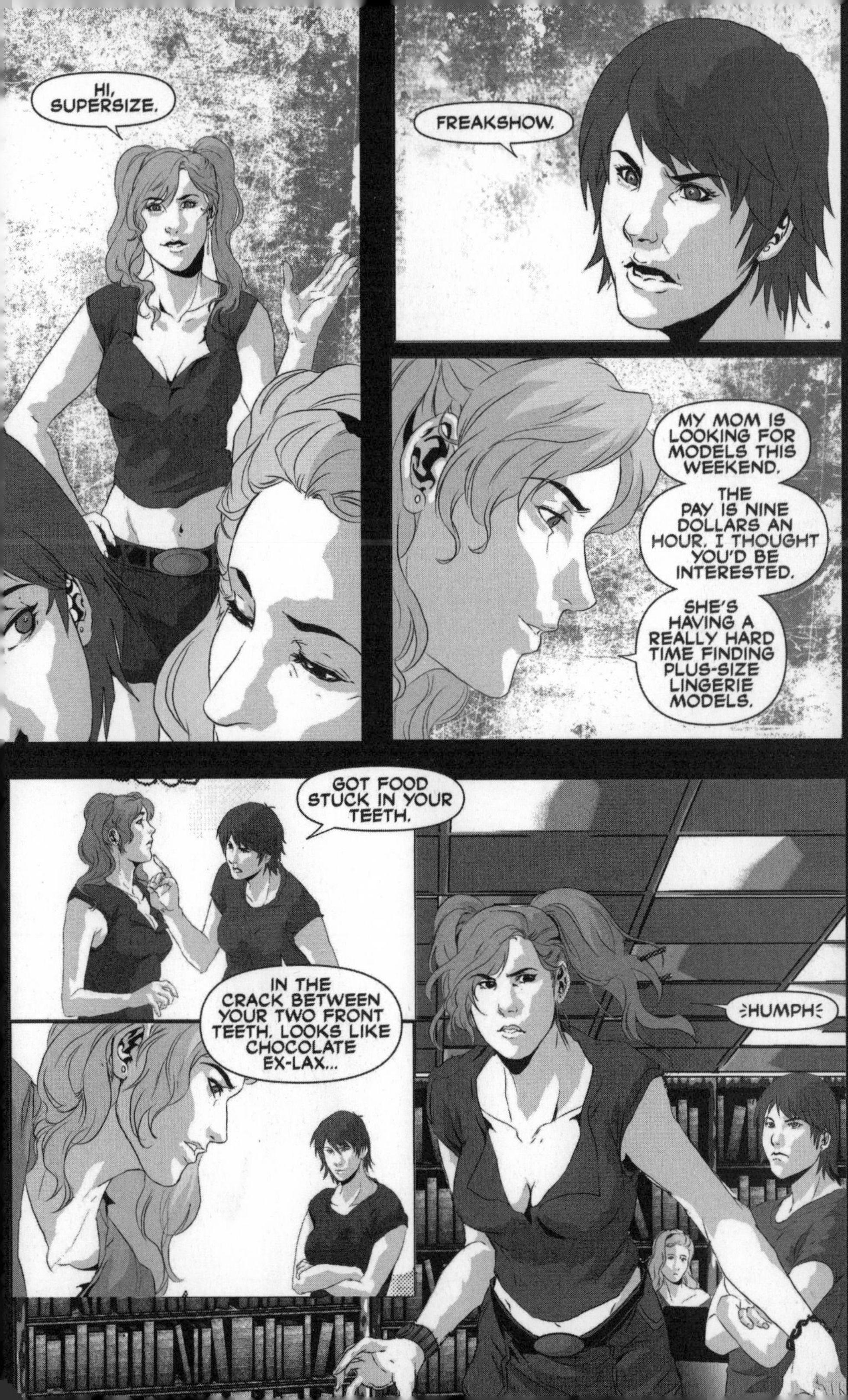
HI, SUPERSIZE.
FREAKSHOW.
MY MOM IS LOOKING FOR MODELS THIS WEEKEND.
THE PAY IS NINE DOLLARS AN HOUR. I THOUGHT YOU'D BE INTERESTED.
SHE'S HAVING A REALLY HARD TIME FINDING PLUS-SIZE LINGERIE MODELS.
GOT FOOD STUCK IN YOUR TEETH.
IN THE CRACK BETWEEN YOUR TWO FRONT TEETH. LOOKS LIKE CHOCOLATE EX-LAX...
HUMPH

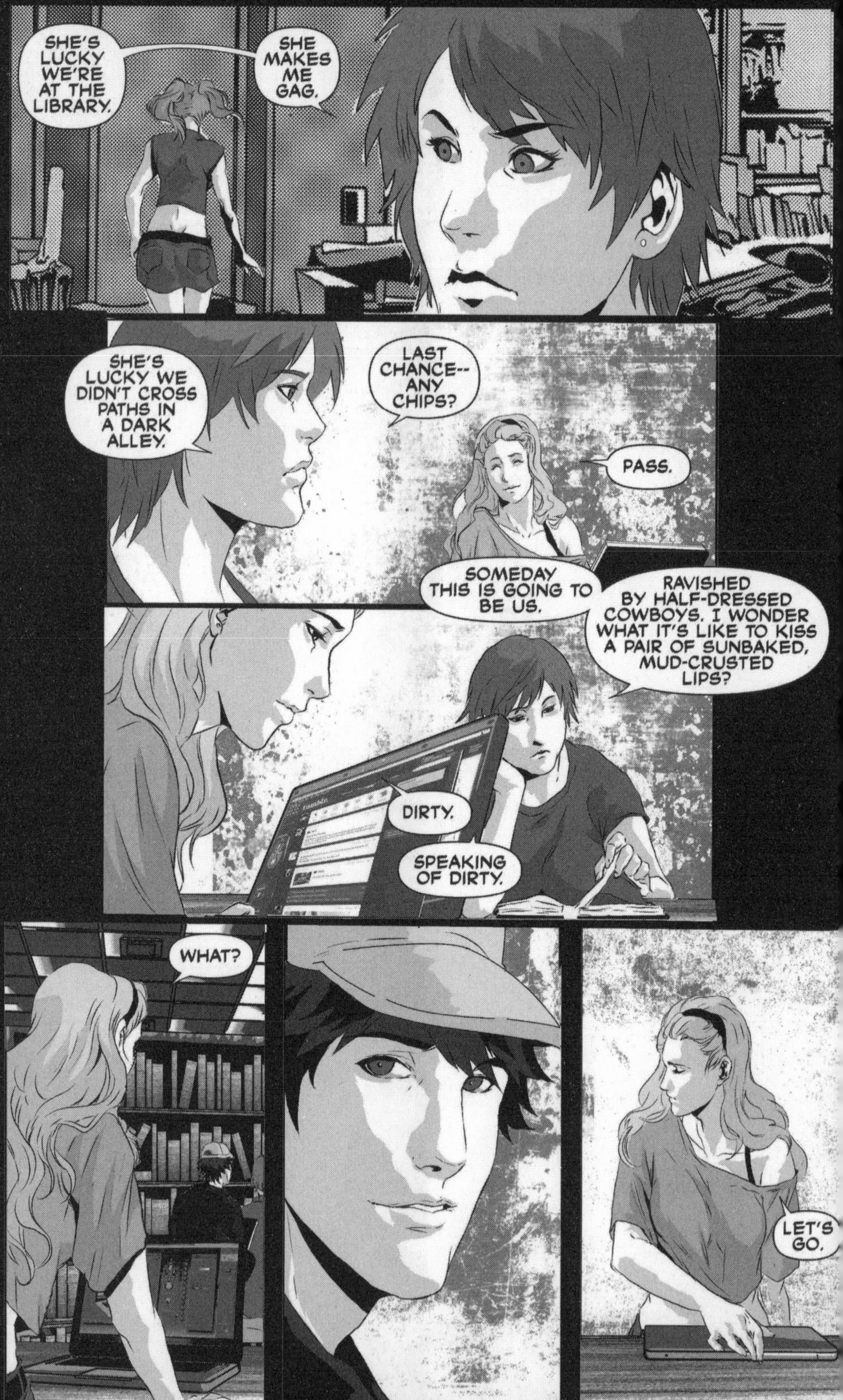
SHE'S LUCKY WE'RE AT THE LIBRARY.
SHE MAKES ME GAG.
SHE'S LUCKY WE DIDN'T CROSS PATHS IN A DARK ALLEY.
LAST CHANCE-- ANY CHIPS?
PASS.
SOMEDAY THIS IS GOING TO BE US.
RAVISHED BY HALF-DRESSED COWBOYS. I WONDER WHAT IT'S LIKE TO KISS A PAIR OF SUNBAKED, MUD-CRUSTED LIPS?
DIRTY.
SPEAKING OF DIRTY.
WHAT?
LET'S GO.

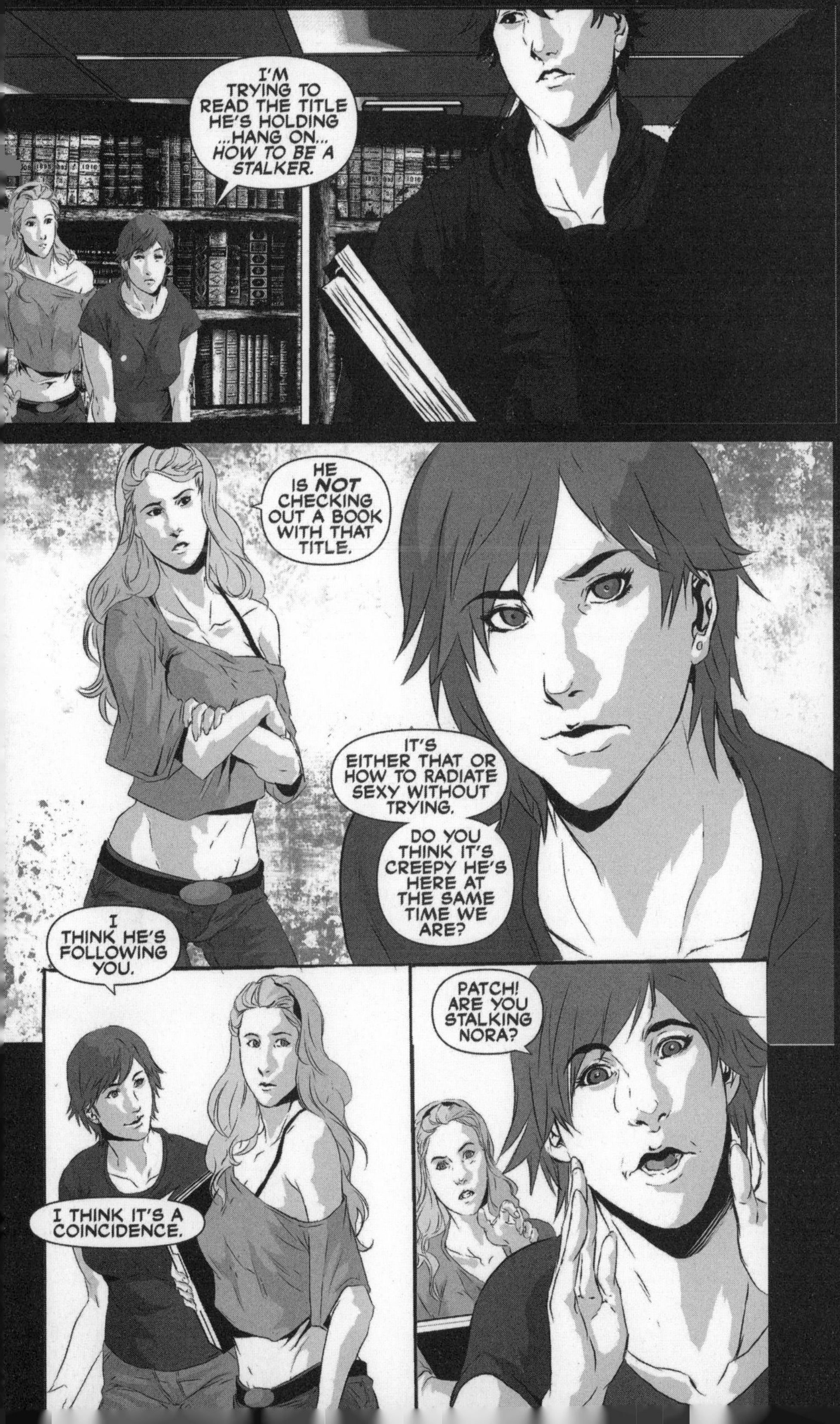

I'M TRYING TO READ THE TITLE HE'S HOLDING ...HANG ON... *HOW TO BE A STALKER.*
HE IS **NOT** CHECKING OUT A BOOK WITH THAT TITLE.
IT'S EITHER THAT OR *HOW TO RADIATE SEXY WITHOUT TRYING.*
DO YOU THINK IT'S CREEPY HE'S HERE AT THE SAME TIME WE ARE?
I THINK HE'S FOLLOWING YOU.
I THINK IT'S A COINCIDENCE.
PATCH! ARE YOU STALKING NORA?

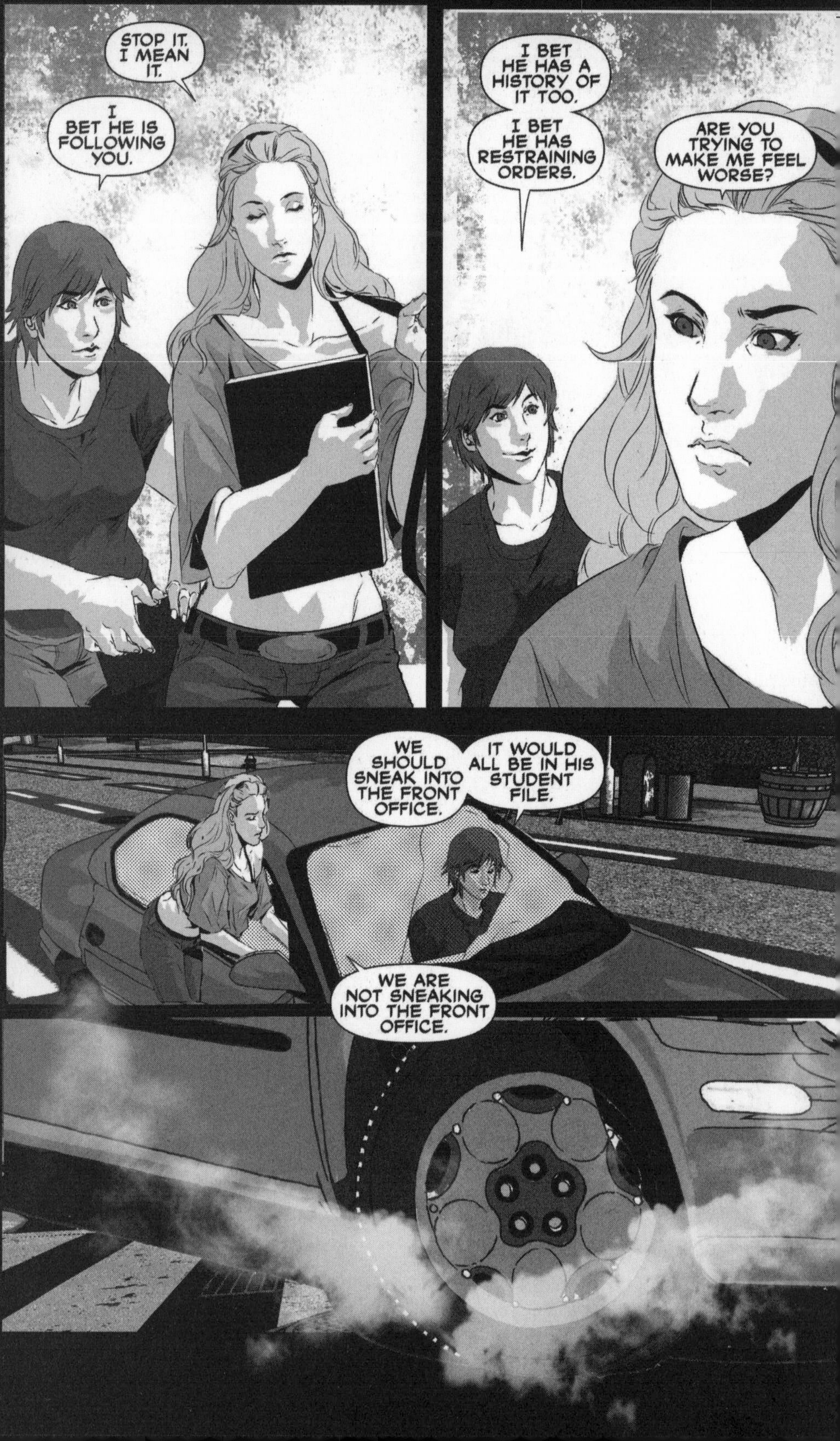
STOP IT. I MEAN IT.
I BET HE IS FOLLOWING YOU.
I BET HE HAS A HISTORY OF IT TOO.
I BET HE HAS RESTRAINING ORDERS.
ARE YOU TRYING TO MAKE ME FEEL WORSE?
WE SHOULD SNEAK INTO THE FRONT OFFICE.
IT WOULD ALL BE IN HIS STUDENT FILE.
WE ARE NOT SNEAKING INTO THE FRONT OFFICE.

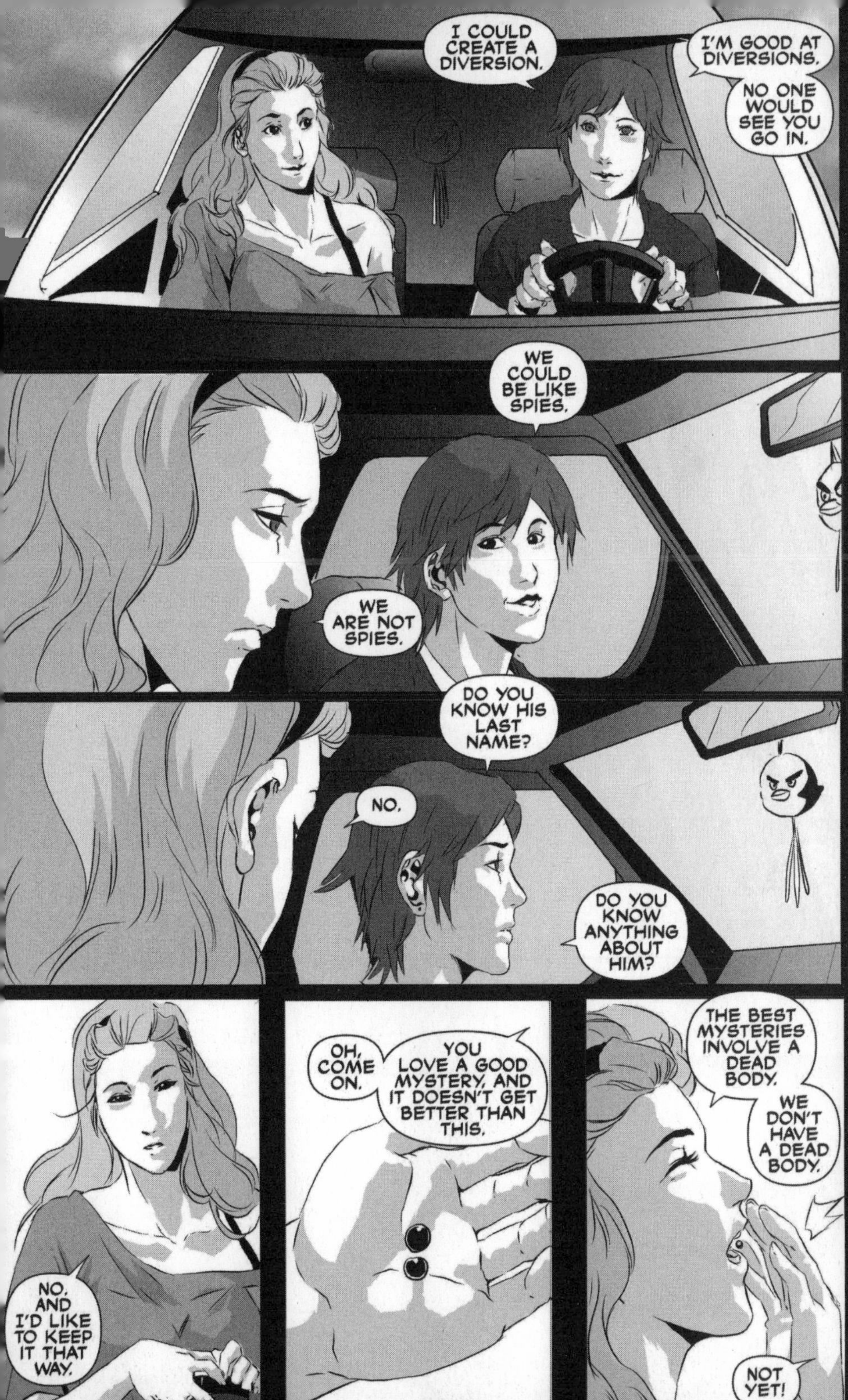
I COULD CREATE A DIVERSION.
I'M GOOD AT DIVERSIONS.
NO ONE WOULD SEE YOU GO IN.
WE COULD BE LIKE SPIES.
WE ARE NOT SPIES.
DO YOU KNOW HIS LAST NAME?
NO.
DO YOU KNOW ANYTHING ABOUT HIM?
NO. AND I'D LIKE TO KEEP IT THAT WAY.
OH, COME ON.
YOU LOVE A GOOD MYSTERY, AND IT DOESN'T GET BETTER THAN THIS.
THE BEST MYSTERIES INVOLVE A DEAD BODY.
WE DON'T HAVE A DEAD BODY.
NOT YET!

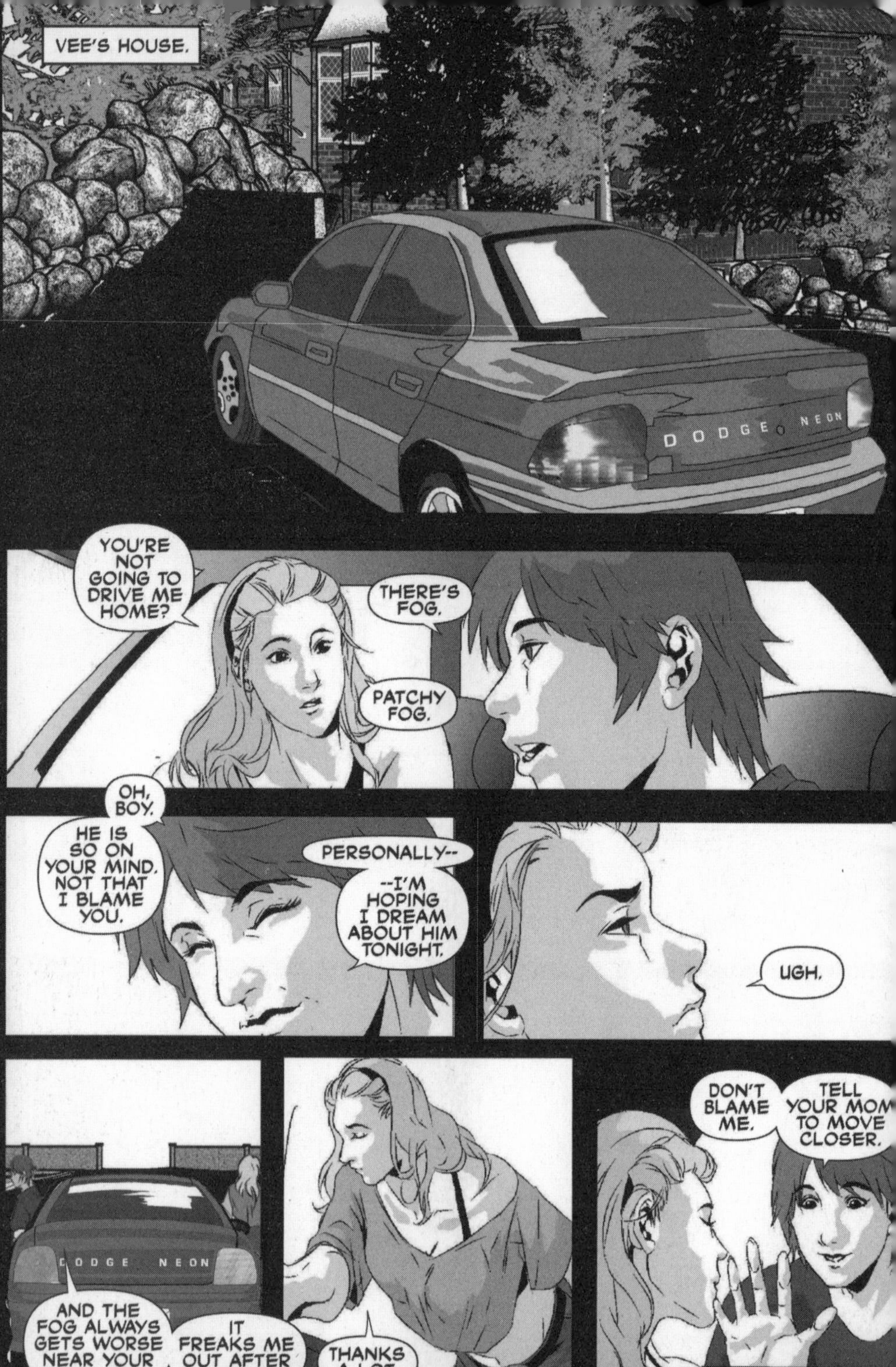

VEE'S HOUSE.
DODGE NEON
YOU'RE NOT GOING TO DRIVE ME HOME?
THERE'S FOG.
PATCHY FOG.
OH, BOY.
HE IS SO ON YOUR MIND. NOT THAT I BLAME YOU.
PERSONALLY--
--I'M HOPING I DREAM ABOUT HIM TONIGHT.
UGH.
DODGE NEON
AND THE FOG ALWAYS GETS WORSE NEAR YOUR HOUSE.
IT FREAKS ME OUT AFTER DARK.
THANKS A LOT.
DON'T BLAME ME.
TELL YOUR MOM TO MOVE CLOSER.

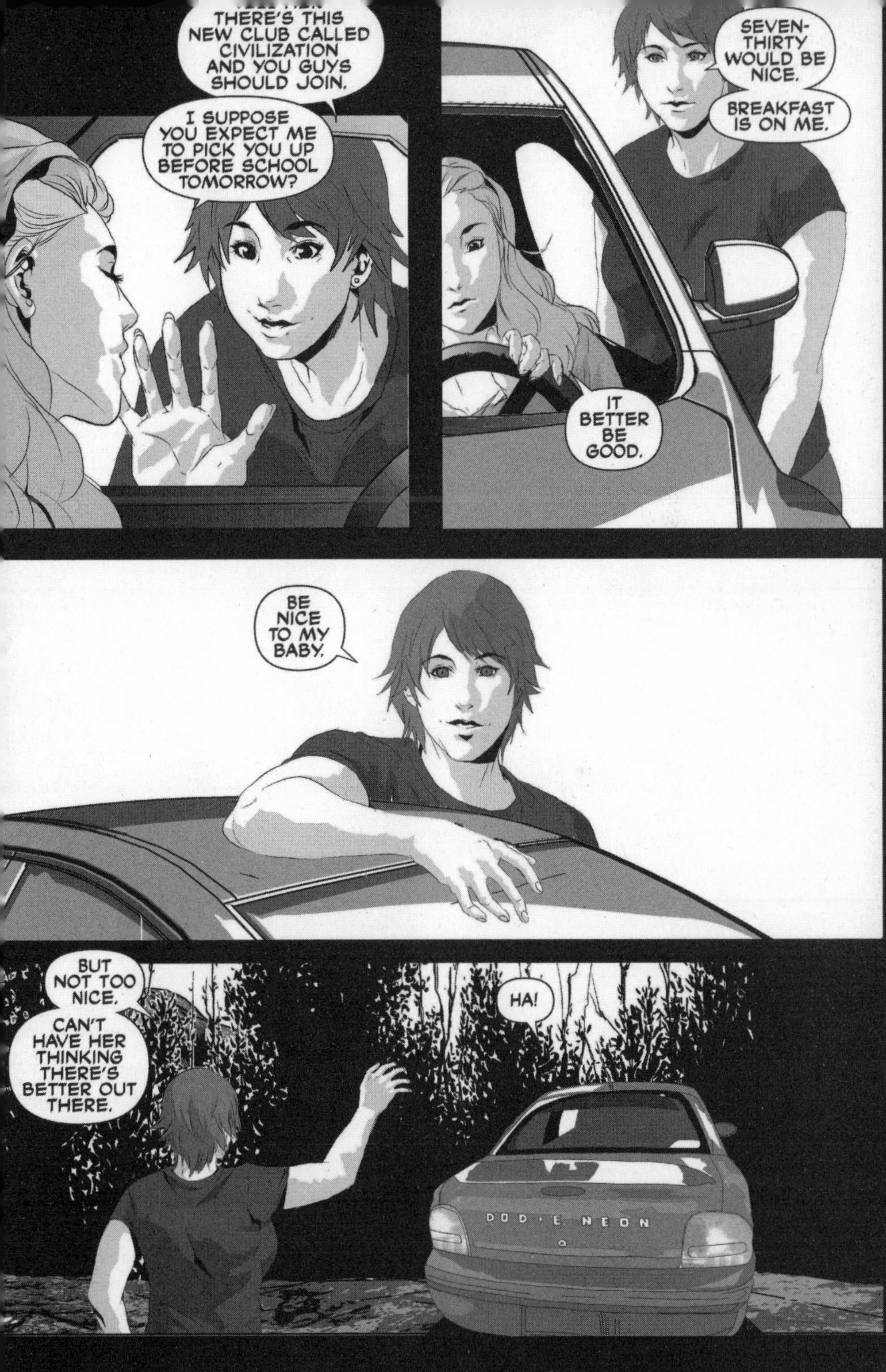
THERE'S THIS NEW CLUB CALLED CIVILIZATION AND YOU GUYS SHOULD JOIN.
I SUPPOSE YOU EXPECT ME TO PICK YOU UP BEFORE SCHOOL TOMORROW?
SEVEN-THIRTY WOULD BE NICE.
BREAKFAST IS ON ME.
IT BETTER BE GOOD.
BE NICE TO MY BABY.
BUT NOT TOO NICE.
CAN'T HAVE HER THINKING THERE'S BETTER OUT THERE.
HA!

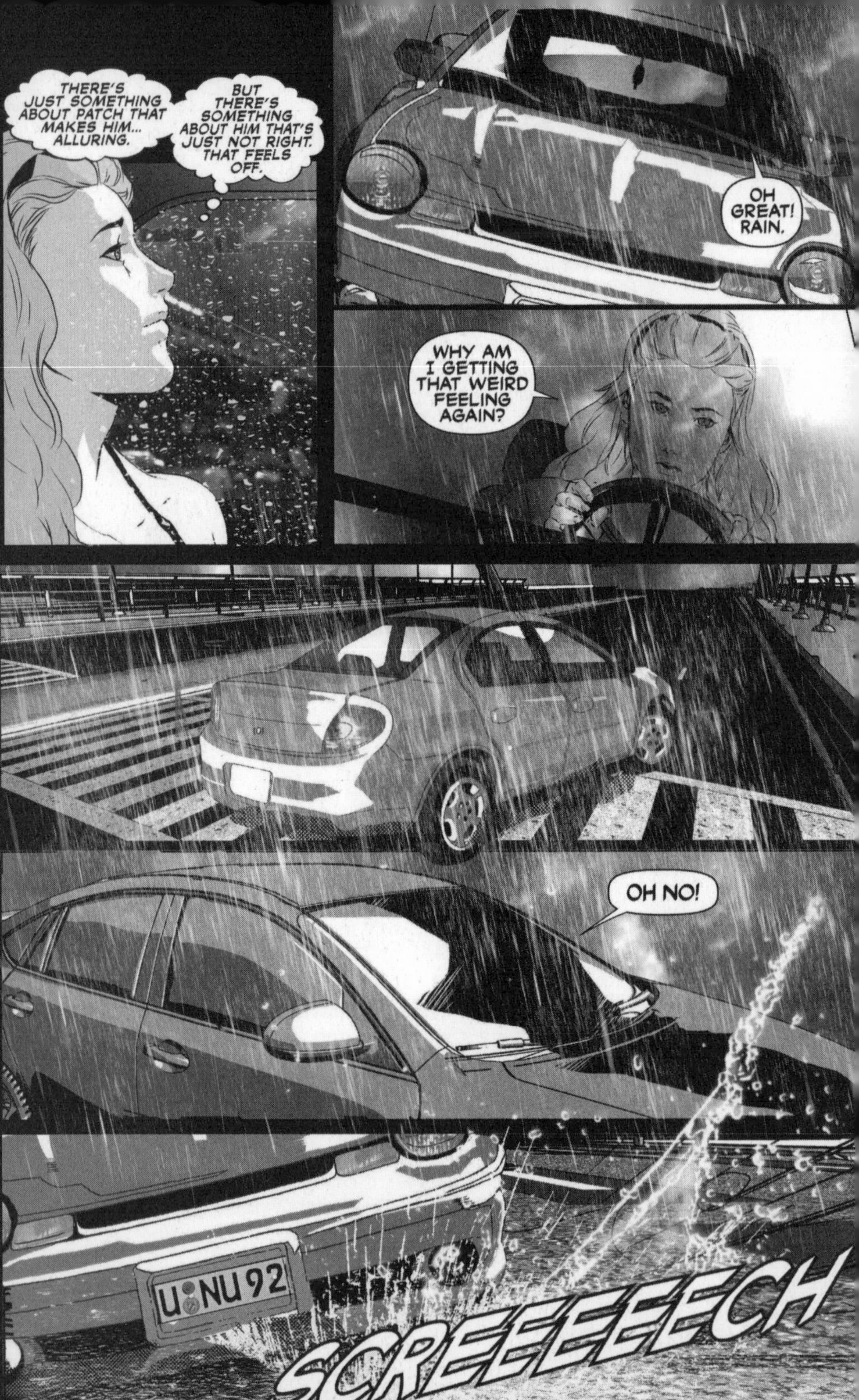
THERE'S JUST SOMETHING ABOUT PATCH THAT MAKES HIM... ALLURING.
BUT THERE'S SOMETHING ABOUT HIM THAT'S JUST NOT RIGHT. THAT FEELS OFF.
OH GREAT! RAIN.
WHY AM I GETTING THAT WEIRD FEELING AGAIN?
OH NO!
U NU 92
SCREEEEEEECH

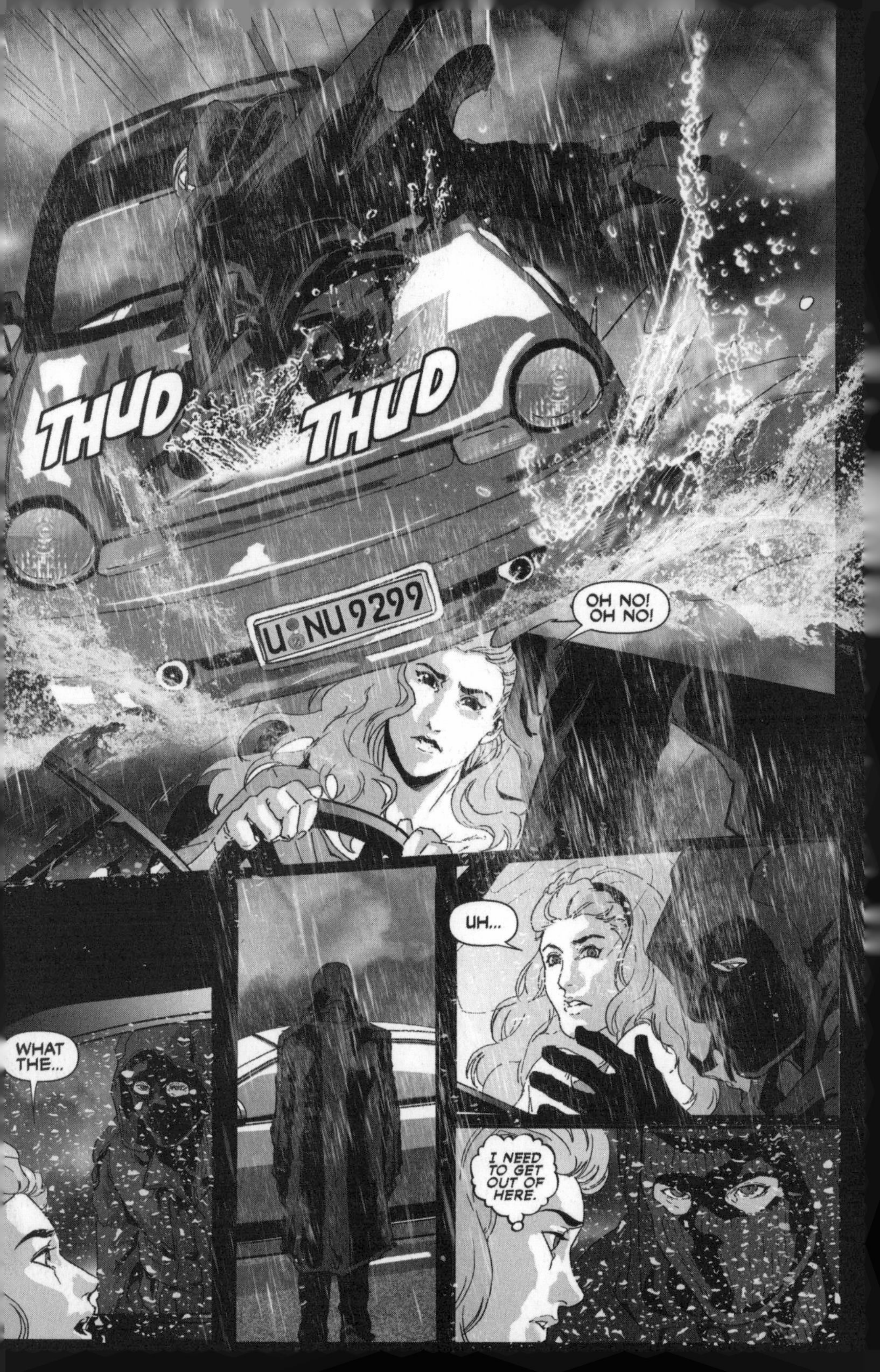
THUD
THUD
U NU 9299
OH NO! OH NO!
UH...
WHAT THE...
I NEED TO GET OUT OF HERE.

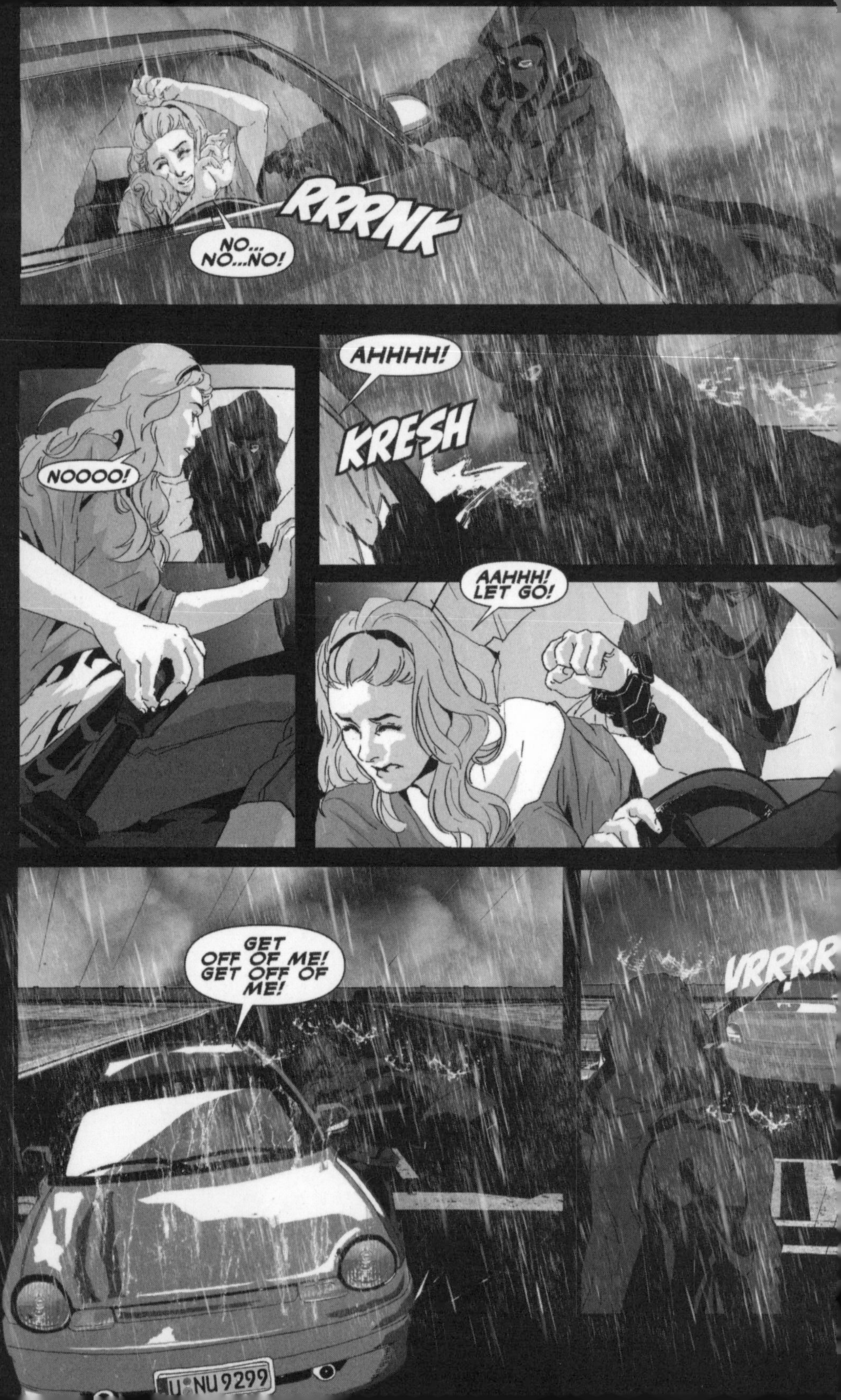
RRRNK
NO... NO...NO!
NOOOO!
AHHHH!
KRESH
AAHHH! LET GO!
GET OFF OF ME! GET OFF OF ME!
VRRRR
U NU 9299

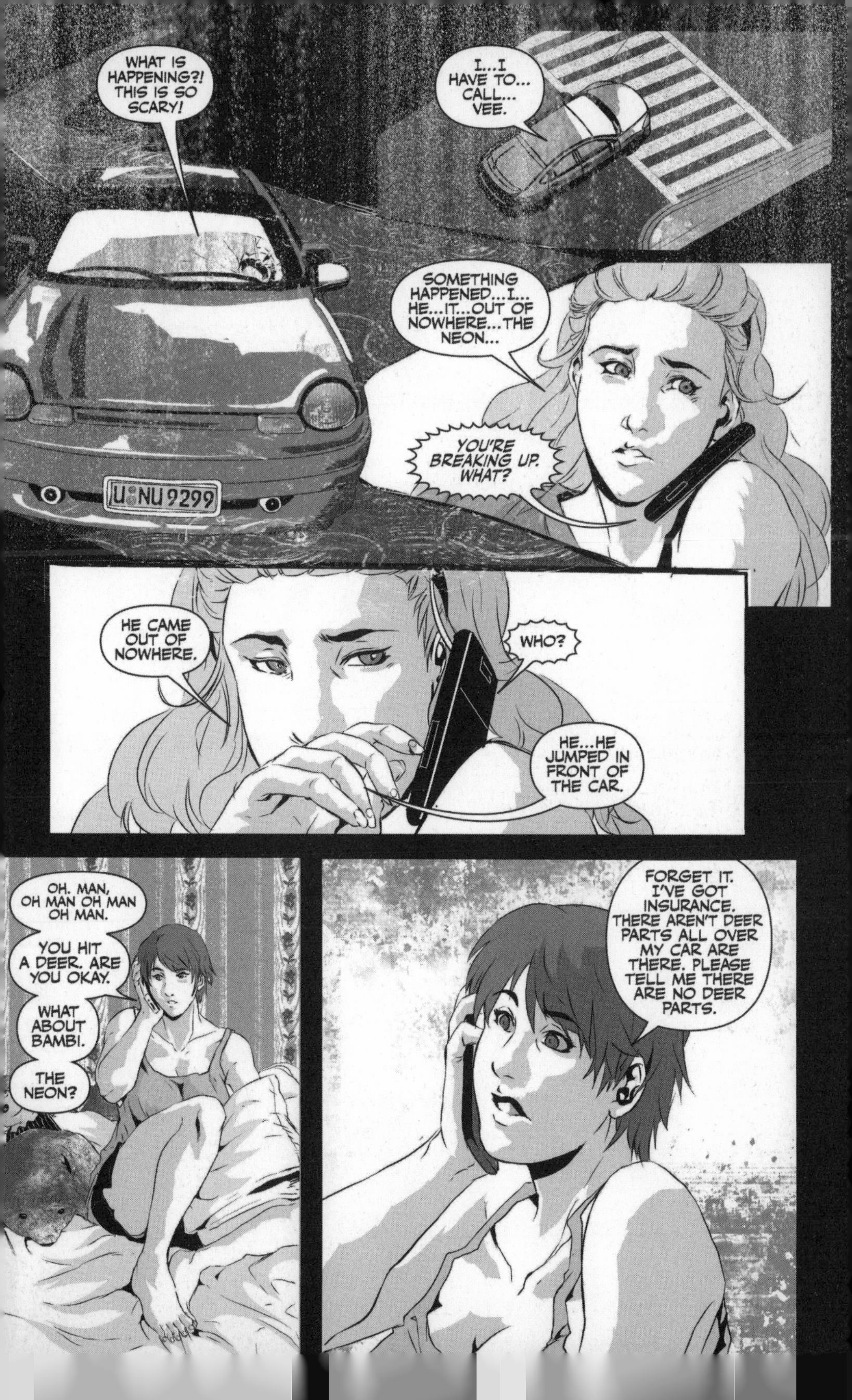
WHAT IS HAPPENING?! THIS IS SO SCARY!
I...I HAVE TO... CALL... VEE.
U NU 9299
SOMETHING HAPPENED...I... HE...IT...OUT OF NOWHERE...THE NEON...
YOU'RE BREAKING UP. WHAT?
HE CAME OUT OF NOWHERE.
WHO?
HE...HE JUMPED IN FRONT OF THE CAR.
OH. MAN, OH MAN OH MAN OH MAN.
YOU HIT A DEER. ARE YOU OKAY.
WHAT ABOUT BAMBI.
THE NEON?
FORGET IT. I'VE GOT INSURANCE. THERE AREN'T DEER PARTS ALL OVER MY CAR ARE THERE. PLEASE TELL ME THERE ARE NO DEER PARTS.

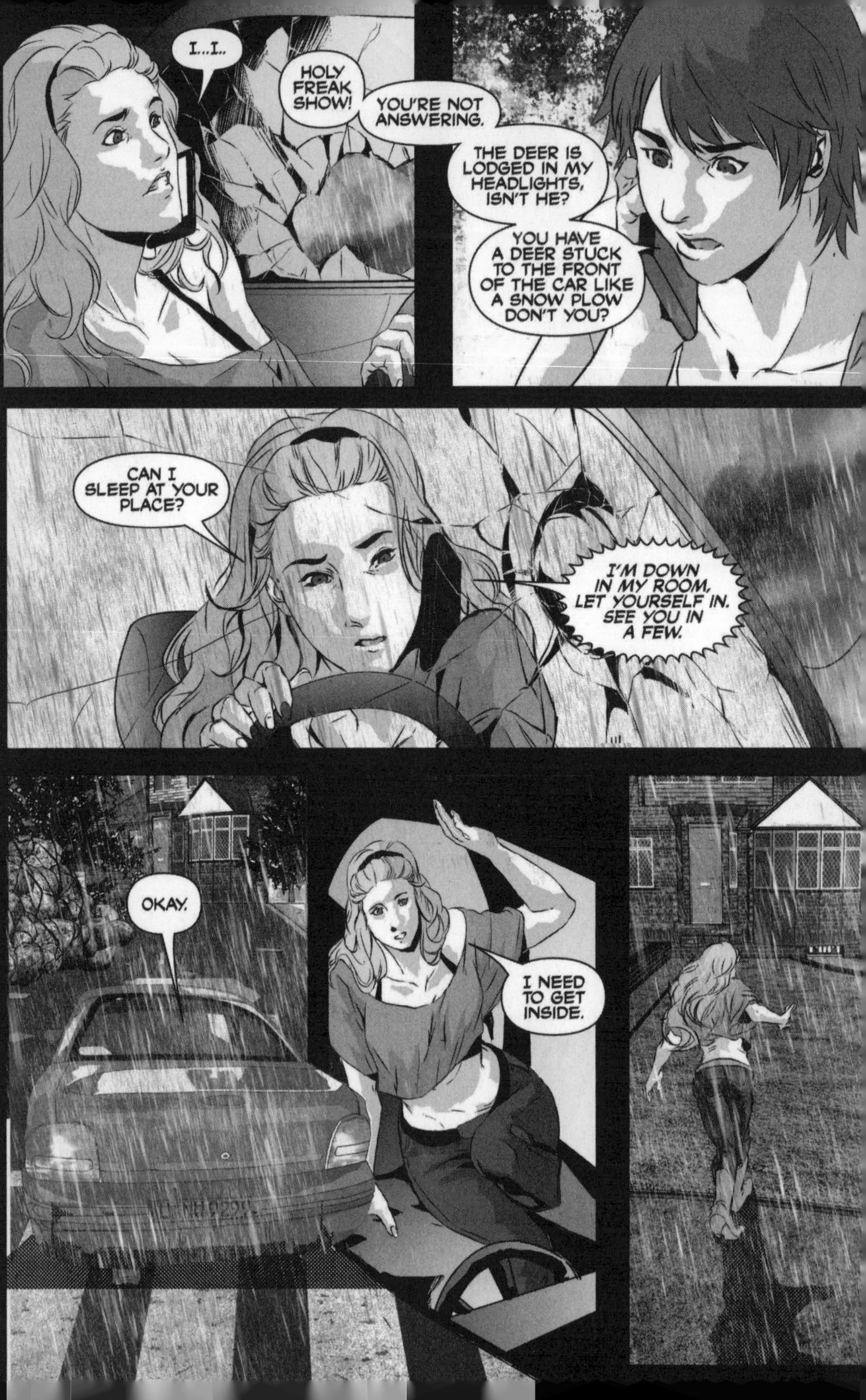

I...I..
HOLY FREAK SHOW!
YOU'RE NOT ANSWERING.
THE DEER IS LODGED IN MY HEADLIGHTS, ISN'T HE?
YOU HAVE A DEER STUCK TO THE FRONT OF THE CAR LIKE A SNOW PLOW DON'T YOU?
CAN I SLEEP AT YOUR PLACE?
I'M DOWN IN MY ROOM, LET YOURSELF IN. SEE YOU IN A FEW.
OKAY.
I NEED TO GET INSIDE.

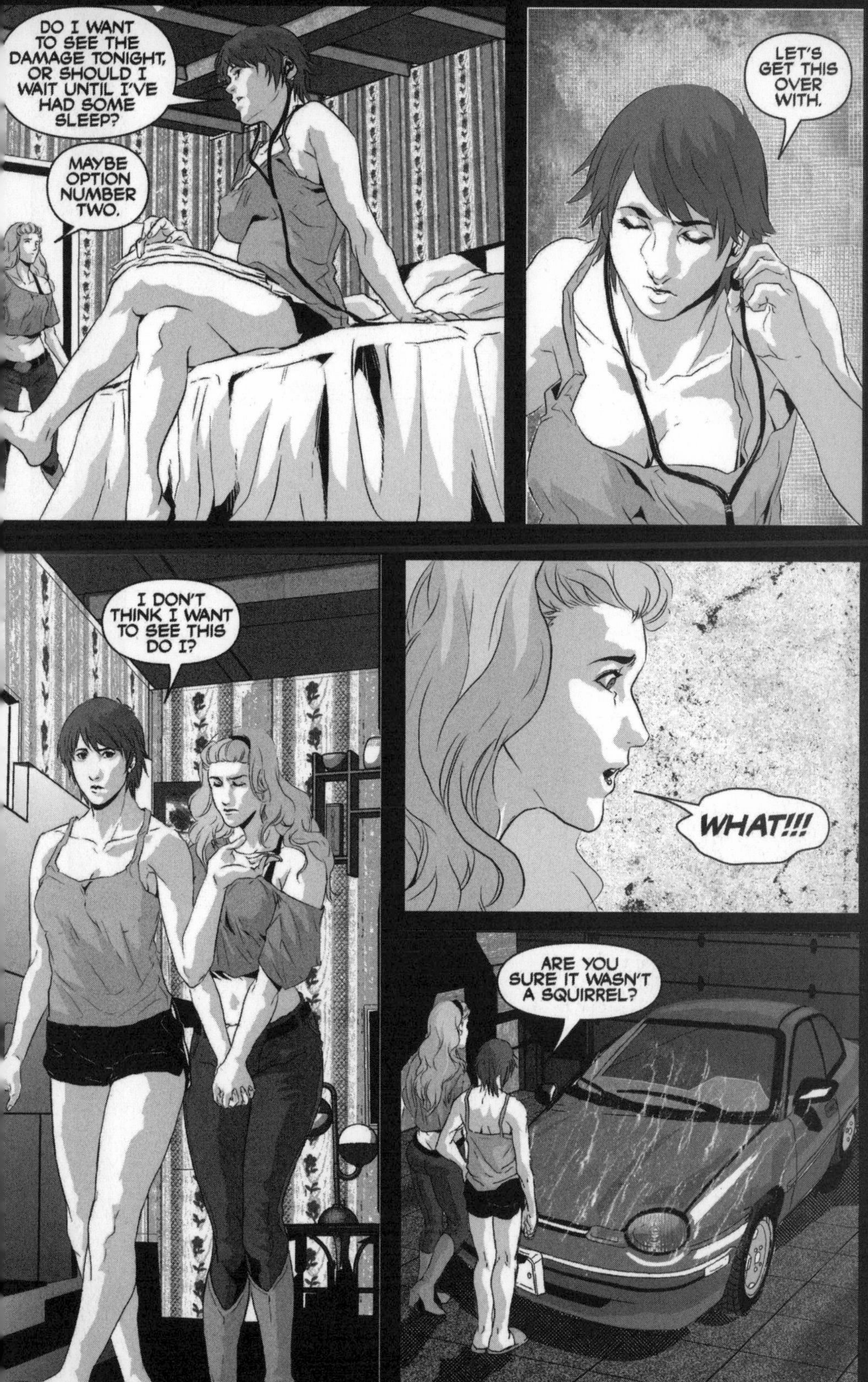
DO I WANT TO SEE THE DAMAGE TONIGHT, OR SHOULD I WAIT UNTIL I'VE HAD SOME SLEEP?
MAYBE OPTION NUMBER TWO.
LET'S GET THIS OVER WITH.
I DON'T THINK I WANT TO SEE THIS DO I?
WHAT!!!
ARE YOU SURE IT WASN'T A SQUIRREL?

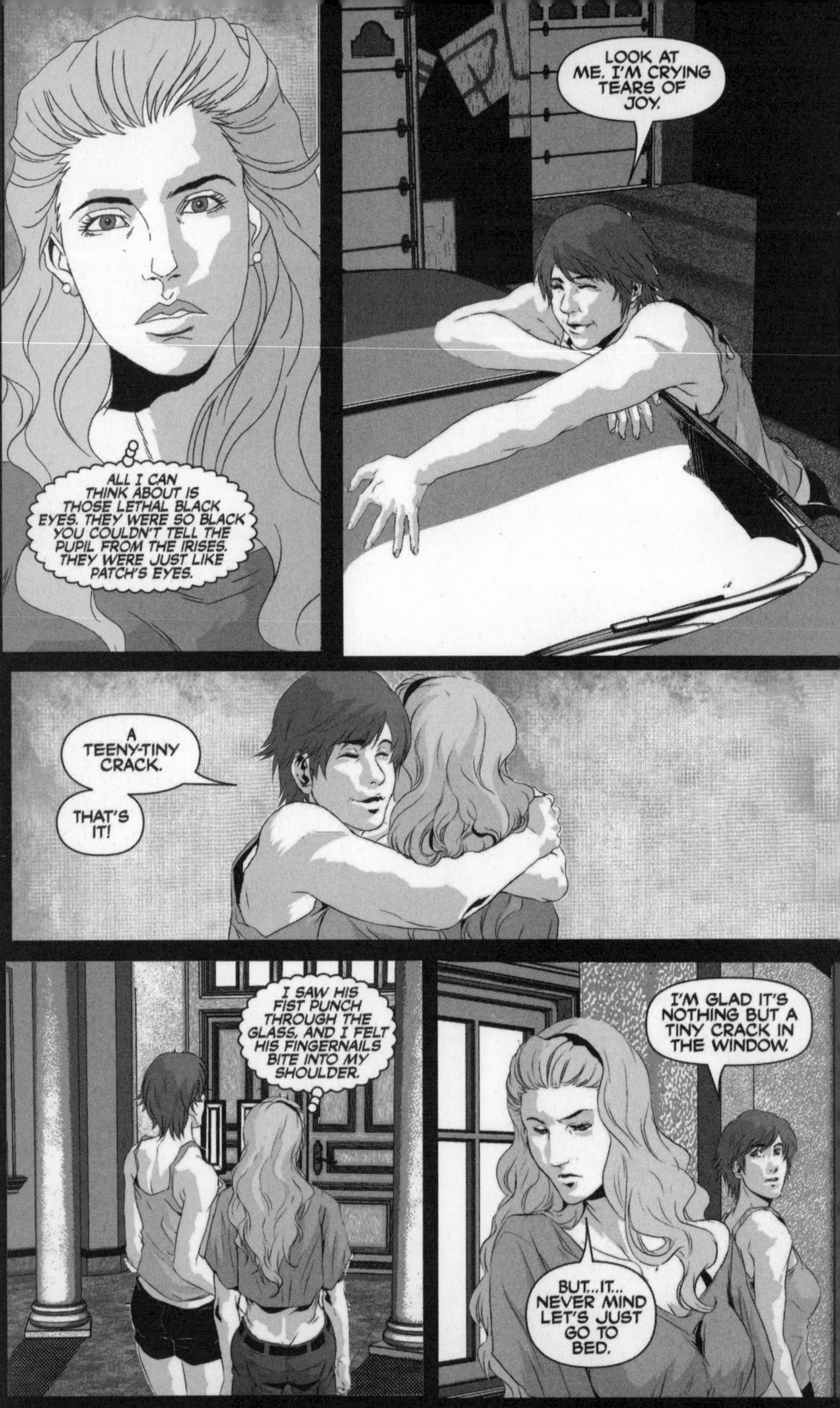
ALL I CAN THINK ABOUT IS THOSE LETHAL BLACK EYES. THEY WERE SO BLACK YOU COULDN'T TELL THE PUPIL FROM THE IRISES. THEY WERE JUST LIKE PATCH'S EYES.
LOOK AT ME. I'M CRYING TEARS OF JOY.
A TEENY-TINY CRACK.
THAT'S IT!
I SAW HIS FIST PUNCH THROUGH THE GLASS, AND I FELT HIS FINGERNAILS BITE INTO MY SHOULDER.
I'M GLAD IT'S NOTHING BUT A TINY CRACK IN THE WINDOW.
BUT...IT... NEVER MIND LET'S JUST GO TO BED.

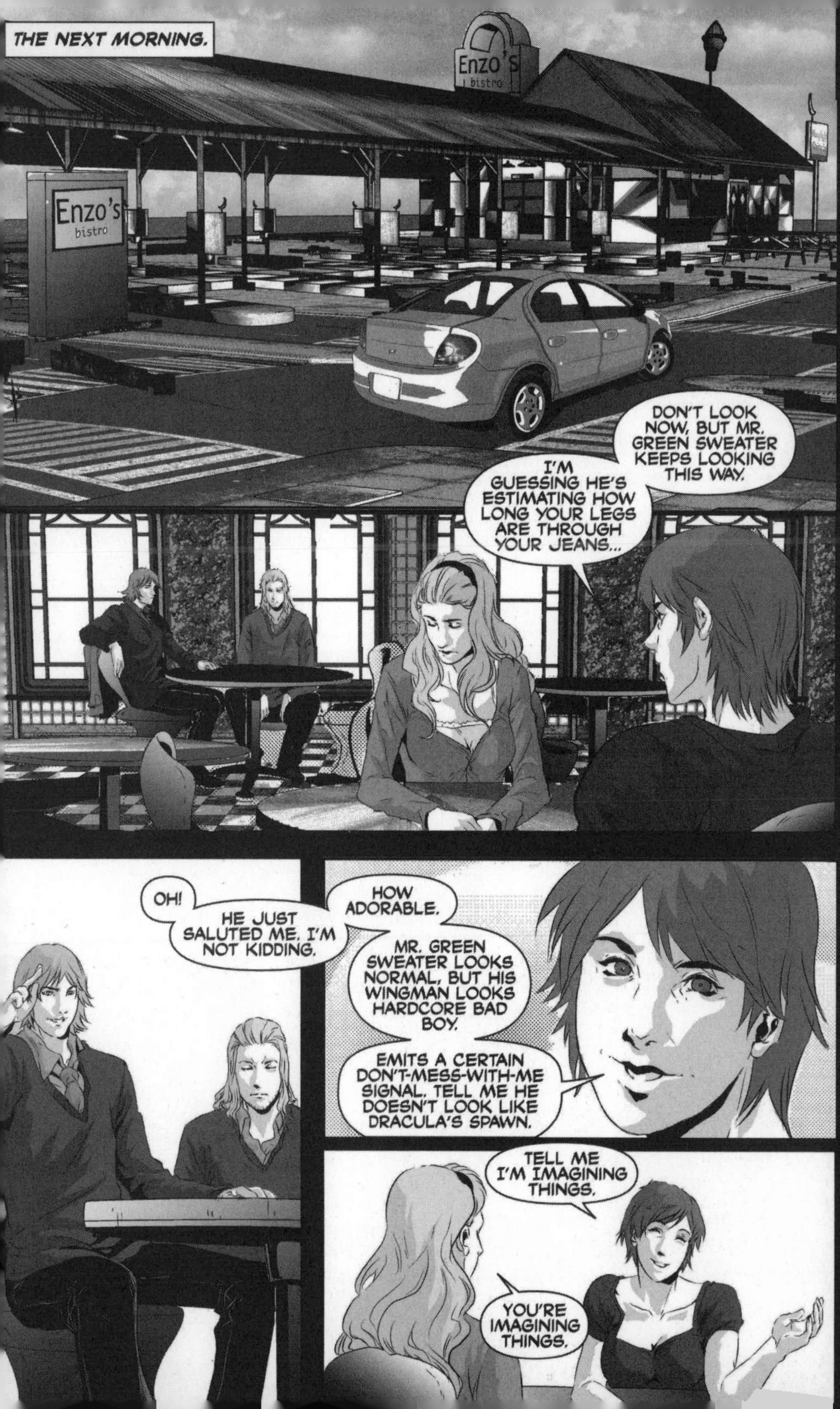
THE NEXT MORNING.
Enzo's bistro
Enzo's bistro
DON'T LOOK NOW, BUT MR. GREEN SWEATER KEEPS LOOKING THIS WAY.
I'M GUESSING HE'S ESTIMATING HOW LONG YOUR LEGS ARE THROUGH YOUR JEANS...
OH!
HE JUST SALUTED ME. I'M NOT KIDDING.
HOW ADORABLE.
MR. GREEN SWEATER LOOKS NORMAL, BUT HIS WINGMAN LOOKS HARDCORE BAD BOY.
EMITS A CERTAIN DON'T-MESS-WITH-ME SIGNAL. TELL ME HE DOESN'T LOOK LIKE DRACULA'S SPAWN.
TELL ME I'M IMAGINING THINGS.
YOU'RE IMAGINING THINGS.

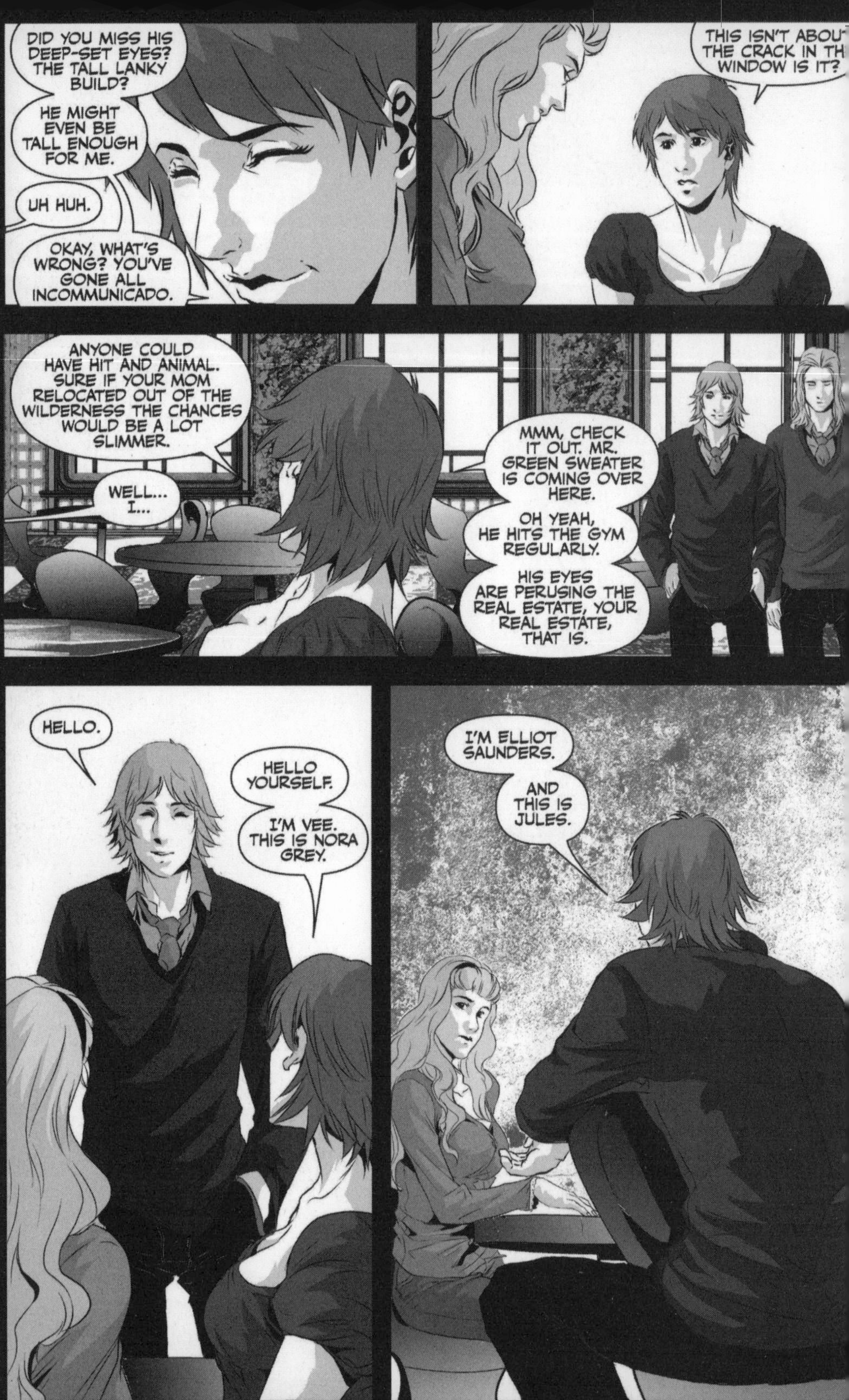
DID YOU MISS HIS DEEP-SET EYES? THE TALL LANKY BUILD?
HE MIGHT EVEN BE TALL ENOUGH FOR ME.
UH HUH.
OKAY, WHAT'S WRONG? YOU'VE GONE ALL INCOMMUNICADO.
THIS ISN'T ABOU THE CRACK IN TH WINDOW IS IT?
ANYONE COULD HAVE HIT AND ANIMAL. SURE IF YOUR MOM RELOCATED OUT OF THE WILDERNESS THE CHANCES WOULD BE A LOT SLIMMER.
WELL... I...
MMM, CHECK IT OUT. MR. GREEN SWEATER IS COMING OVER HERE.
OH YEAH, HE HITS THE GYM REGULARLY.
HIS EYES ARE PERUSING THE REAL ESTATE, YOUR REAL ESTATE, THAT IS.
HELLO.
HELLO YOURSELF.
I'M VEE. THIS IS NORA GREY.
I'M ELLIOT SAUNDERS.
AND THIS IS JULES.

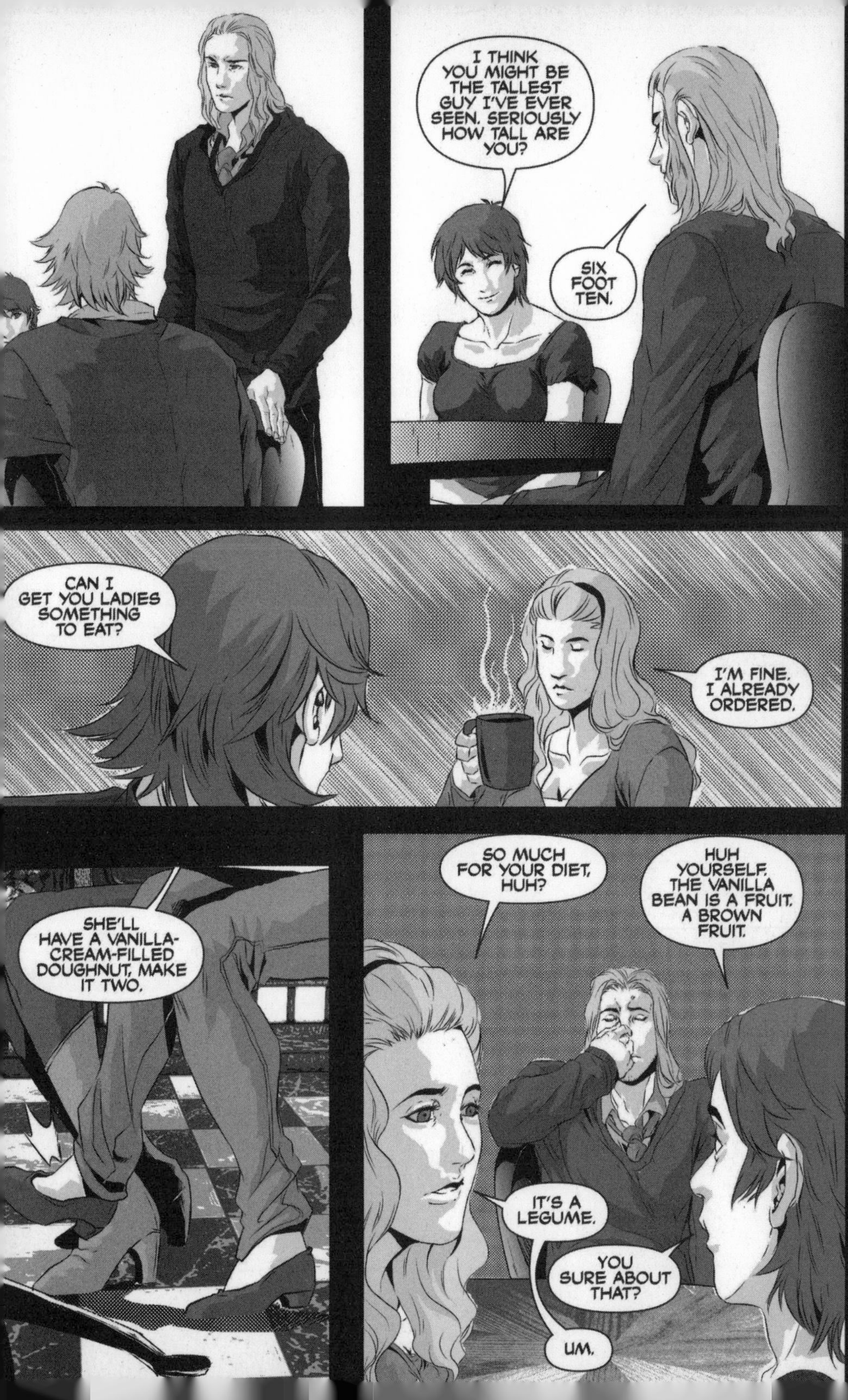
I THINK YOU MIGHT BE THE TALLEST GUY I'VE EVER SEEN. SERIOUSLY HOW TALL ARE YOU?
SIX FOOT TEN.
CAN I GET YOU LADIES SOMETHING TO EAT?
I'M FINE. I ALREADY ORDERED.
SHE'LL HAVE A VANILLA-CREAM-FILLED DOUGHNUT, MAKE IT TWO.
SO MUCH FOR YOUR DIET, HUH?
HUH YOURSELF. THE VANILLA BEAN IS A FRUIT. A BROWN FRUIT.
IT'S A LEGUME.
YOU SURE ABOUT THAT?
UM.

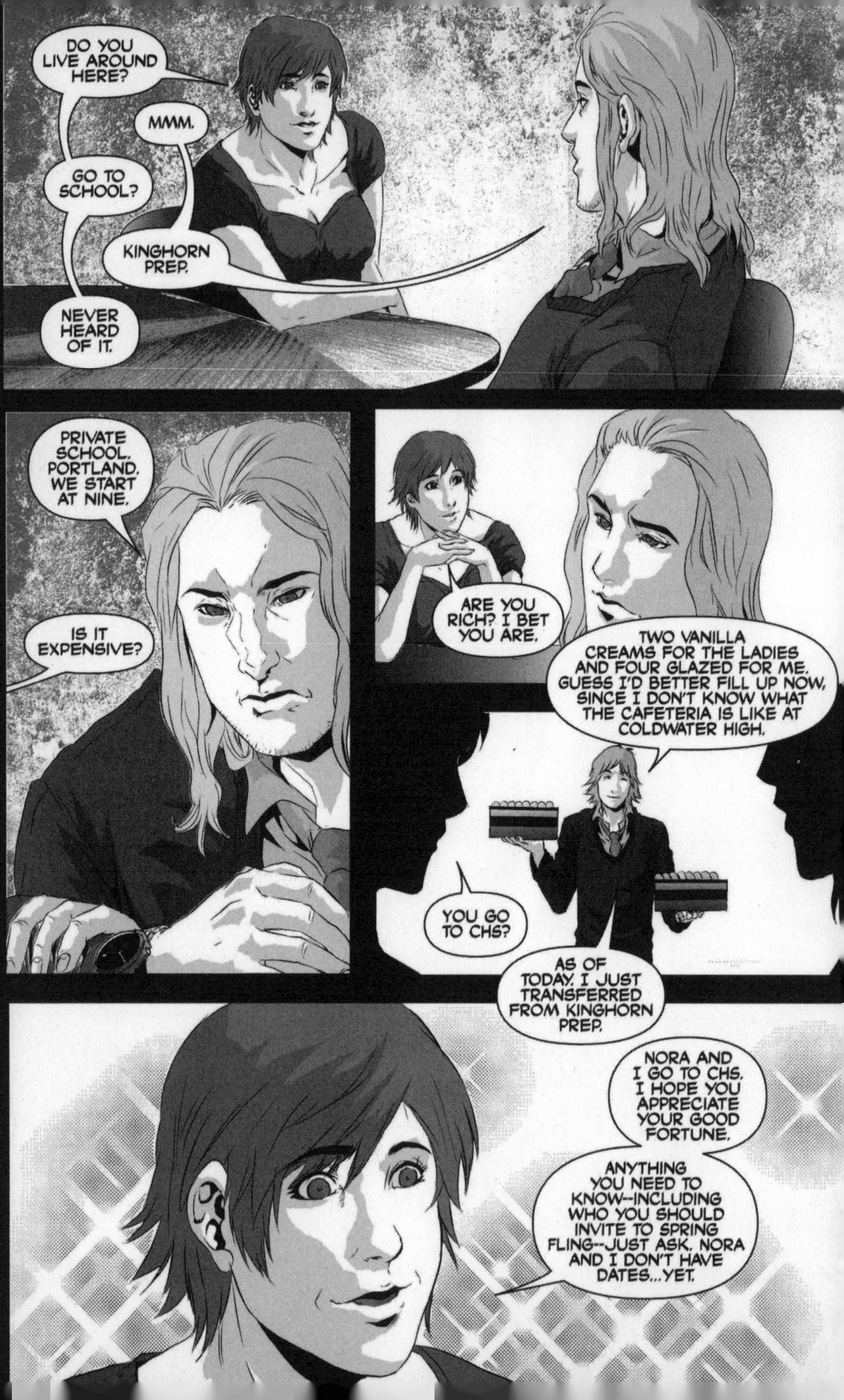
DO YOU LIVE AROUND HERE?
MMM.
GO TO SCHOOL?
KINGHORN PREP.
NEVER HEARD OF IT.
PRIVATE SCHOOL, PORTLAND. WE START AT NINE.
IS IT EXPENSIVE?
ARE YOU RICH? I BET YOU ARE.
TWO VANILLA CREAMS FOR THE LADIES AND FOUR GLAZED FOR ME. GUESS I'D BETTER FILL UP NOW, SINCE I DON'T KNOW WHAT THE CAFETERIA IS LIKE AT COLDWATER HIGH.
YOU GO TO CHS?
AS OF TODAY. I JUST TRANSFERRED FROM KINGHORN PREP.
NORA AND I GO TO CHS. I HOPE YOU APPRECIATE YOUR GOOD FORTUNE.
ANYTHING YOU NEED TO KNOW--INCLUDING WHO YOU SHOULD INVITE TO SPRING FLING--JUST ASK. NORA AND I DON'T HAVE DATES...YET.

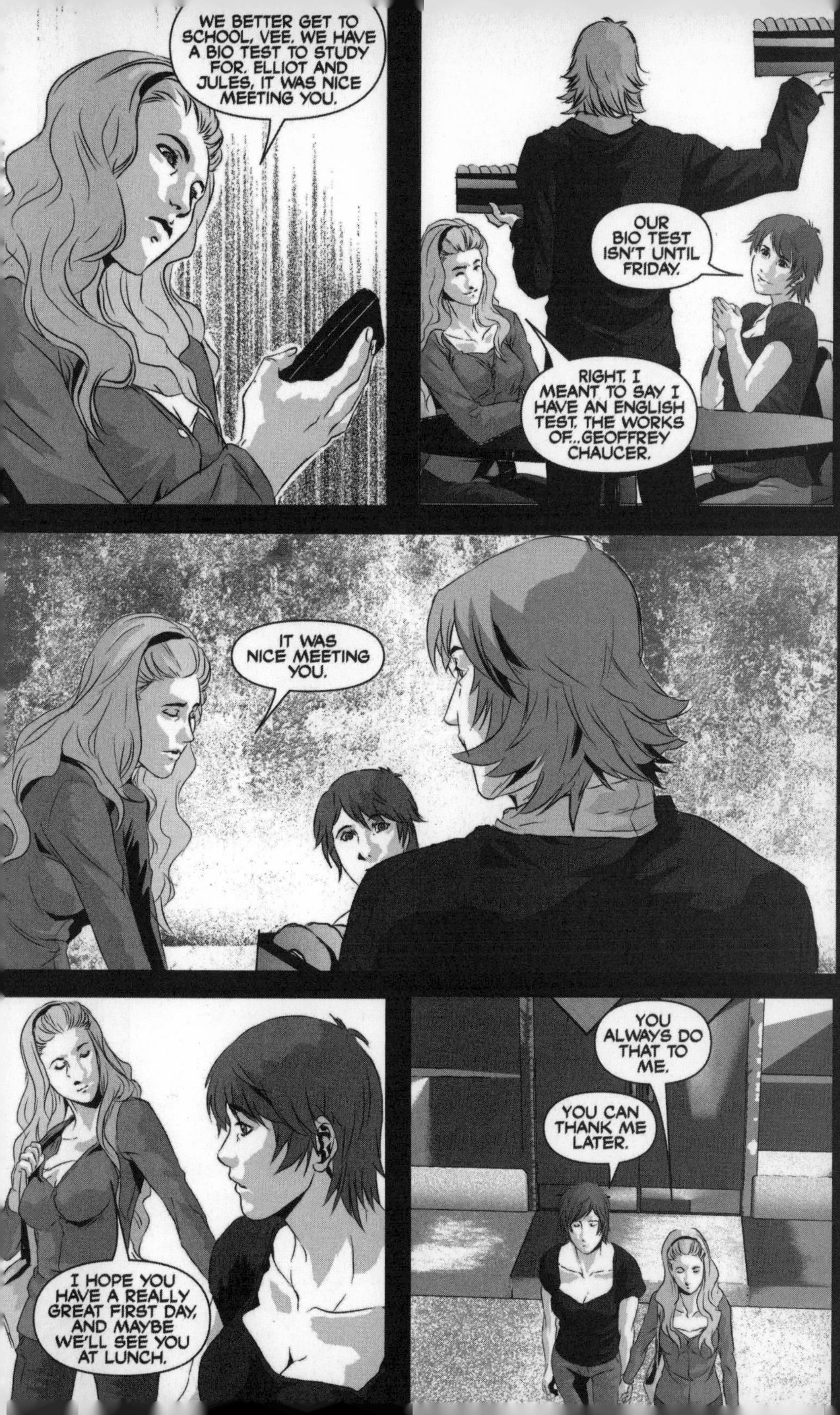
WE BETTER GET TO SCHOOL, VEE. WE HAVE A BIO TEST TO STUDY FOR. ELLIOT AND JULES, IT WAS NICE MEETING YOU.
OUR BIO TEST ISN'T UNTIL FRIDAY.
RIGHT. I MEANT TO SAY I HAVE AN ENGLISH TEST. THE WORKS OF...GEOFFREY CHAUCER.
IT WAS NICE MEETING YOU.
I HOPE YOU HAVE A REALLY GREAT FIRST DAY, AND MAYBE WE'LL SEE YOU AT LUNCH.
YOU ALWAYS DO THAT TO ME.
YOU CAN THANK ME LATER.

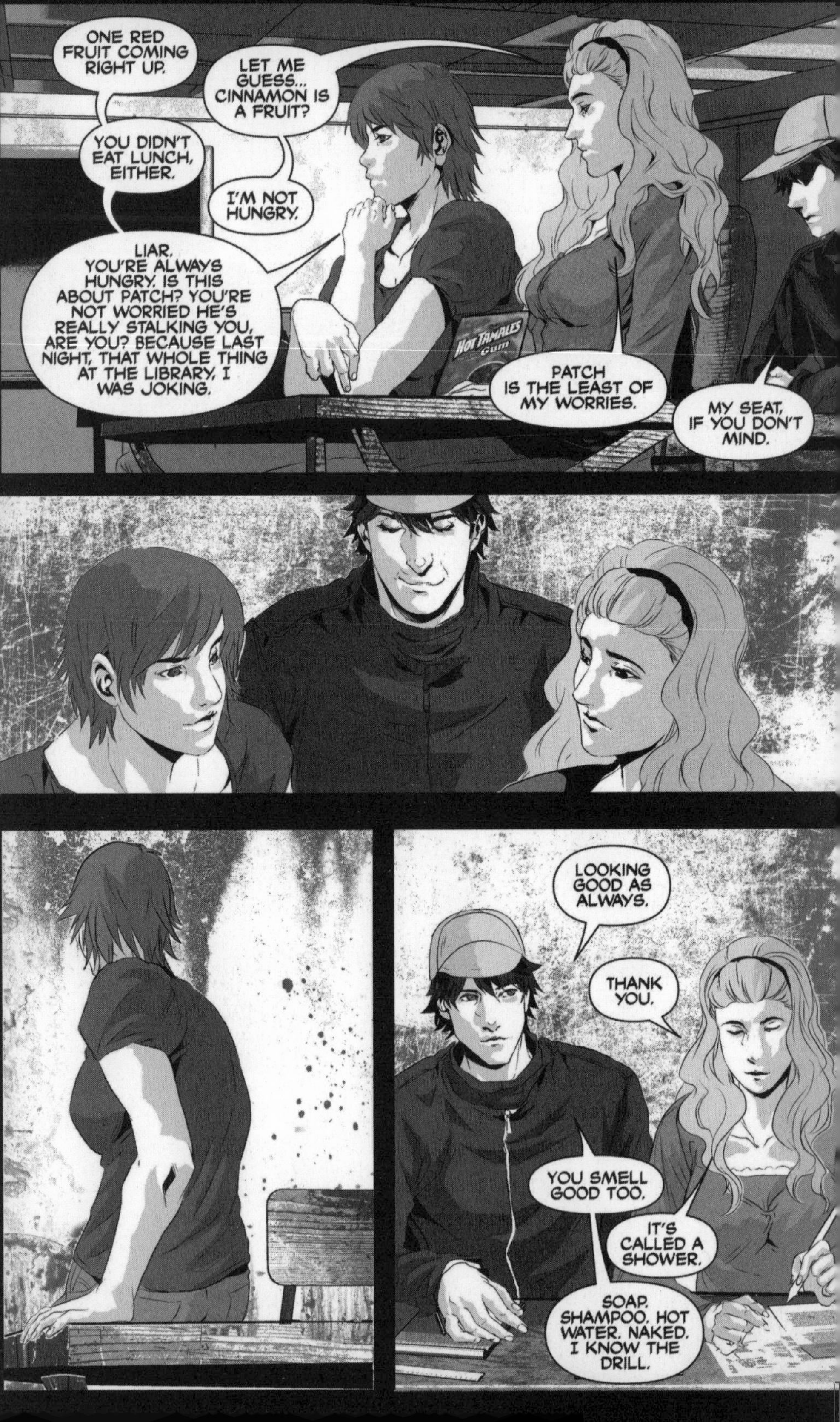
ONE RED FRUIT COMING RIGHT UP.
LET ME GUESS... CINNAMON IS A FRUIT?
YOU DIDN'T EAT LUNCH, EITHER.
I'M NOT HUNGRY.
LIAR. YOU'RE ALWAYS HUNGRY. IS THIS ABOUT PATCH? YOU'RE NOT WORRIED HE'S REALLY STALKING YOU, ARE YOU? BECAUSE LAST NIGHT, THAT WHOLE THING AT THE LIBRARY, I WAS JOKING.
HOT TAMALES Gum
PATCH IS THE LEAST OF MY WORRIES.
MY SEAT, IF YOU DON'T MIND.
LOOKING GOOD AS ALWAYS.
THANK YOU.
YOU SMELL GOOD TOO.
IT'S CALLED A SHOWER.
SOAP. SHAMPOO. HOT WATER. NAKED. I KNOW THE DRILL.

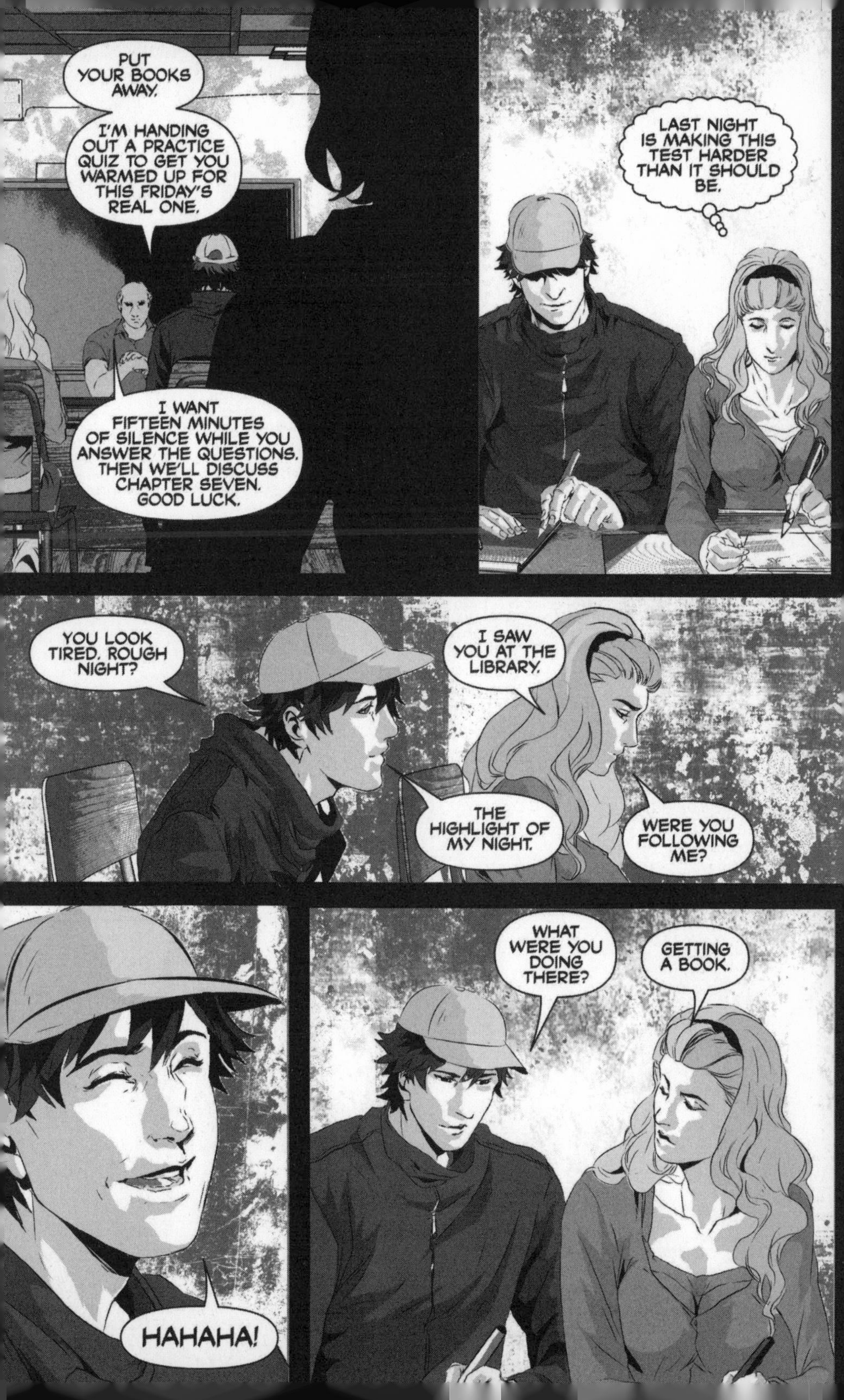
PUT YOUR BOOKS AWAY.
I'M HANDING OUT A PRACTICE QUIZ TO GET YOU WARMED UP FOR THIS FRIDAY'S REAL ONE.
I WANT FIFTEEN MINUTES OF SILENCE WHILE YOU ANSWER THE QUESTIONS. THEN WE'LL DISCUSS CHAPTER SEVEN. GOOD LUCK.
LAST NIGHT IS MAKING THIS TEST HARDER THAN IT SHOULD BE.
YOU LOOK TIRED. ROUGH NIGHT?
I SAW YOU AT THE LIBRARY.
THE HIGHLIGHT OF MY NIGHT.
WERE YOU FOLLOWING ME?
HAHAHA!
WHAT WERE YOU DOING THERE?
GETTING A BOOK.

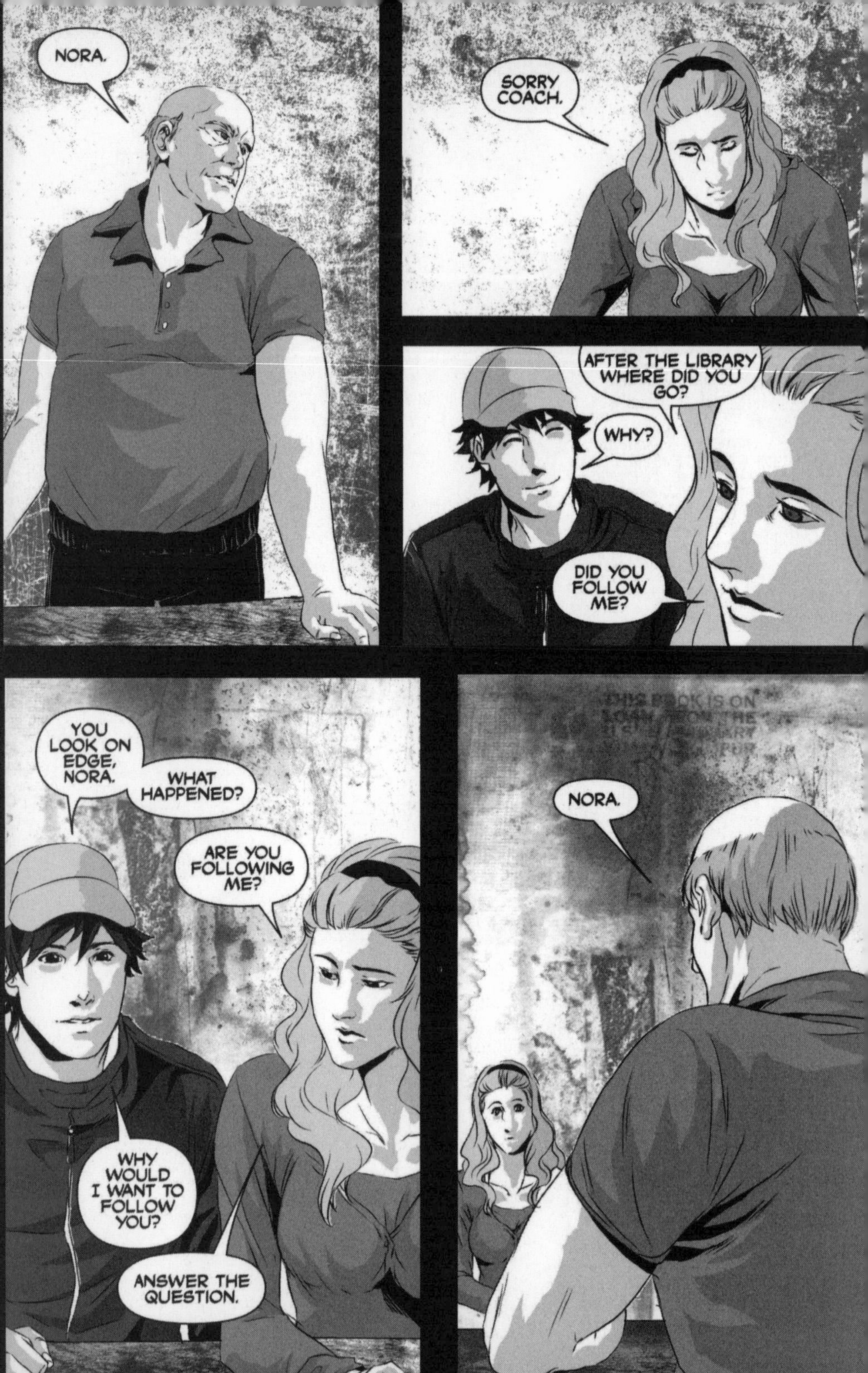
NORA.
SORRY COACH.
AFTER THE LIBRARY WHERE DID YOU GO?
WHY?
DID YOU FOLLOW ME?
YOU LOOK ON EDGE, NORA.
WHAT HAPPENED?
ARE YOU FOLLOWING ME?
WHY WOULD I WANT TO FOLLOW YOU?
ANSWER THE QUESTION.
NORA.

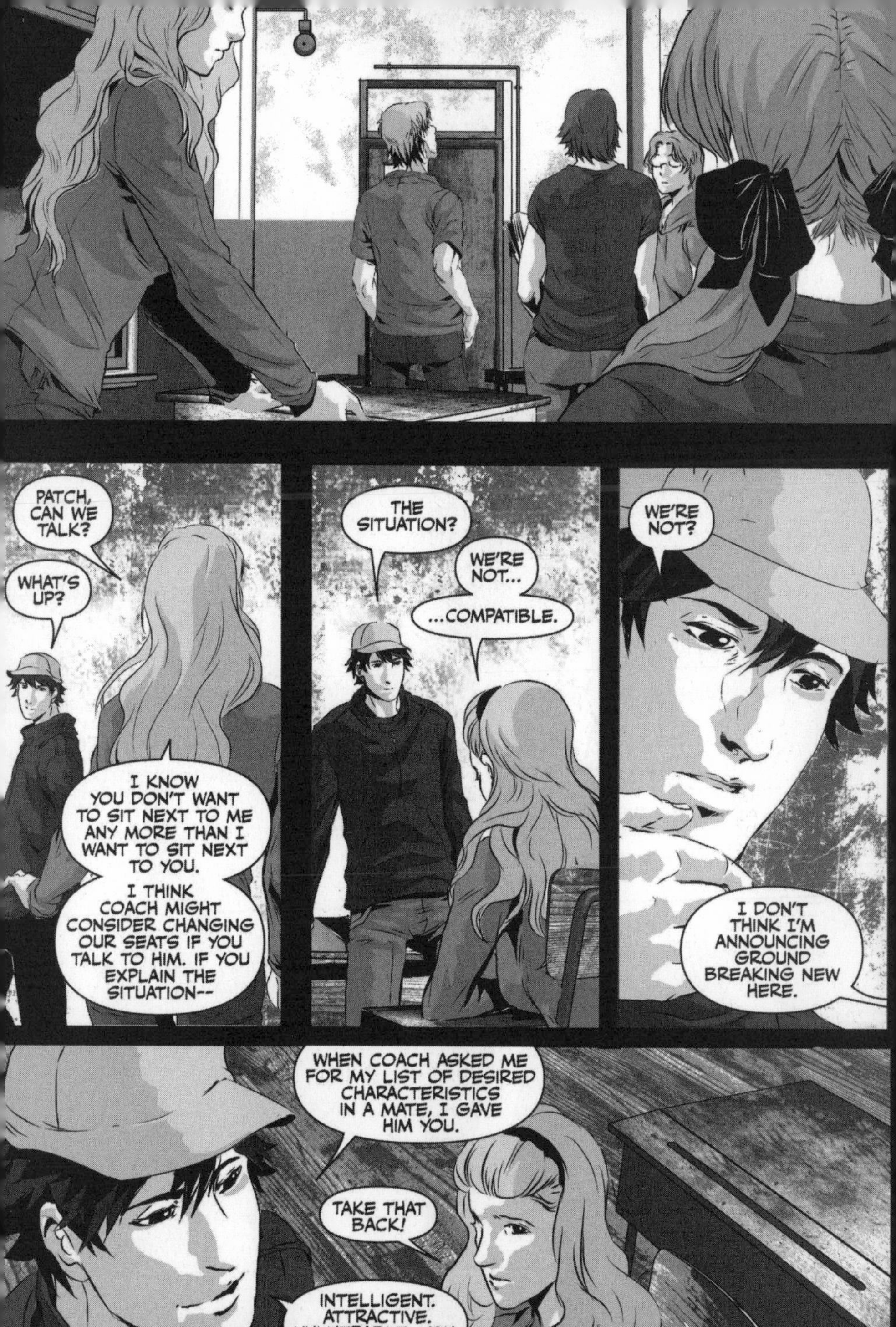
PATCH, CAN WE TALK?
WHAT'S UP?
I KNOW YOU DON'T WANT TO SIT NEXT TO ME ANY MORE THAN I WANT TO SIT NEXT TO YOU.
I THINK COACH MIGHT CONSIDER CHANGING OUR SEATS IF YOU TALK TO HIM. IF YOU EXPLAIN THE SITUATION--
THE SITUATION?
WE'RE NOT...
...COMPATIBLE.
WE'RE NOT?
I DON'T THINK I'M ANNOUNCING GROUND BREAKING NEW HERE.
WHEN COACH ASKED ME FOR MY LIST OF DESIRED CHARACTERISTICS IN A MATE, I GAVE HIM YOU.
TAKE THAT BACK!
INTELLIGENT. ATTRACTIVE. VULNERABLE. YOU DISAGREE?

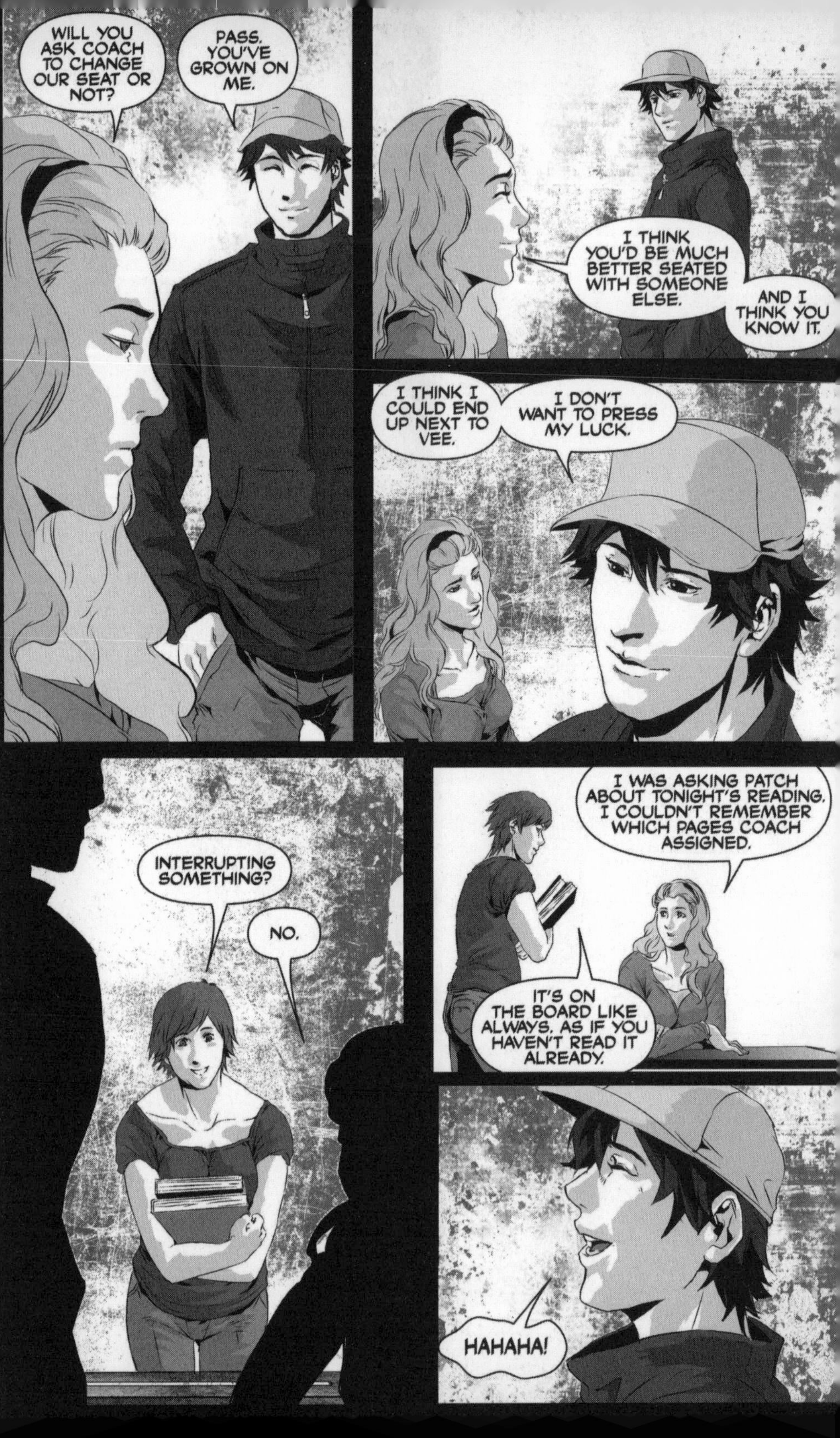
WILL YOU ASK COACH TO CHANGE OUR SEAT OR NOT?
PASS. YOU'VE GROWN ON ME.
I THINK YOU'D BE MUCH BETTER SEATED WITH SOMEONE ELSE.
AND I THINK YOU KNOW IT.
I THINK I COULD END UP NEXT TO VEE.
I DON'T WANT TO PRESS MY LUCK.
INTERRUPTING SOMETHING?
NO.
I WAS ASKING PATCH ABOUT TONIGHT'S READING. I COULDN'T REMEMBER WHICH PAGES COACH ASSIGNED.
IT'S ON THE BOARD LIKE ALWAYS, AS IF YOU HAVEN'T READ IT ALREADY.
HAHAHA!

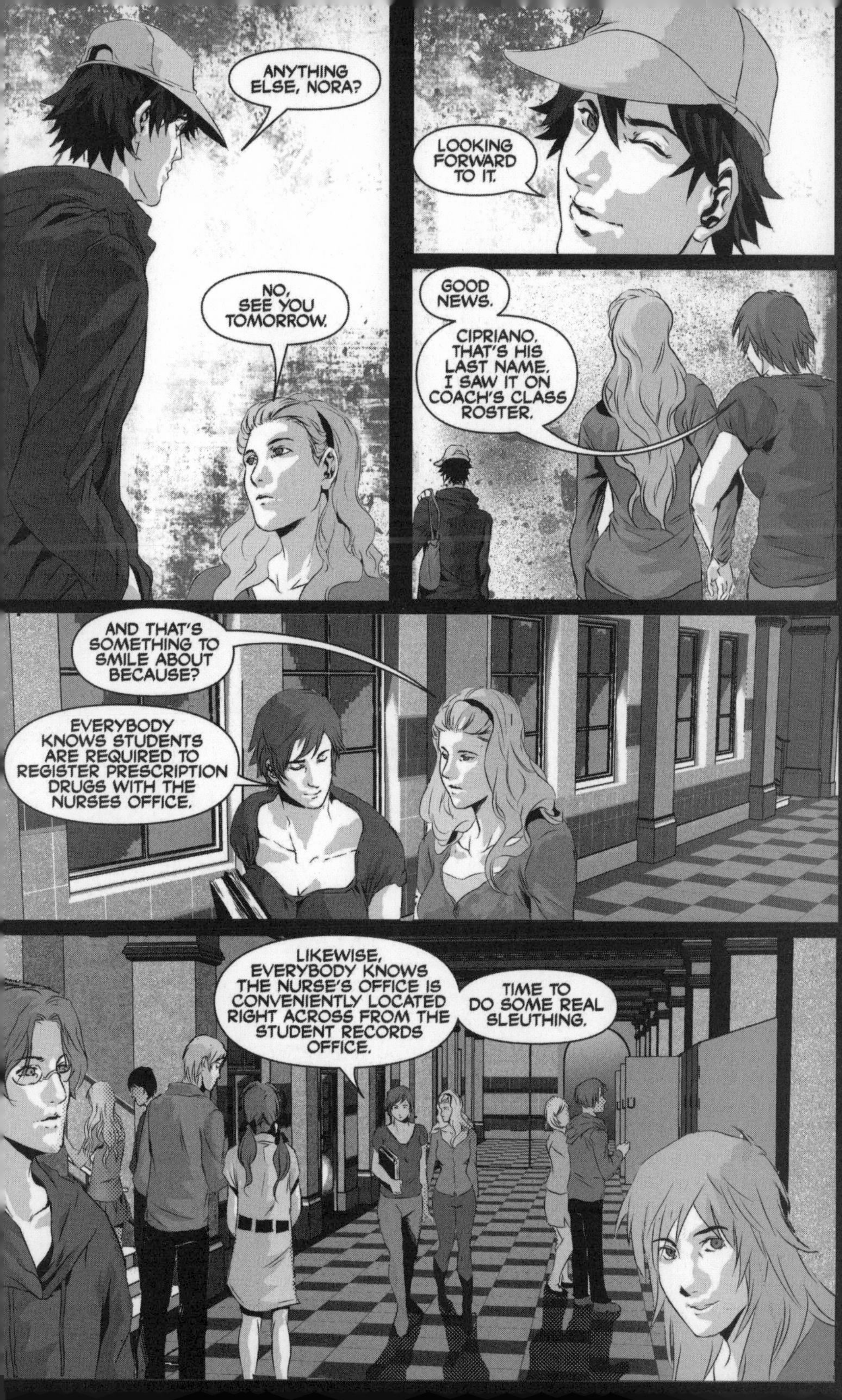
ANYTHING ELSE, NORA?
LOOKING FORWARD TO IT.
NO, SEE YOU TOMORROW.
GOOD NEWS.
CIPRIANO, THAT'S HIS LAST NAME. I SAW IT ON COACH'S CLASS ROSTER.
AND THAT'S SOMETHING TO SMILE ABOUT BECAUSE?
EVERYBODY KNOWS STUDENTS ARE REQUIRED TO REGISTER PRESCRIPTION DRUGS WITH THE NURSES OFFICE.
LIKEWISE, EVERYBODY KNOWS THE NURSE'S OFFICE IS CONVENIENTLY LOCATED RIGHT ACROSS FROM THE STUDENT RECORDS OFFICE.
TIME TO DO SOME REAL SLEUTHING.

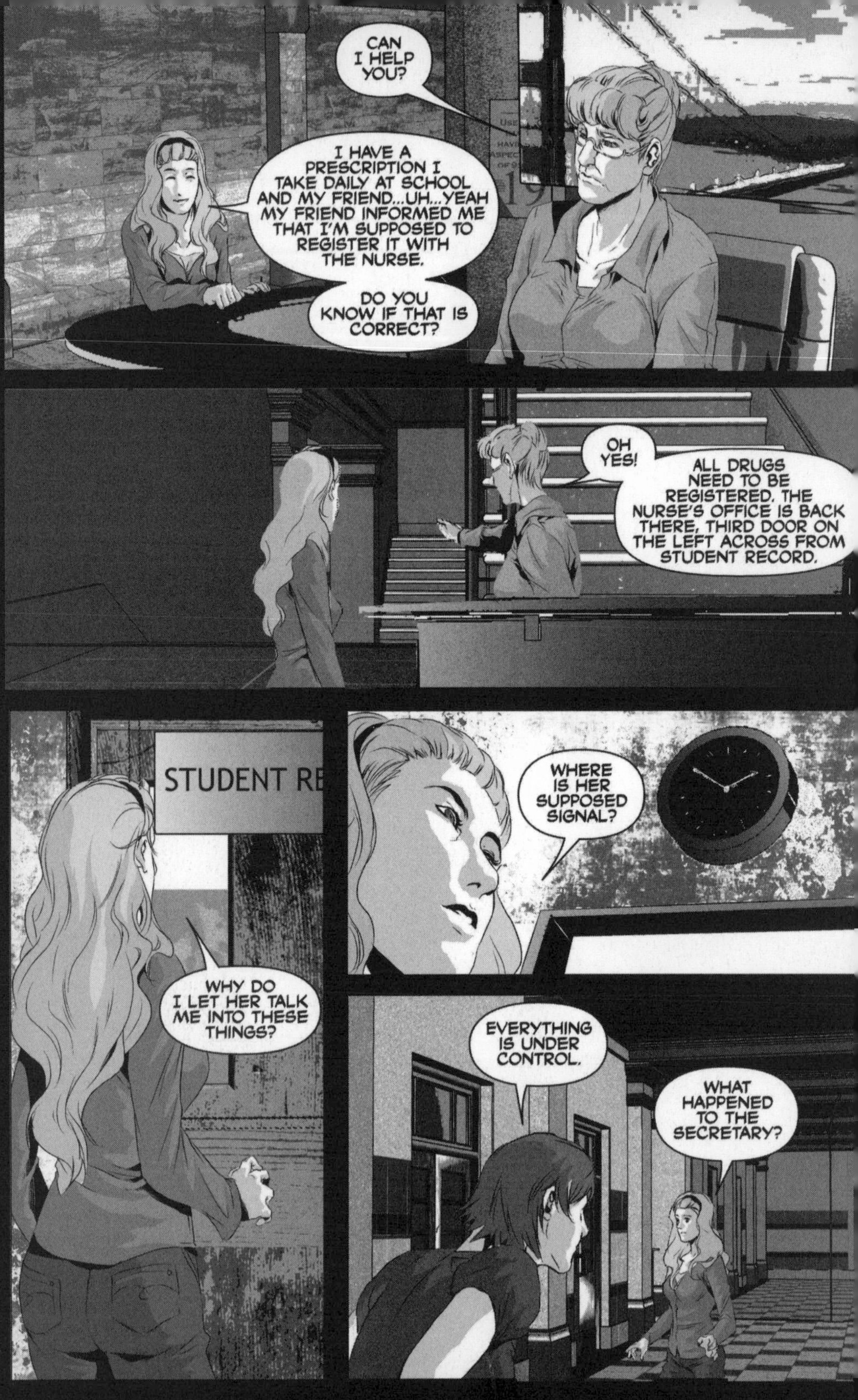
CAN I HELP YOU?
I HAVE A PRESCRIPTION I TAKE DAILY AT SCHOOL AND MY FRIEND...UH...YEAH MY FRIEND INFORMED ME THAT I'M SUPPOSED TO REGISTER IT WITH THE NURSE.
DO YOU KNOW IF THAT IS CORRECT?
OH YES!
ALL DRUGS NEED TO BE REGISTERED. THE NURSE'S OFFICE IS BACK THERE, THIRD DOOR ON THE LEFT ACROSS FROM STUDENT RECORD.
STUDENT RE
WHY DO I LET HER TALK ME INTO THESE THINGS?
WHERE IS HER SUPPOSED SIGNAL?
EVERYTHING IS UNDER CONTROL.
WHAT HAPPENED TO THE SECRETARY?

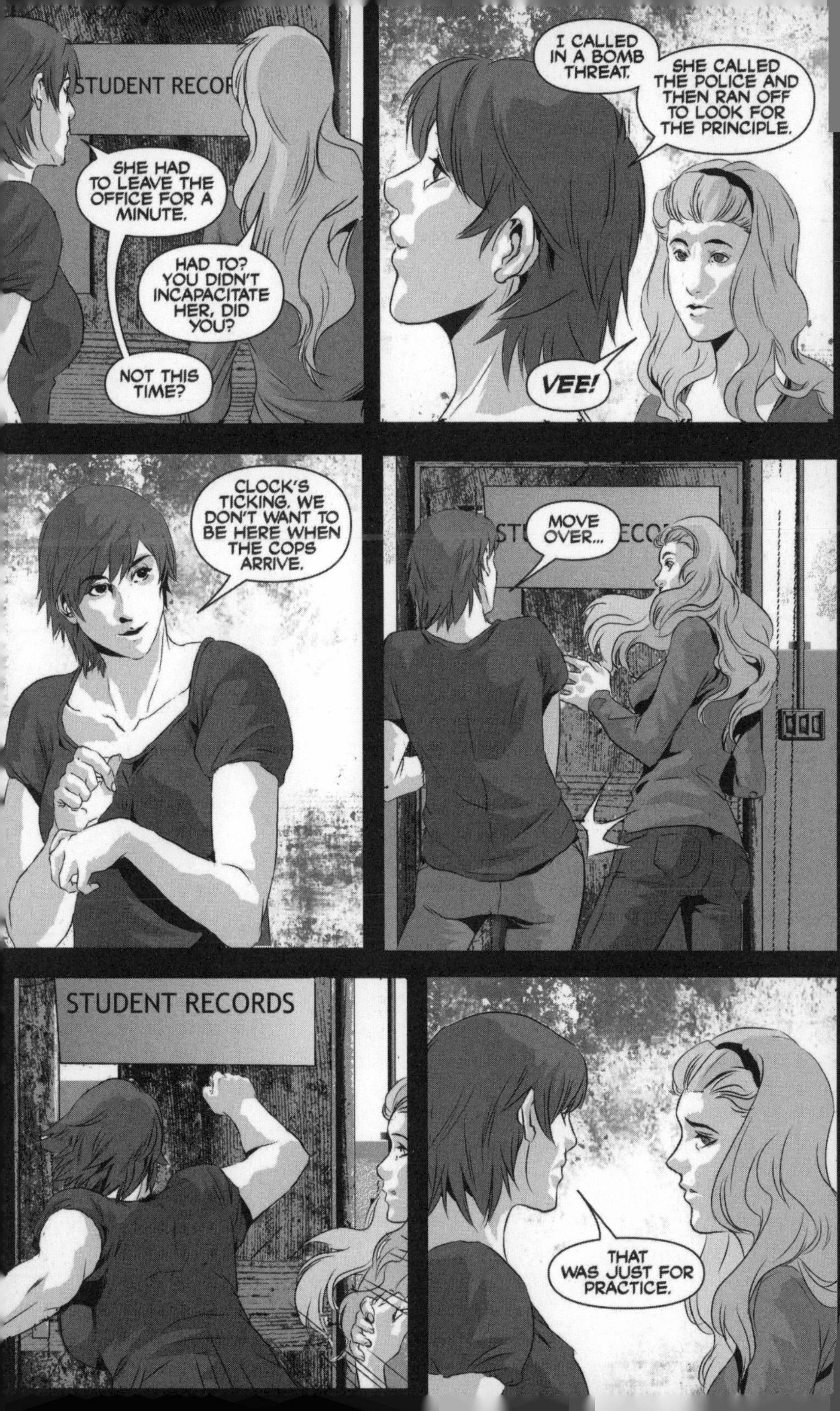
STUDENT RECOR
SHE HAD TO LEAVE THE OFFICE FOR A MINUTE.
HAD TO? YOU DIDN'T INCAPACITATE HER, DID YOU?
NOT THIS TIME?
I CALLED IN A BOMB THREAT.
SHE CALLED THE POLICE AND THEN RAN OFF TO LOOK FOR THE PRINCIPLE.
VEE!
CLOCK'S TICKING. WE DON'T WANT TO BE HERE WHEN THE COPS ARRIVE.
MOVE OVER...
STUDENT RECORDS
THAT WAS JUST FOR PRACTICE.

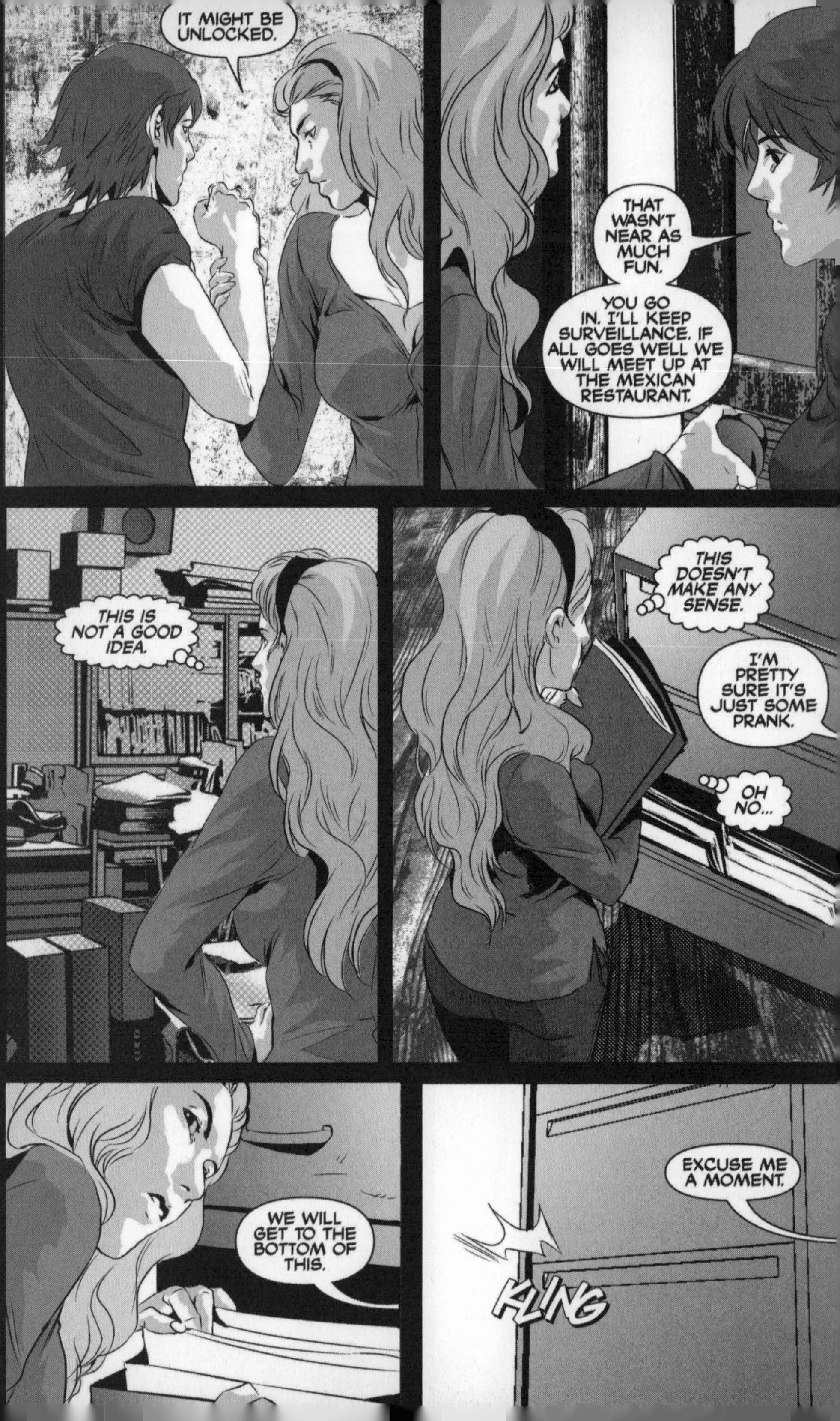
IT MIGHT BE UNLOCKED.
THAT WASN'T NEAR AS MUCH FUN.
YOU GO IN. I'LL KEEP SURVEILLANCE. IF ALL GOES WELL WE WILL MEET UP AT THE MEXICAN RESTAURANT.
THIS IS NOT A GOOD IDEA.
THIS DOESN'T MAKE ANY SENSE.
I'M PRETTY SURE IT'S JUST SOME PRANK.
OH NO...
WE WILL GET TO THE BOTTOM OF THIS.
EXCUSE ME A MOMENT.
KLING

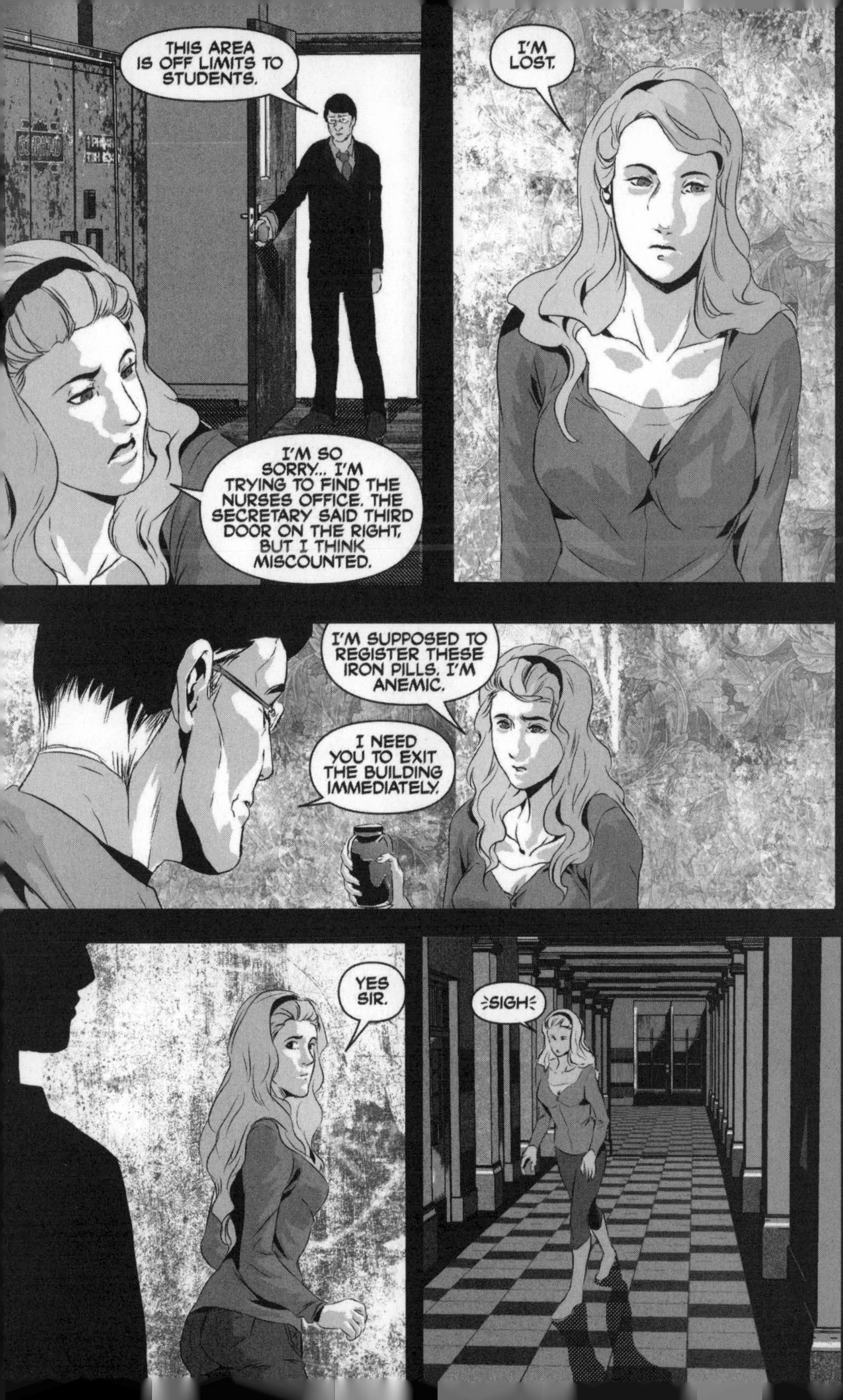
THIS AREA IS OFF LIMITS TO STUDENTS.
I'M SO SORRY... I'M TRYING TO FIND THE NURSES OFFICE. THE SECRETARY SAID THIRD DOOR ON THE RIGHT, BUT I THINK MISCOUNTED.
I'M LOST.
I'M SUPPOSED TO REGISTER THESE IRON PILLS. I'M ANEMIC.
I NEED YOU TO EXIT THE BUILDING IMMEDIATELY.
YES SIR.
SIGH

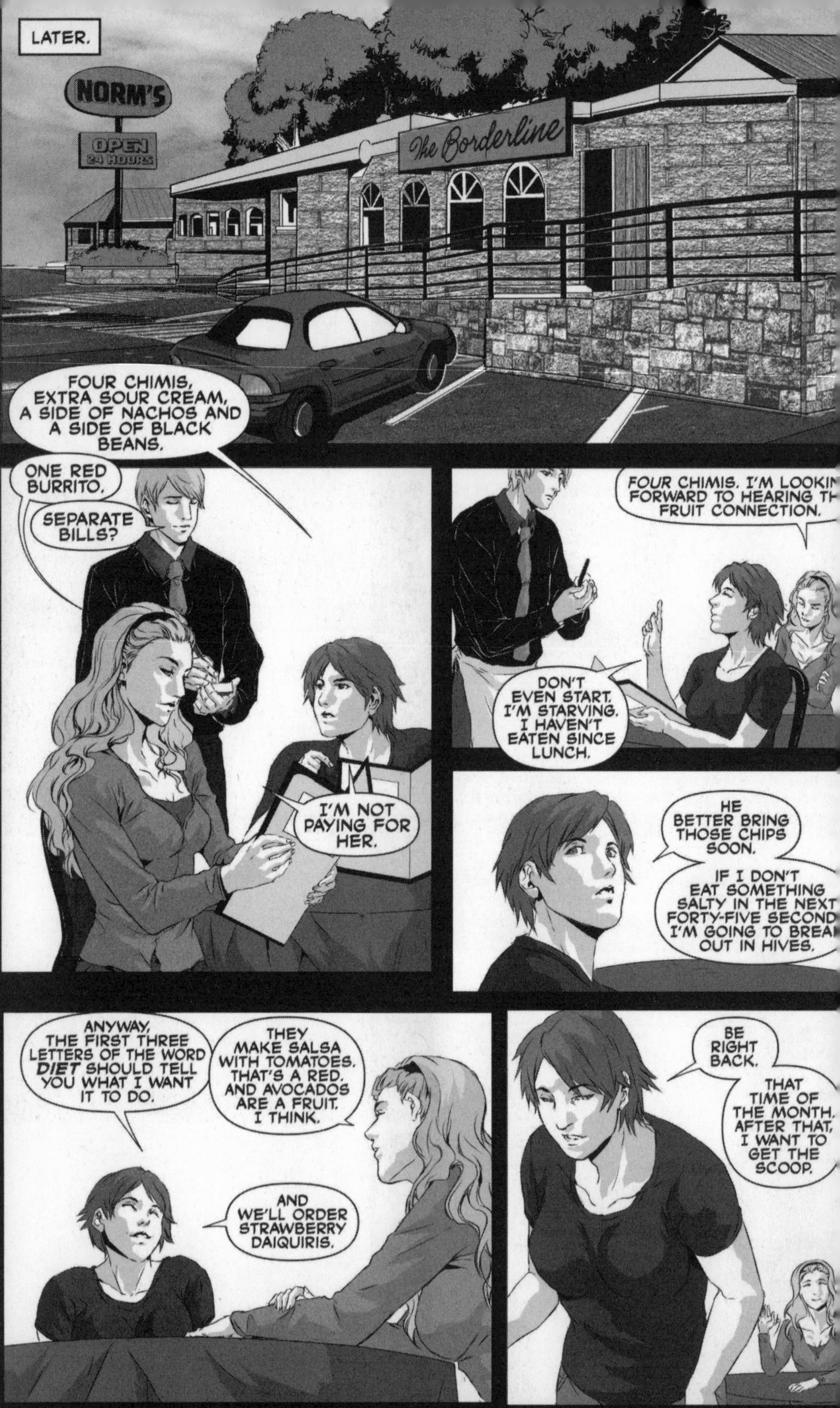
LATER.
NORM'S
OPEN 24 HOURS
The Borderline
FOUR CHIMIS, EXTRA SOUR CREAM, A SIDE OF NACHOS AND A SIDE OF BLACK BEANS.
ONE RED BURRITO.
SEPARATE BILLS?
I'M NOT PAYING FOR HER.
FOUR CHIMIS. I'M LOOKIN FORWARD TO HEARING TH FRUIT CONNECTION.
DON'T EVEN START. I'M STARVING. I HAVEN'T EATEN SINCE LUNCH.
HE BETTER BRING THOSE CHIPS SOON.
IF I DON'T EAT SOMETHING SALTY IN THE NEXT FORTY-FIVE SECOND I'M GOING TO BREA OUT IN HIVES.
THEY MAKE SALSA WITH TOMATOES. THAT'S A RED. AND AVOCADOS ARE A FRUIT. I THINK.
AND WE'LL ORDER STRAWBERRY DAIQUIRIS.
ANYWAY, THE FIRST THREE LETTERS OF THE WORD *DIET* SHOULD TELL YOU WHAT I WANT IT TO DO.
BE RIGHT BACK.
THAT TIME OF THE MONTH. AFTER THAT, I WANT TO GET THE SCOOP.

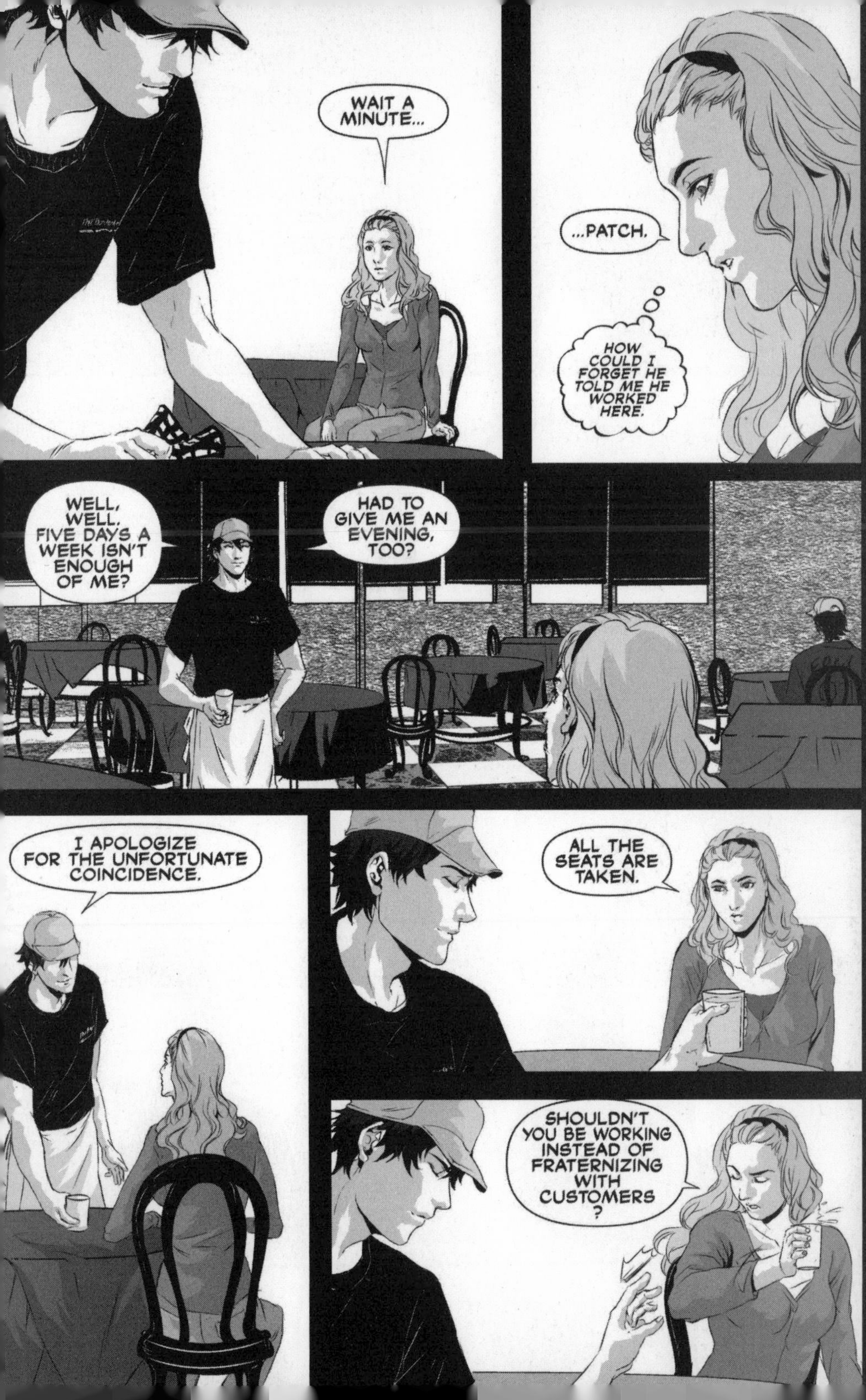
WAIT A MINUTE...
...PATCH.
HOW COULD I FORGET HE TOLD ME HE WORKED HERE.
WELL, WELL. FIVE DAYS A WEEK ISN'T ENOUGH OF ME?
HAD TO GIVE ME AN EVENING, TOO?
I APOLOGIZE FOR THE UNFORTUNATE COINCIDENCE.
ALL THE SEATS ARE TAKEN.
SHOULDN'T YOU BE WORKING INSTEAD OF FRATERNIZING WITH CUSTOMERS?

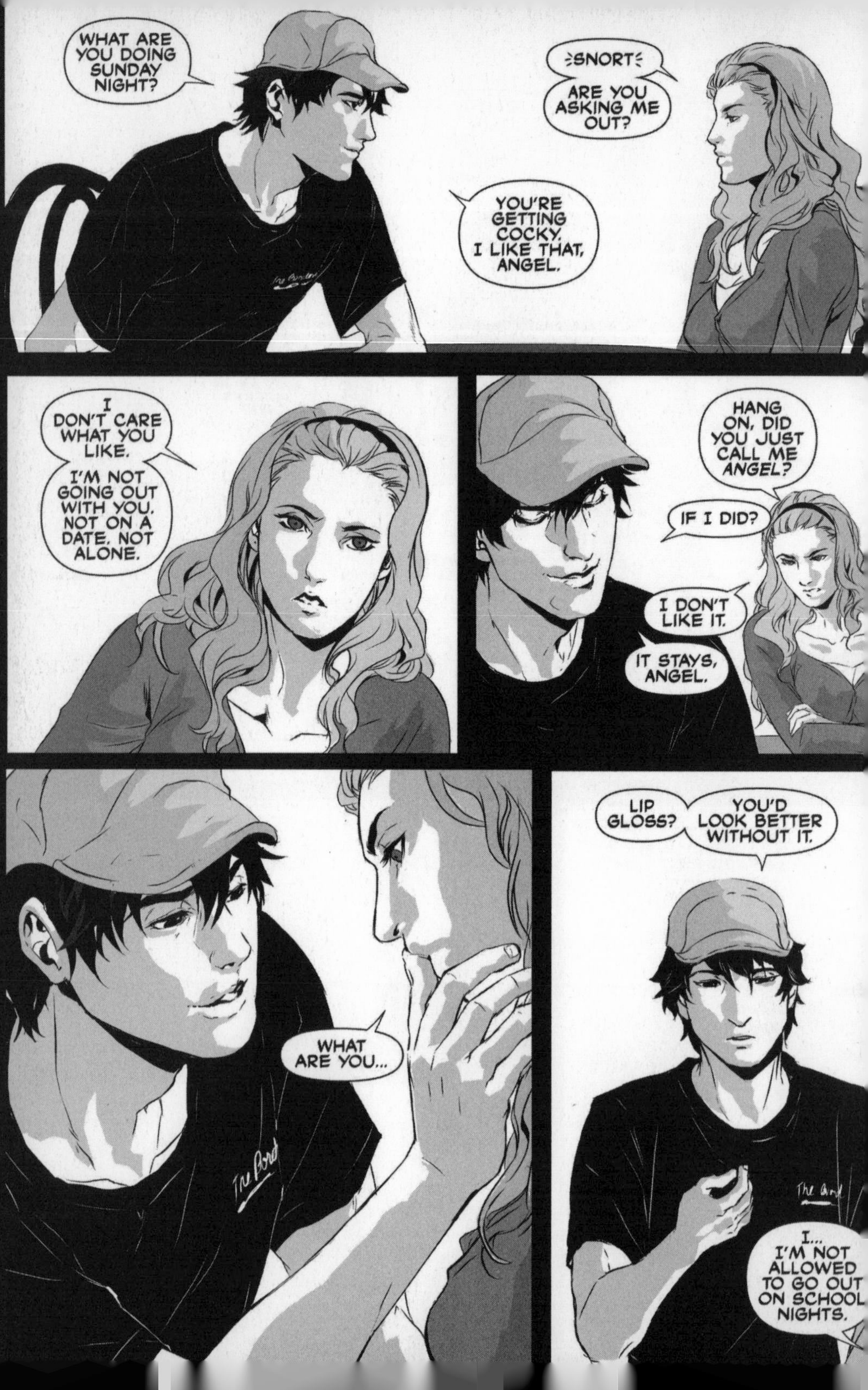
WHAT ARE YOU DOING SUNDAY NIGHT?
:SNORT:
ARE YOU ASKING ME OUT?
YOU'RE GETTING COCKY. I LIKE THAT, ANGEL.
I DON'T CARE WHAT YOU LIKE.
I'M NOT GOING OUT WITH YOU. NOT ON A DATE. NOT ALONE.
HANG ON, DID YOU JUST CALL ME ANGEL?
IF I DID?
I DON'T LIKE IT.
IT STAYS, ANGEL.
WHAT ARE YOU...
LIP GLOSS?
YOU'D LOOK BETTER WITHOUT IT.
I... I'M NOT ALLOWED TO GO OUT ON SCHOOL NIGHTS.

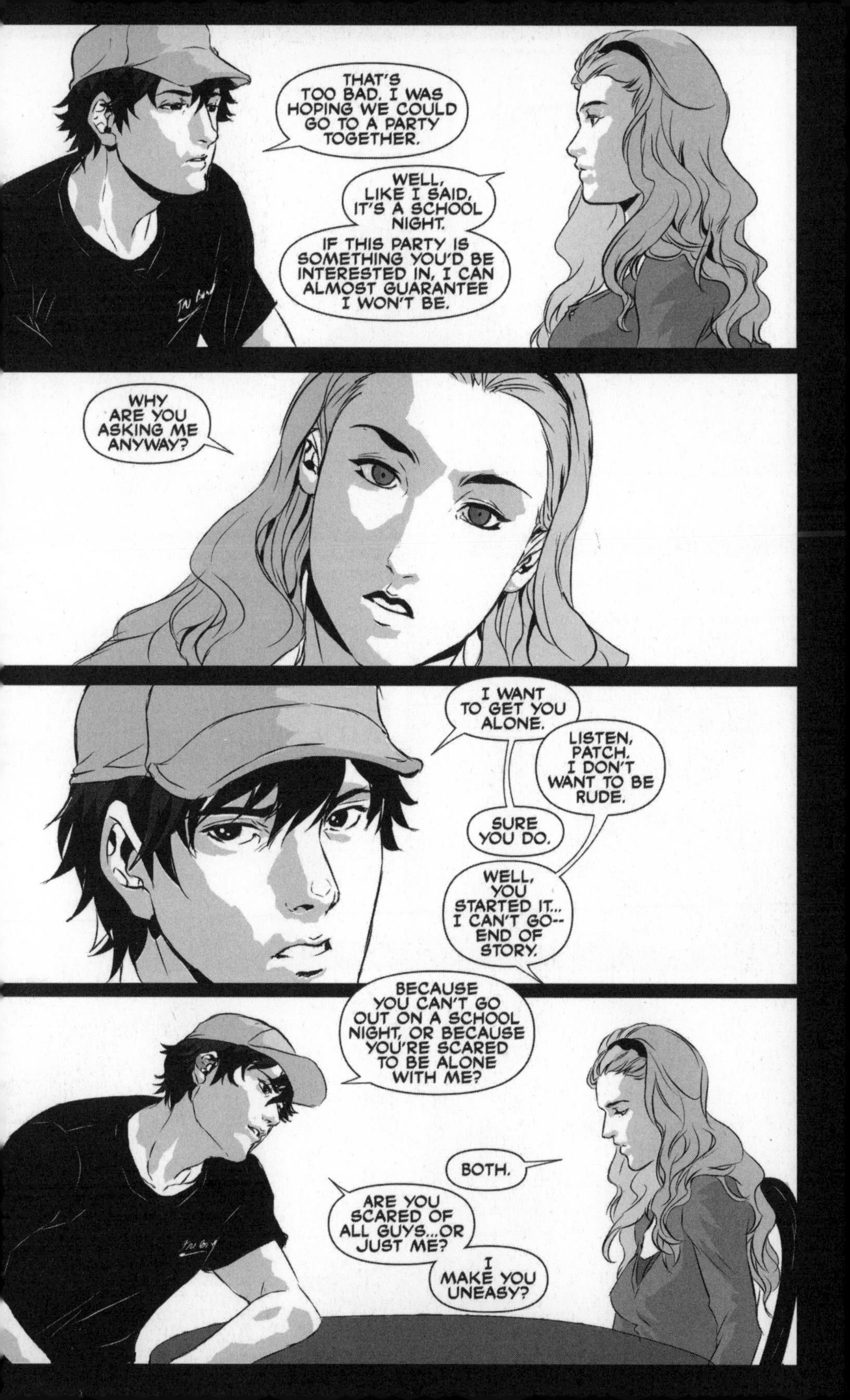
THAT'S TOO BAD. I WAS HOPING WE COULD GO TO A PARTY TOGETHER.
WELL, LIKE I SAID, IT'S A SCHOOL NIGHT.
IF THIS PARTY IS SOMETHING YOU'D BE INTERESTED IN, I CAN ALMOST GUARANTEE I WON'T BE.
WHY ARE YOU ASKING ME ANYWAY?
I WANT TO GET YOU ALONE.
LISTEN, PATCH. I DON'T WANT TO BE RUDE.
SURE YOU DO.
WELL, YOU STARTED IT... I CAN'T GO-- END OF STORY.
BECAUSE YOU CAN'T GO OUT ON A SCHOOL NIGHT, OR BECAUSE YOU'RE SCARED TO BE ALONE WITH ME?
BOTH.
ARE YOU SCARED OF ALL GUYS...OR JUST ME?
I MAKE YOU UNEASY?

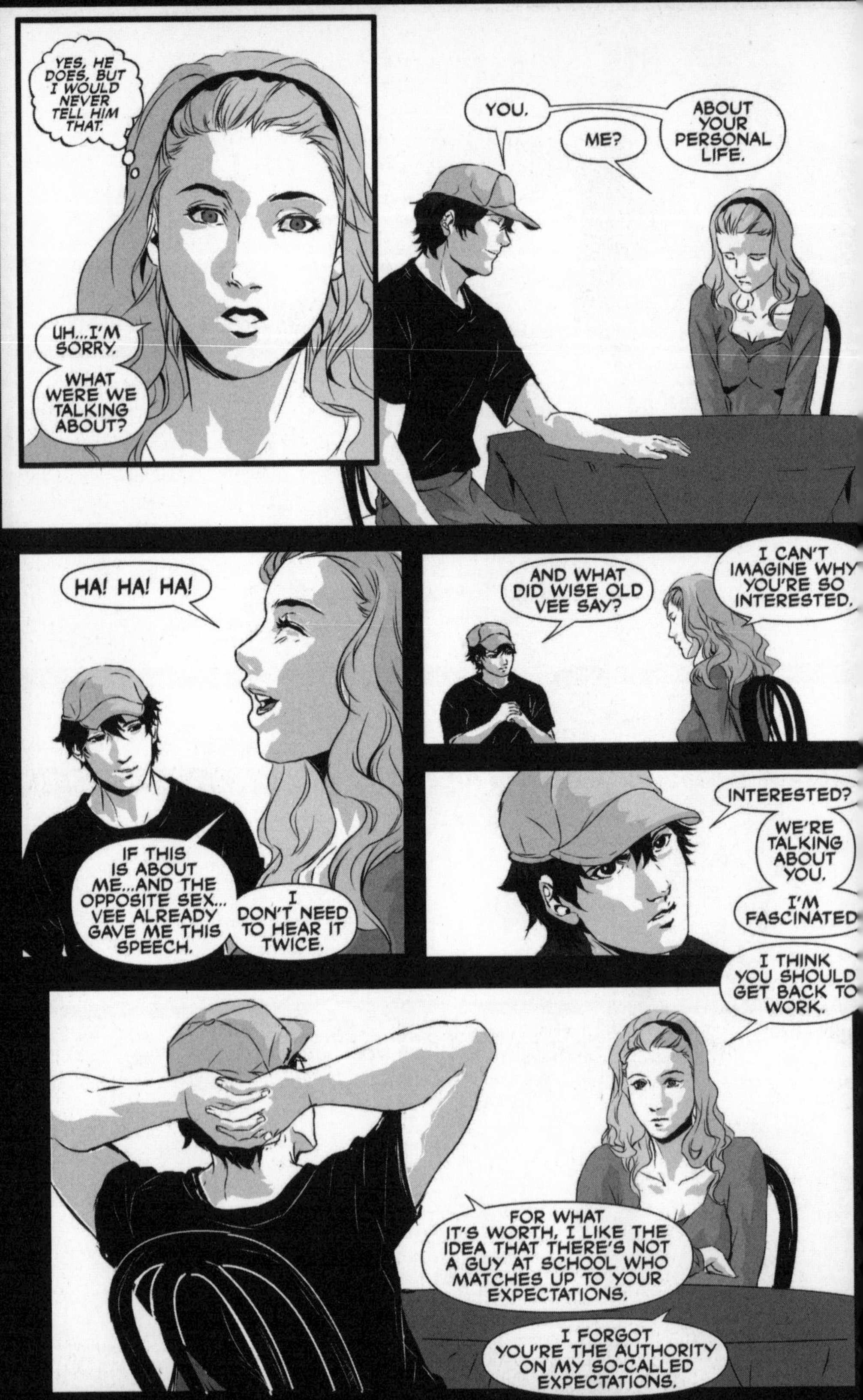
YES, HE DOES, BUT I WOULD NEVER TELL HIM THAT.
UH...I'M SORRY.
WHAT WERE WE TALKING ABOUT?
YOU.
ME?
ABOUT YOUR PERSONAL LIFE.
HA! HA! HA!
IF THIS IS ABOUT ME...AND THE OPPOSITE SEX... VEE ALREADY GAVE ME THIS SPEECH.
I DON'T NEED TO HEAR IT TWICE.
AND WHAT DID WISE OLD VEE SAY?
I CAN'T IMAGINE WHY YOU'RE SO INTERESTED.
INTERESTED?
WE'RE TALKING ABOUT YOU.
I'M FASCINATED.
I THINK YOU SHOULD GET BACK TO WORK.
FOR WHAT IT'S WORTH, I LIKE THE IDEA THAT THERE'S NOT A GUY AT SCHOOL WHO MATCHES UP TO YOUR EXPECTATIONS.
I FORGOT YOU'RE THE AUTHORITY ON MY SO-CALLED EXPECTATIONS.

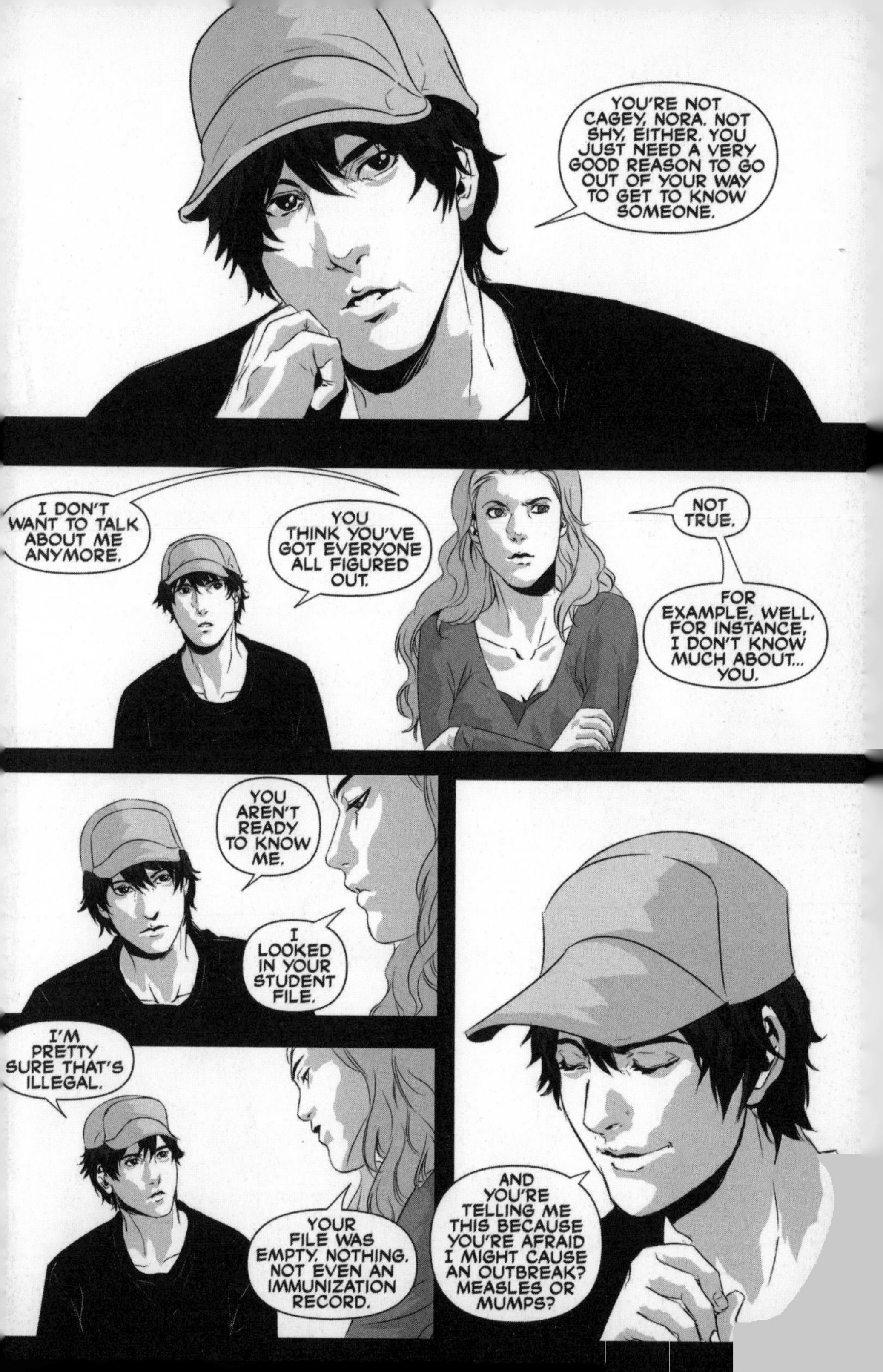

YOU'RE NOT CAGEY, NORA. NOT SHY, EITHER. YOU JUST NEED A VERY GOOD REASON TO GO OUT OF YOUR WAY TO GET TO KNOW SOMEONE.
I DON'T WANT TO TALK ABOUT ME ANYMORE.
YOU THINK YOU'VE GOT EVERYONE ALL FIGURED OUT.
NOT TRUE.
FOR EXAMPLE, WELL, FOR INSTANCE, I DON'T KNOW MUCH ABOUT... YOU.
YOU AREN'T READY TO KNOW ME.
I LOOKED IN YOUR STUDENT FILE.
I'M PRETTY SURE THAT'S ILLEGAL.
YOUR FILE WAS EMPTY. NOTHING. NOT EVEN AN IMMUNIZATION RECORD.
AND YOU'RE TELLING ME THIS BECAUSE YOU'RE AFRAID I MIGHT CAUSE AN OUTBREAK? MEASLES OR MUMPS?

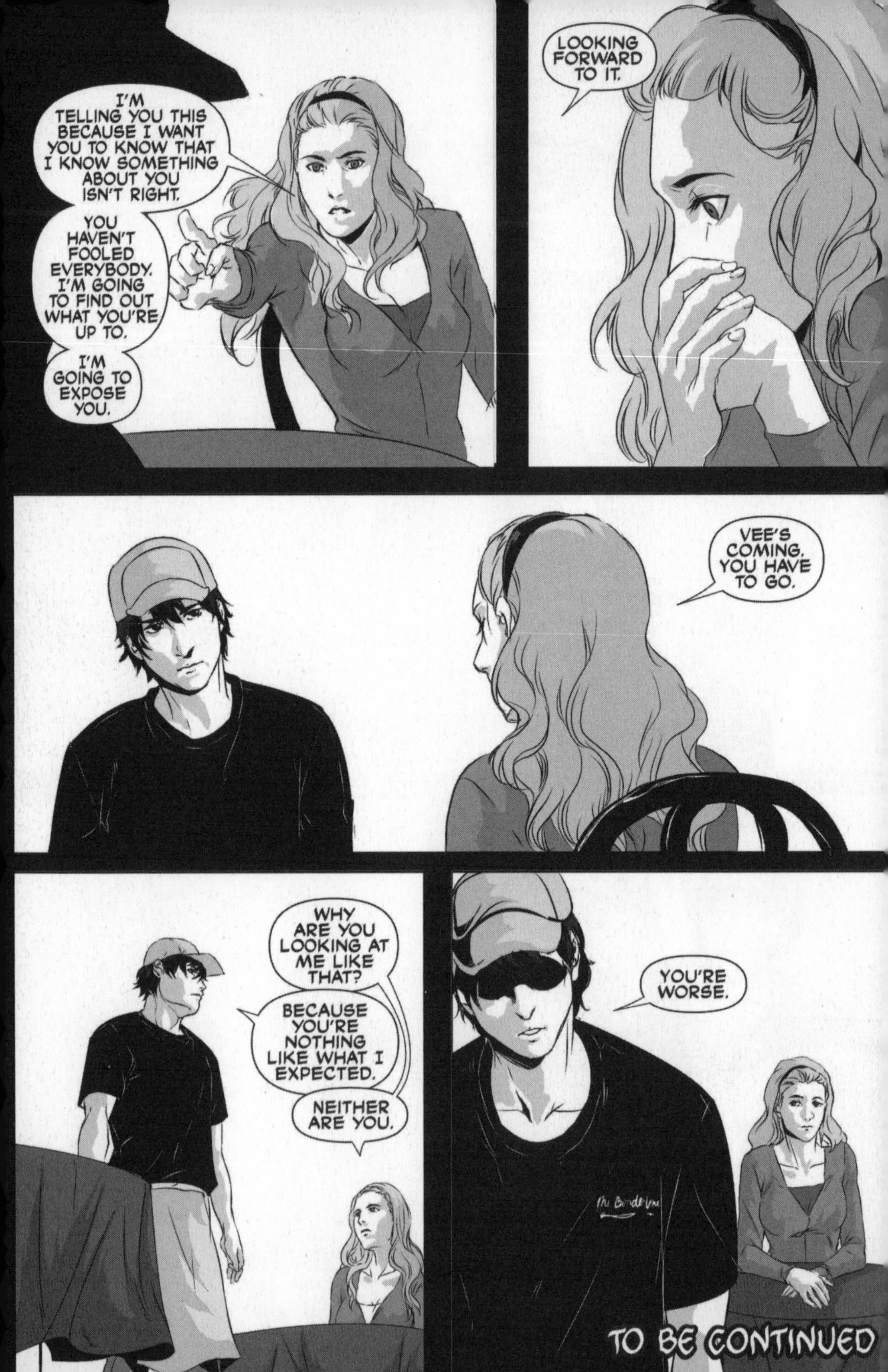

I'M TELLING YOU THIS BECAUSE I WANT YOU TO KNOW THAT I KNOW SOMETHING ABOUT YOU ISN'T RIGHT.
YOU HAVEN'T FOOLED EVERYBODY. I'M GOING TO FIND OUT WHAT YOU'RE UP TO.
I'M GOING TO EXPOSE YOU.
LOOKING FORWARD TO IT.
VEE'S COMING. YOU HAVE TO GO.
WHY ARE YOU LOOKING AT ME LIKE THAT?
BECAUSE YOU'RE NOTHING LIKE WHAT I EXPECTED.
NEITHER ARE YOU.
YOU'RE WORSE.
TO BE CONTINUED

hush, hush

Graphic Novel

BONUS MATERIAL

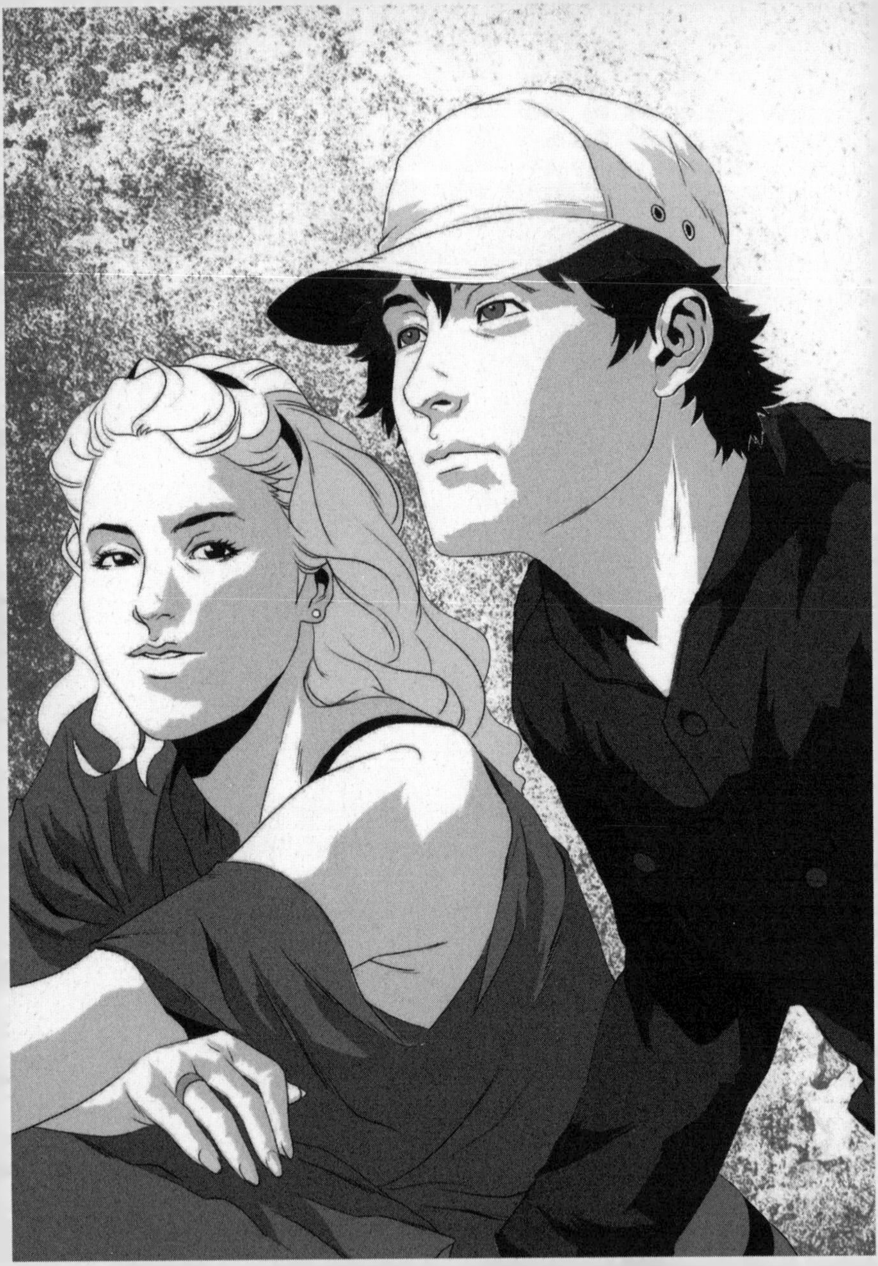

An
Original

hush hush

Story
by

Becca Fitzpatrick

Chapter 1

NORA

It was an unseasonably hot afternoon at Old Orchard Beach. Colorful umbrellas poked

out of the sand, and the humidity was on the rise. I was stretched out on a beach towel,

the sun baking so fiercely I could feel sweat beading behind my knees, in the crooks of

my elbows, and on my nose where my sunglasses rested. If I didn't move into the shade

soon, I was going to get a headache.

I heard Patch approach before I saw him. He was whistling the main score to

Disney's *Robin Hood*. I loved when he did that. It meant he was in a good mood. Of

course, I hadn't seen Patch in anything but a good mood for weeks. Chauncey Langeais

was dead, there was a pleasant shortage of vengeful killers pursuing us, and my end-of-year finals were over as of two hours ago. What more could a girl ask for?

Patch balanced an ice-cold can of Minute Maid Lemonade on my stomach, and I squealed.

"Thirsty?" he asked, grinning as he stretched out on the sand beside me. I had on a turquoise tankini, but Patch looked completely out of place at the beach. Dark jeans, dark T-shirt, dark eyes. Just like always.

I swept my hair into a ponytail, trying to coax a breeze along my neck. "I'm so hot I think the only cure at this point is a swim." I looked longingly at the ocean, sparkling a blue so dazzling it hurt my eyes, but I knew better. This far north, the Atlantic didn't creep above frigid until August . . . just in time for jellyfish to arrive.

"You *are* that hot," Patch murmured, and the way he gazed at me left no doubt he wasn't talking about the temperature. He traced a heart on my thigh, then kissed the spot. "What are we doing tonight?"

"End-of-school party at Enzo's," I reminded him.

Patch rolled onto his back and groaned.

"I promised Vee we'd be there. She's on the decorating committee. This is important to her."

"I had other ideas. You, me, and a picnic under the stars. Right here on the beach." He looked sideways at me, the corners of his mouth tilting up like a pirate's. "It's hot enough that clothing would be optional."

Romantic date on the beach. Just the two of us. Patch's proposal sounded *very* enticing. Just one small problem. "I can't back out. Vee has been dropping all kinds of hints that I'm spending way too much time with you."

"That's a bad thing?"

"No," I said, bending down to kiss him. His skin was warm from sun and his stubble tickled my lips. "But I do feel like I'm playing Switzerland here. We'll go to the party for an hour, then head back to my place, deal? My mom's on the road until tomorrow. We'll have the house to ourselves," I added in a voice meant to entice.

Patch raised himself up on one elbow. "Five minutes at the party."

I gave his shoulder a jab. "Five minutes doesn't count, silly!"

"Ten," he bargained.

"One *hour*. I'm not budging. We have the whole summer to spend together. Half the school will be there tonight. You'll love it. I know how much you enjoy working the crowd," I teased. Patch wasn't reserved, and he definitely wasn't shy, but he didn't go out of his way to make people feel comfortable, either. In fact, most people instinctively recoiled when he stepped into a room. At six-two, he had a long and lean and lethal build. His wardrobe was black, always black. He had hard-bitten features and an unapproachable expression, and at any given moment, he looked like he was hunting for trouble.

Patch had a reputation for fighting and gambling. Since I'd known him, he'd swapped priorities, and I knew he took his job as my guardian angel seriously. Lately I'd seen a secret side to him. Tender, romantic, playful. Protective. The rest of the world just hadn't gotten the memo yet.

Patch stroked his chin as though plotting a scheme. "Vee needs a distraction. A boyfriend."

"Vee *had* a boyfriend. And he nearly killed me. I think she's going to be laying off the crushes for the next little while." I wasn't sure if it was the glare of sun, or the memory of Chauncey, but I shut my eyes to get a grip on my sudden light-headedness. I felt *this close* to passing out.

"Starting to look a little flushed, Angel."

"It shouldn't be this hot in May," I complained, pulling myself up to sitting. No shade in sight. None available, anyway. I wished I'd thought to bring my own umbrella. I could always hold my towel above my head like a canopy—

Before I could finish the thought, Patch lifted me up and slung me over his shoulder.

"Patch!" I shrieked. "Put me down *now!*"

I could feel his shoulders shake with laughter, and before I knew it, I was laughing too, in between yelps of protest. I hammered my palms against his back, but there wasn't a lot of conviction behind it; Patch started kissing the bare skin of my thigh, just in reach of his mouth as he jogged me over the sand, and it made me dizzy with pleasure.

He strode into the surf and launched me on top of a wave. The icy water rushed at me from every direction, driving into my skin like a thousand tiny needles. Patch dove in headfirst behind me, clothes and all, wrapping me in his embrace. I was encircled by sensation; warm relief where he touched me, and blasting cold. The water was so clear I could see him through it. Our legs kicking together, our fingers entwined. The tide pushed and pulled at us, but Patch kept me anchored to him.

I broke the water's surface, wiping water out of my eyes and hoping my mascara hadn't smeared.

"Cooled off?" Patch asked.

I splashed water at him. "Yes!" I said, feigning affront.

"That makes one of us." Patch tugged off his shirt, lassoed it around my waist, and pulled me into a slippery, salty kiss. The waves broke, thundering into us with an intensity that could never rival my love for Patch.

This was how we would be forever. Together.

Chapter 2

PATCH

I'd promised Nora I'd pick her up for the party at eight. I was on my bike, speeding along
a winding back road, and it was starting to get dark. I'd taken this route a hundred times
before and never passed another driver. The trees formed a canopy over the road, making
it seem later than it was. I couldn't hear anything over the whine of my engine, and when
I came around a bend, she was standing in the middle of the road, asking to be hit.

I braked, swerving to miss her. I leaned sharply to my right, then straightened.
Another few inches and I would've plowed into her. Parking the bike, I strode back to her,
tugging off my helmet.

"What was that?" I asked Dabria angrily.

"I wanted to get your attention."

"Well, congratulations. You got it."

"How's Nora?"

I didn't answer right away. My breath came out harshly between my teeth. It felt like a trick question. Dabria had an angle, always. She twirled her hair around her finger, her eyes glinting with mischief. "If I thought you cared, I might tell you," I said at last.

"I didn't realize silly little schoolgirls were your type."

"It's taken you this long to realize there's very little you know about me." A statement, not a question.

Dabria rolled her eyes so far back in her head they almost disappeared. "Don't be so *grumpy*. It doesn't suit you."

I shook my head. "Not grumpy. Straightforward. So believe me when I tell you, whatever game you're playing? It's going to backfire. Leave Nora alone. And while you're at it, pay me the same courtesy."

Before I could bat her hand away, she reached up and straightened my collar. *Just like old times,* the gesture said, and it aggravated me even more. "This is a game you just might want to play," she said. "It's called 'I Know Something You Don't.'"

"Wrong. Not interested."

"What if I said it's about . . . the archangels?"

"What about them?" I said calmly and with cold indifference. My history with the archangels, the most powerful and authoritative branch of angels in heaven, wasn't secret. Weeks ago, they'd elevated me from fallen to guardian angel. A lifetime ago, before I fell,

I'd been one of them. My involvement with them was cut-and-dried, and I'd put it behind me. Dabria knew this.

"They might have made you Nora's guardian angel because they were bound by their own laws, but don't be naive. You tricked them. They don't forgive and they don't forget—not our kind. I have a source who tells me they're going to do away with you. Quietly, of course. They're laying a trap for you, and you won't see it coming."

"What kind of trap?" I asked in a low, menacing voice.

Her mouth twisted into a taunting smile. "If I thought you cared, I might tell you," she mimicked.

I shook my head again, but this time there was nothing casual in the gesture. It was deliberate and threatening. "Tell me what you know," I told Dabria in a voice that lacked tolerance. "You found me tonight because that's what you want. So get it out."

"After what you did to me? You tore out my wings," she shot back, her eyes giving away the only flash of anger or betrayal. The rest of her—her whimsical smile, her lazy posture, her bored voice—spoke of aloof immunity to what I'd done.

"I don't regret it. You would have done the same."

"I loved you. I loved you more than you deserved," she stated simply.

I looked her in the eye, but I didn't answer. I couldn't return the sentiment. It would be a lie, for one. And I wasn't in the mood to placate, for two. "The archangels," I reminded her.

"Nora isn't the only girl out there who needs a guardian angel."

"Explain."

"That's all I know. You can thank me for the heads-up later," she singsonged.

I watched her walk away, a bad feeling stirring inside me. I read between her words, and instantly a few guesses jumped to mind, none of them good. I'd known all along the archangels weren't going to let what I'd done slide. I'd conspired to get a human body. I'd plotted a girl's death. I'd fallen in love with her before I carried it out, but that's not how the archangels saw things. I'd broken their laws, and they'd make me pay.

They were going to send me to hell, and I had a few guesses how.

Chapter 3

NORA

I knew something was off the moment he picked me up. I opened the front door to find

Patch wearing a distracted expression, as though he'd been thinking about something

besides me on the ride over.

"You're late," I teased him, but I was a little annoyed. He'd kept me waiting

nearly thirty minutes and hadn't bothered to call.

"I had a few errands to run," he said without so much as a kiss or a comment on

my dress—a white eyelet sundress that was his favorite. "I had to go back to my place

and trade out the bike for the Jeep."

"Nothing like last-minute errands," I said, trying not to sound cranky.

"The worst," Patch agreed absently.

We drove to Enzo's in almost perfect silence. Patch sat forward in his seat, arms draped over the wheel, eyes watching the road as if he expected to catch a deer in his headlights around the next bend. He didn't seem to notice five minutes had passed without a single word spoken between us. His thumb tapped the wheel, and the set of his jaw seemed almost rigid.

"Is something wrong?" I asked.

He flashed me a quick reassuring smile. "Nope. Been looking forward to this all day."

"Liar."

"How's Vee? Decorations up and ready?"

Patch never asked about Vee. And he never made small talk.

"Seriously, are you sure nothing's wrong?" I asked.

He gave my knee a quick squeeze. "You look incredible in that dress. I can't take my eyes off you."

My mood lifted. "You noticed."

"It's my favorite."

I let go of a breath I hadn't realized I'd been holding, and returned Patch's smile. I rolled the window down, letting the wind chase through my hair. The air didn't feel hot and muggy now, but refreshing and breathable. Funny how it could change so fast.

Just like a moment.

Chapter 4

PATCH

Every time I walked inside Enzo's, I got a funny feeling. It was one of those uncomfortable wrenches in your gut, reminding you of being someplace when you'd rather be anywhere else. Months before Nora knew who I was, I'd sat at a table in the back of Enzo's, watching her. I'd studied her schedule, her personality, her mannerisms. I'd learned everything I could about her, because I was going to use that information to get close to her, and then sacrifice her for a human body. I'd never told her how long I'd followed her or how meticulously I'd planned. I was trying to forget the memory. I wasn't the same guy I'd been back then, but I didn't know if she'd see it that way.

"There she is," Nora said, grabbing my hand and pulling me forward into the crowd. I sidestepped an unidentifiable ice sculpture, and there was Vee.

"Well?" Vee asked, pointing overhead at hundreds of red and black balloons twisted together to form a wide snake that dangled from the ceiling. "What do you think?"

"It looks amazing," Nora answered. "Really, truly amazing. I'm blown away."

Vee raised her eyebrows at me. She wasn't asking my opinion. She was daring me to say what I really thought. "Well, Patch?"

Nora vised my hand threateningly, and I smiled. "Nice work."

"I'm manning the punch station," Vee said, turning her body to shut me out of the conversation. "My shift lasts an hour. Come find me and we'll hang." And she left.

"Where do you want to sit?" Nora asked me, scanning the tables. "Over there?" She pointed to a table in the back, where the light didn't reach properly. The same table I'd sat at multiple times while watching her from a distance. It was the last place I wanted to sit. I didn't want to be here in the first place. Dabria's words echoed at the back of my mind. The archangels were laying a trap. If I wasn't careful, I'd walk straight into it. I took a good look at the faces around me, skeptical of them all. Was I being tailed? Probably. The archangels wouldn't like that I was becoming so intimately involved in Nora's life. I was new to this, and the rules were old, barely intact memories. I felt my uncertainty rise.

"Here's just as good," I said, striding to the nearest empty table and pulling out her chair. I took the adjacent seat and stole a look at my watch under the table. Fifty-five minutes and counting. "I'll grab us something to drink," I offered. I was on my feet, anxious to do something.

I thought about telling Nora everything. I thought about telling her the archangels were a serious threat. They were powerful, and they had us outnumbered. But I didn't want to alarm her until I knew for sure. Right now, I was going on Dabria's word. I didn't think she was lying, but I didn't fully trust her either. She had something to gain from this. What, I still didn't know.

Bypassing the punch line, I stepped outside. The doors shut behind me, and the parking lot grew quiet. I walked around the side of the building and called Rixon.

"I need you to do something for me," I told him. "Keep an eye on Dabria."

"Got a bad feeling?" he asked.

"Worse than usual."

"Think she's plotting revenge now that you've demoted her to fallen angel?"

"Could be. But I think there's more. She told me the archangels are holding a grudge and making plans. It's no secret they don't like me, but I'm still trying to figure out how they plan on getting rid of me. Dabria claims she has a source. I want to know who it is, and what they know."

"Consider it done."

I hung up and went over what I knew. If Dabria was telling the truth, the archangels would have to build a case against me to send me to hell—I hoped. If they intended to do it quietly, they could use underground channels and erase their steps. Years ago I would have put the archangels above foul play, but I'd seen enough to change my mind. I'd seen enough *firsthand* to change my mind.

Politics were hard to escape.

Inside Enzo's, I couldn't find Nora. Our table had been taken over by Marcie Millar, the only person I'd ever known Nora to hate. I walked over.

"Lose your girlfriend?" Marcie asked me when I took the chair beside her.

"You wouldn't know anything about that?" I returned calmly, but I fixed her with a dark, measured look.

"How much is it worth to you?" She crossed her legs, bumping my knee as she did. It was no accident.

I said nothing. As the silence thickened, it was clear that Marcie grew more unnerved. To her credit, she hid it well.

She shrugged. "Maybe she doesn't want to be found. If you get tired of looking for her, I could use a drink."

I bent forward in my seat, locking her in an unbreakable gaze. For all intents and purposes, the method—a simple mind-trick—worked as well as hypnosis. *Did you take this table from Nora?* I asked her thoughts directly.

Marcie didn't blink. "I told her you were looking for her. She left without being asked," she confessed freely.

Make it up to her by showing yourself out, I commanded her thoughts. *The party's over.*

Obediently, Marcie rose to her feet, gathered her belongings, and marched out the exit. If the archangels hadn't been weighing on my thoughts, I might have taken satisfaction in getting rid of her.

I stood abruptly when I saw Nora across the room, talking to a guy I didn't know. Her expression was polite and friendly, but she had her arms folded protectively across her chest. Every time he took a step closer, she backed away. She caught me looking and waved me over.

"Patch, this is Anthony Amowitz. He was in my PE class this year. Anthony, this is Patch."

"Her boyfriend," I said, snagging two glasses of punch from the refreshments table and handing one to Nora.

"Cool, man," he said, but I could tell he didn't find it one bit cool. "So. How'd you two meet?"

"Biology," I offered.

He nodded. "Nice, nice. How long have you been together?"

I took a sip of punch. "Long enough."

Nora kicked my shoe discreetly. "About a month," she told the guy brightly.

"I haven't seen you around school," he said, frowning slightly as he examined me head to toe. "Are you new?"

A casual nod.

He laughed, and it was an obnoxious, husky sound. "You got yourself a talker," he told Nora, as if he could share a private joke with her.

"A pleasure talking to you, Andy." I handed him my empty punch glass. "If you'll excuse us, I'd like to dance with my girl."

I led Nora to the open floor at the center of the bistro. Tables and chairs had been pushed along the walls, and couples were already dancing to the music blaring over the speakers.

"Anthony," she giggled into my ear. "His name is Anthony."

I smiled down at her. "I don't like finding you flirting with other men, Angel."

She pulled on a face of mock nuisance. "*That?* So not my idea of flirting."

"What is?"

Her exasperation melted into a slow, provocative curve of her lips. She was beautiful with her face lit up that way. Swaying to the music, I fanned my fingers through her soft curls, watching them spill onto her shoulders. An eyelash had fallen just below her left eye, and I licked my thumb, pressing it to her cheek to catch the eyelash.

"Make a wish," I instructed her.

"Can I say it out loud?"

I shook my head. "It won't come true."

She scrunched her eyes closed and wrinkled her nose. Concentration tightened her face. She peeked, caught me watching, and quickly shut her eyes again. I grinned at her stern, serious expression. I wanted to kiss her, but I didn't want to break her focus.

"Okay," she said at last. She drew a deep breath and blew the eyelash off my thumb. I followed it for one brief moment before it sailed out of sight, into the crowd.

"What did you wish for?" I asked, knowing she wouldn't tell.

"I think you know." She looked up at me then, out from under her eyelashes, gazing at me in a way that dared me to pretend I didn't know.

"I would have wished for the same thing," I told her honestly.

"If we both wish for it, maybe it will come true."

She made it sound possible. She made everything feel within reach. But doubt edged into my mind. I'd faced down many opponents over the years, but none had the strength, influence, and power of the archangels. For the first time, I worried I was out of my league. I would do whatever it took to stay here with Nora, to keep her safe and begin making amends for a lifetime of wrongs, but the challenge felt ominous.

The archangels didn't lose.

Panel one
Nora looking up at Patch.
Nora: I'm busy tonight
Patch: So am I.

Panel two
Nora standing alone by the desk where she and Patch had been sitting. He is already gone.
Nora thought bubble: Did he just eat up all the time so I'd fail? Did he think one flashy grim would redeem him? Yes, he did.
Nora: I won't call! EVER!
Vee from off panel: Have you finished your column for tomorrow's deadline?

Panel three
Nora turns to Vee. Vee is writing note into a notepad.
Vee: I'm thinking of writing mine on the injustice of seating charts.
Vee: I got paired with a girl who said she just finished lice treatment this morning.

Panel four
They are now in the hallway and Nora is pointing at Patch who is farther up the hall.
Nora: My new partner.
Vee : The senior transfer? Guess he didn't study hard enough the first time around. Or the second.

Panel five
Vee Smiling at Nora.
Vee: Third time's a charm.

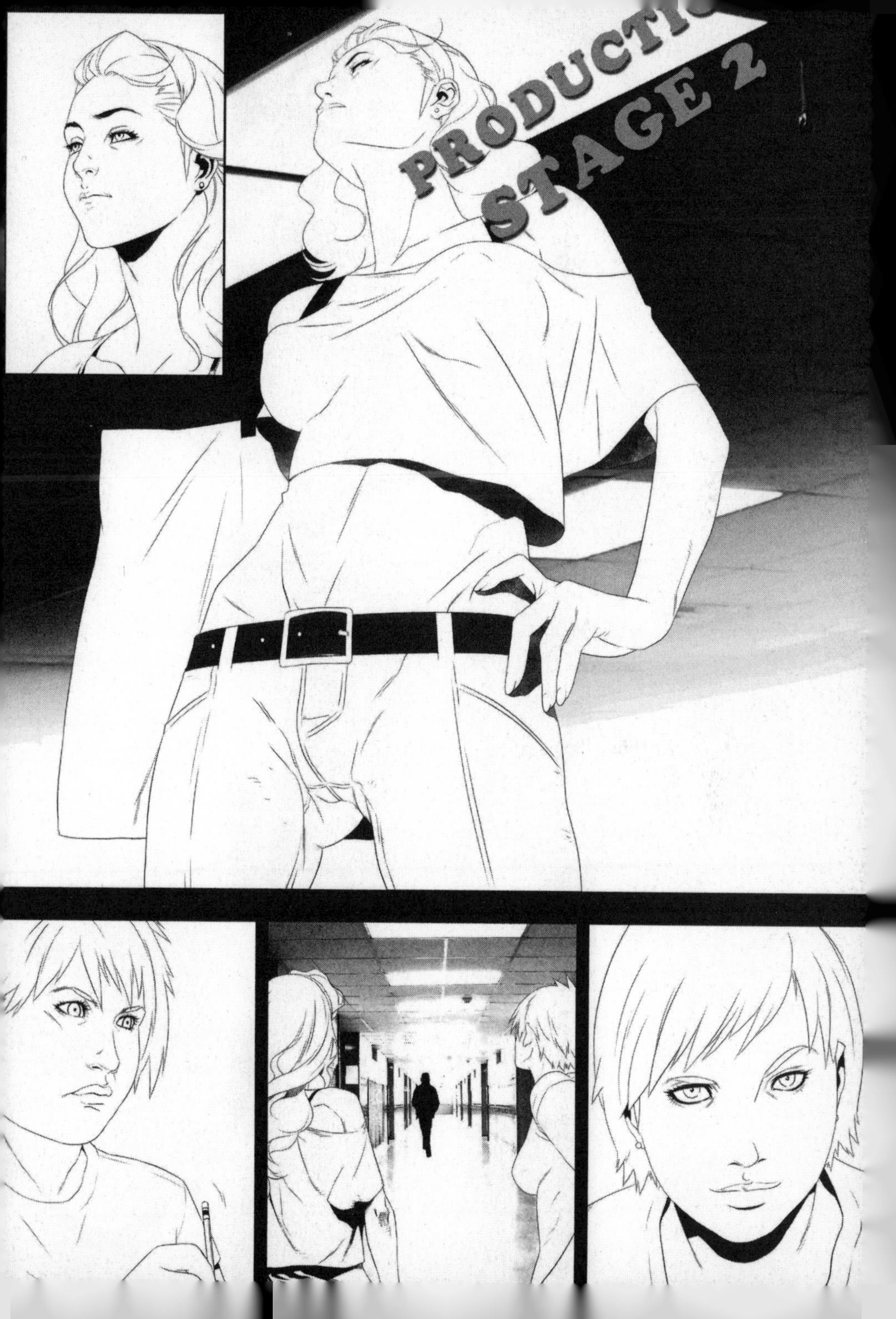
STAGE 2

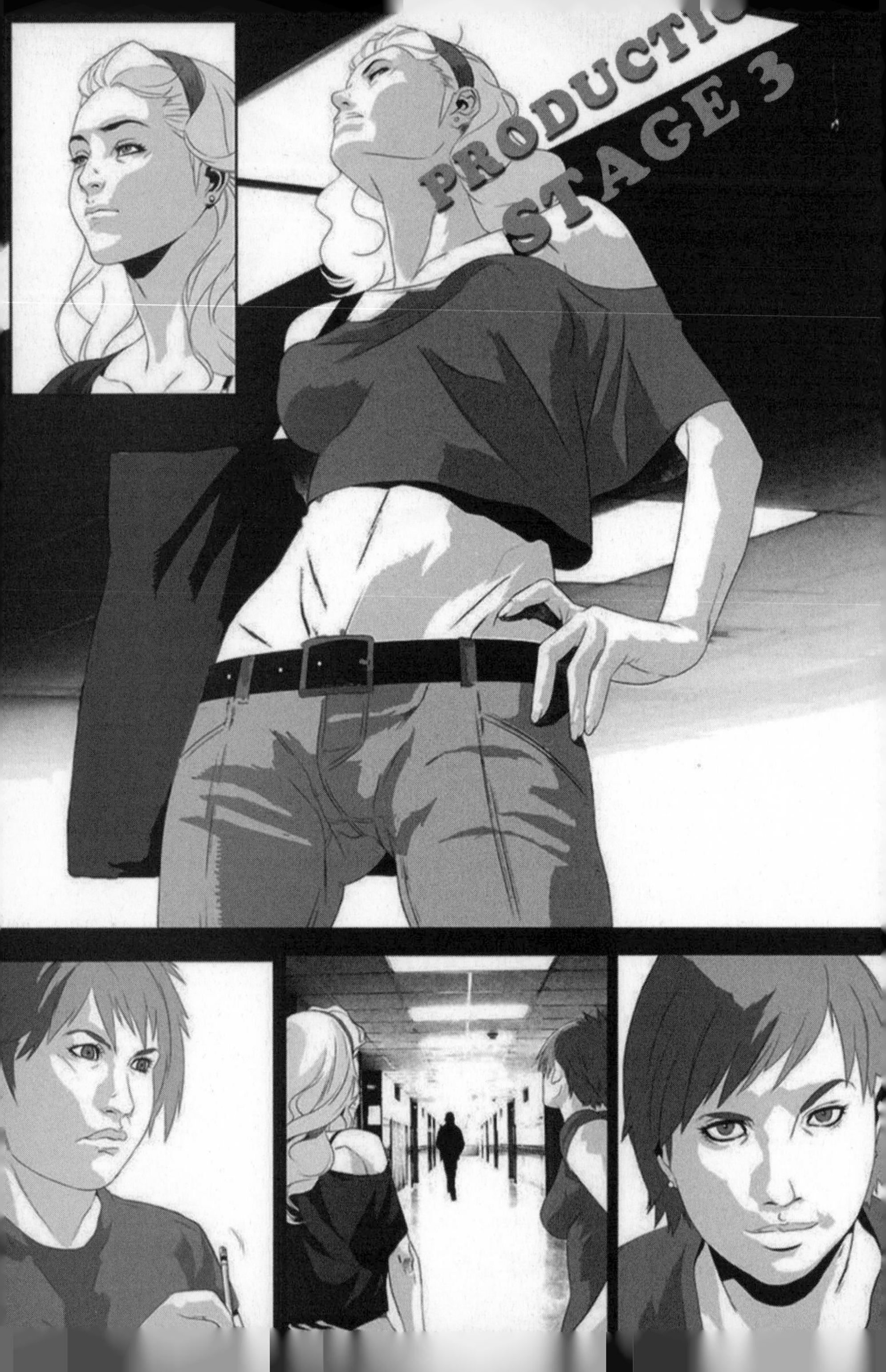

PRODUCTIO
STAGE 3

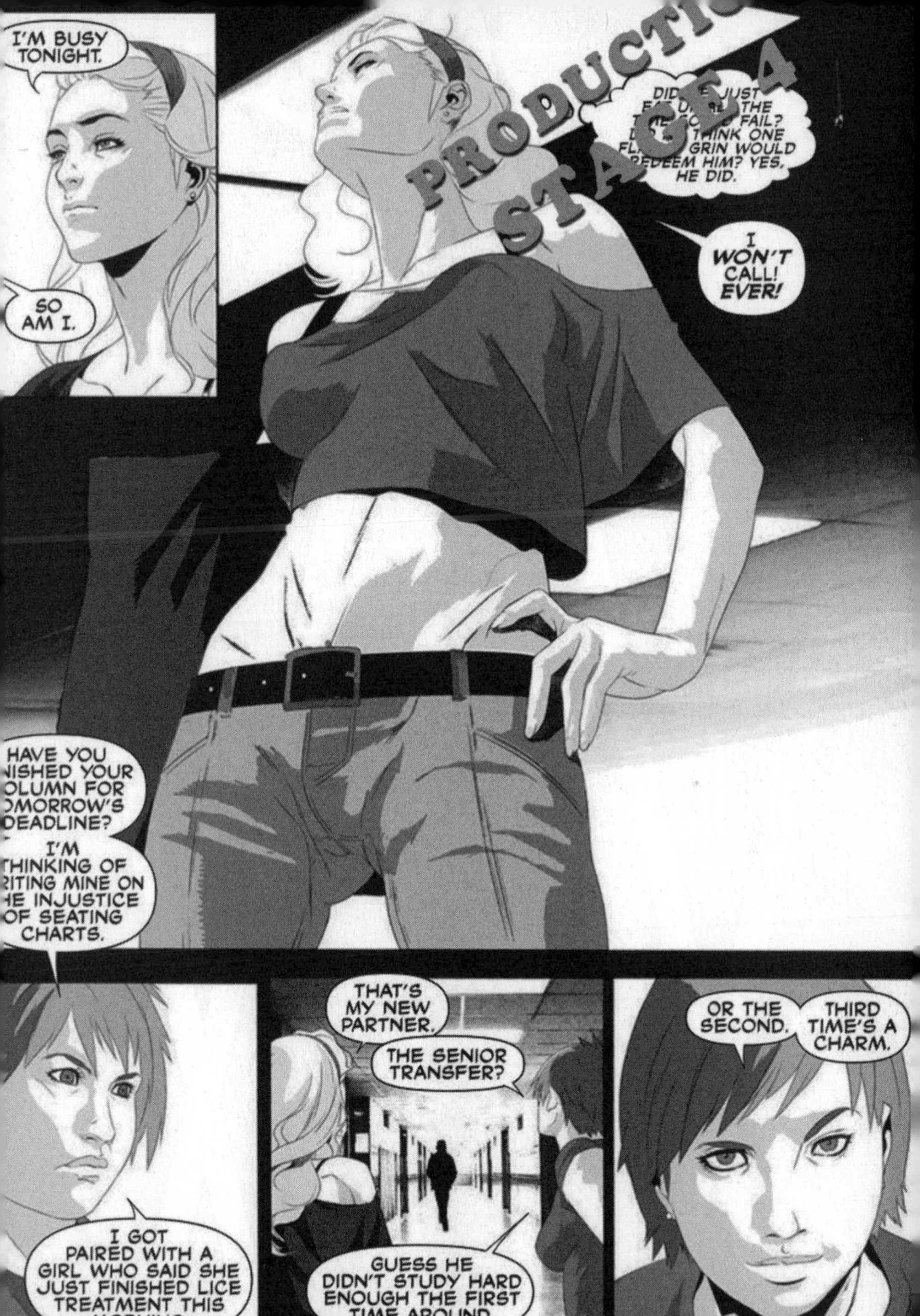
I'M BUSY TONIGHT.
SO AM I.
HE DID.
I *WON'T* CALL! *EVER!*
HAVE YOU NISHED YOUR OLUMN FOR OMORROW'S DEADLINE?
I'M THINKING OF RITING MINE ON HE INJUSTICE OF SEATING CHARTS.
I GOT PAIRED WITH A GIRL WHO SAID SHE JUST FINISHED LICE TREATMENT THIS MORNING.
THAT'S MY NEW PARTNER.
THE SENIOR TRANSFER?
GUESS HE DIDN'T STUDY HARD ENOUGH THE FIRST TIME AROUND.
OR THE SECOND.
THIRD TIME'S A CHARM.

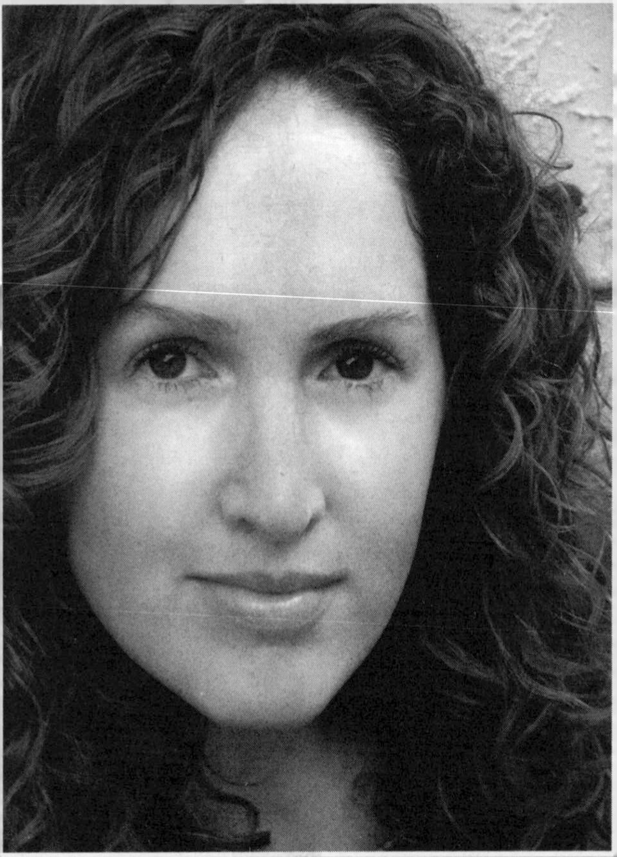

atrick's first book, *Hush, Hush,* debuted as a *New York*
he graduated college with a degree in health, which she
d for storytelling. When not writing, she's most likely r
e racks for shoes, or fulfilling her mission to taste ever
under the sun. She lives in Colorado, the lone girl in a
oys.

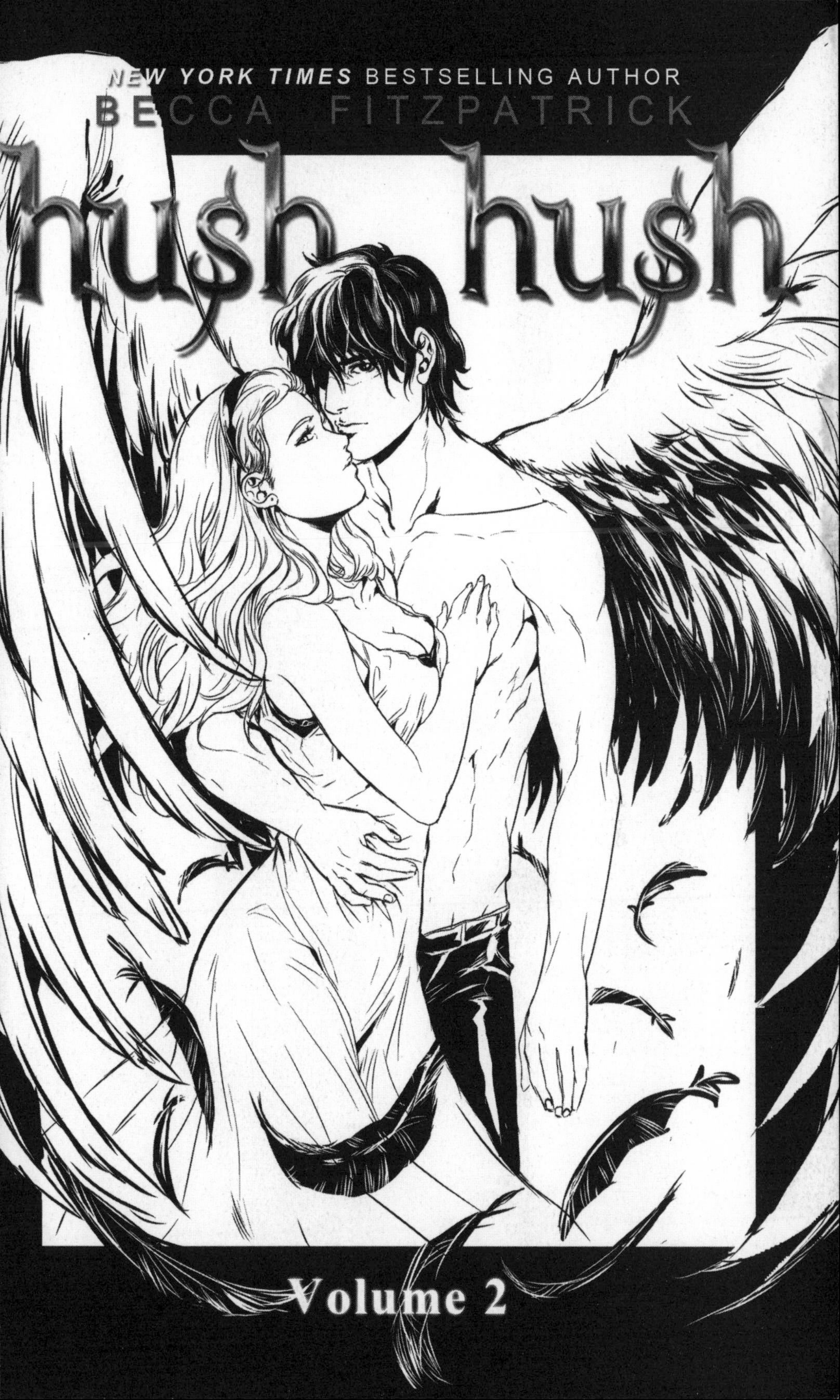
NEW YORK TIMES BESTSELLING AUTHOR
BECCA FITZPATRICK
hush hush
Volume 2

A sacred oath,
a fallen angel,
a forbidden love

YOU WON'T BE ABLE TO
KEEP IT *HUSH, HUSH.*